# At this mystery conference, murder is more than just another plot twist...

Nobody *likes* conferences, but they're part of the job.

Millbrook House senior editor Keiran Chandler has spent years curating the best voices in crime lit, but when an unsolicited manuscript is handed to him at the Noir at the Shore mystery conference, truth collides with fiction. *I Know What You Did* is more than just another slush pile submission— it's a direct threat.

U.N. Owen seems to know what really happened in Steeple Hill all those years ago. Who is Owen? How does he know these things? Clearly the mysterious author is after more than a book deal. But what?

With a potentially career-ending publishing merger on the horizon, the end of his affair with bestselling author and former homicide detective Finn Scott, and not so subtle threats from someone in his past, Keiran has a lot bigger problems than coming up with something witty to say on discussion panels.

# Kill Your
# DARLINGS

_Josh Lanyon_

**VELLICHOR BOOKS**

_An imprint of JustJoshin Publishing, Inc._

**KILL YOUR DARLINGS**
January 2026
Copyright (c) 2025 by Josh Lanyon
Edited by Jennifer Jacobson
All rights reserved

ISBN: 978-1-64931-077-4
Published in the United States of America

JustJoshin Publishing, Inc.
3053 Rancho Vista Blvd.
Suite 116
Palmdale, CA 93551
www.joshlanyon.com

This is a work of fiction. Sadly, any resemblance to persons living or dead is entirely coincidental.

*This is a work of fiction. Sadly, any resemblance to persons living or dead is entirely coincidental.*

*To J.J.J. —*

*who makes the hard parts better*
*and the good parts shine.*

*Writing a novel is like driving a car at night. You can only see as far as your headlights, but you can make the whole trip that way.*

**E. L. Doctorow**

# Chapter One

"Regarding Adrien English…"

I automatically glanced from Rachel—Rachel Ving, Ving the Merciless in New York publishing circles—to the panel discussion table where Adrien English was still chatting with Christopher Holmes.

"What about him?" I glanced back at Rachel and did a doubletake. "Do you represent him?" Because that would be news.

"I do now." Rachel smiled. It was a cat that got the cream sort of smile, which surprised me. Nice for Adrien to finally have serious representation, but he wasn't what one would call a heavy hitter in mystery fiction, the occasional tabloid-worthy film option notwithstanding.

I said wryly, "Now I understand the reason behind the delays in signing the new contract."

"I told Adrien to sign *nothing* until we spoke."

Presumably Rachel meant until she and Adrien spoke. She and I spoke on a regular basis.

I said neutrally, "I appreciate your steadfast commitment to your clients' best interests, but we both know things are a little different now."

"You mean with the merger between Millbrook and Wheaton & Woodhouse?" Her shrug was dismissive.

I'd have loved to be able to shrug off that new reality, too. I said, "Despite the press release in *PW*, it's more of a buy-out than a merger."

I hoped that didn't sound as bitter as I felt—as bitter as we all felt now at Millbrook House.

Rachel's dark eyes studied me shrewdly. She said softly, and with equally uncharacteristic frankness, "*You'll* be all right, Keiran. Chin up."

"Oh, hell yeah," I said as quickly as if I really believed it. I regretted saying as much as I had, but the fact was, W&W was already talking about "trimming the fat" from our lists.

"Great panel!" said a woman in the kind of hat you'd expect to see at Ascot—or maybe in *My Fair Lady*.

I smiled in reflex. "Thank you."

On my right, Rachel was saying, "As a matter of fact, you—and your editorial list—were probably a major incentive in W&W's decision to bail out Millbrook."

My laugh was caustic. "I doubt it." Given W&W's neo-pulp, er, *sensibility*, that was pretty unlikely.

"*Nonsense.* While, he may have the literary taste of a Neanderthal, Vaughn Woodhouse is no fool. He wants W&W to start winning awards again. You've spent years curating one of the most respected author portfolios in crime fiction. You'd better believe he wants to get his hands on that list."

My list maybe. Not necessarily me. In fact, during my first official meeting with Vaughn and Lila Penderak, my counterpart at W&W, Vaughn had informed me the "game plan" was to divide my editorial list between Lila and myself.

Lila had all but licked her chops.

Was there a little bit of payback there? I'd started my career in publishing as an intern reading the slush pile at Wheaton & Woodhouse. I'd quickly worked my way up to editorial assistant to Lila, then assistant editor, then editor before I'd left to take the senior editor slot at Millbrook House.

"Even when W&W does win awards, it's largely thanks to you," Rachel was saying.

She was referring to the Miss Butterwith cozy mystery series which, after a brief lull, had brought home the Agatha Award for best novel at this year's Malice Domestic. Christopher Holmes had been my discovery way back in the day, so Rachel was once again being uncharacteristically, unnervingly kind. She must truly think my days at Millbrook were numbered.

I said, "I think Christopher gets the credit there."

"*That* goes without saying." Rachel cast a benign, if proprietorial, glance at her most successful client, now shepherding Adrien toward the exit, and—unless I missed my guess— the hotel bar.

"He's very much looking forward to working with you again."

"Likewise," I said automatically.

In fact, before the ink had dried on Millbrook's intellectual property and contract transfers, Christopher—well, Rachel—had requested that he be moved from Lila's stable to mine. Which, come to think of it—and through no fault of Christopher's—might actually have proved the inciting incident leading to that unpleasant "orientation" meeting with Vaughn and Lila. Four minutes in, Lila had joking-not-joking suggested she'd trade Christopher Holmes for Finn Scott.

And I'd joking-not-joking replied, "Over my dead body."

Nothing against Christopher. I loved the idea of working with him again. But Finn was...

Not only had the Finn Scott releases kept Millbrook House afloat for the last two years, Finn was my—Finn was a friend and the closest thing I had to a regular sexual partner.

In fact, there had been a time when I'd worried he'd—well, anyway, lately we seemed to be on the same page as far as spending a little extra time together. Casual. Nothing complicated.

Starting with this weekend.

"You're going to want to read this!" A tall, skinny guy with spiky silver hair, a lot of piercings and an assortment of colorful tattoos, materialized from the wall-to-wall carpet of conference attendees to shove what looked like a manuscript in a clear binder into my hands.

I opened my mouth to state the obvious: *This isn't how you do it*. But he had already turned away and vanished in the milling crowd. A hit and run submission. I stared down at the title page—typed in Bookman Old Style font, no less.

*I Know What You Did*

Now there was a catchy title—back in 1973. Granted, the full title of Lois Duncan's classic suspense novel was *I Know What You Did Last Summer*, but the abbreviated version had popped up in publishing at least a dozen times since then. You can't copyright a title, which some writers mistake as encouragement from the universe to go right ahead and do what's already been done to death.

And not just when it came to choosing titles.

"*Keiran*!" Rachel's protest was so loud, several people turned to look our way. "Did you just accept an *unsolicited* manuscript?"

"I didn't *accept* it," I said hastily, probably guiltily. "I'm *holding* it, yes, but only because—"

"Get *rid* of it," she commanded in the tone of an epidemiologist trying to stave off a pandemic. "*Bin it*."

"Well, I mean…" I glanced around uncomfortably. Several audience members were watching us.

Rachel was right, of course. Neither Millbrook nor W&W accepted unsolicited manuscripts. Only agented submissions made it over the transom. Unsolicited manuscripts went straight to the circular filing cabinet.

But it's one thing to toss what amounts to junk mail when you're behind closed doors—or, more accurately—to have your PA toss junk mail when *she's* behind closed doors. It's another to trash someone's plastic-bound blood, sweat, and tears in front of a room full of hopeful authors.

I shrugged, said vaguely, "It won't hurt to glance through it."

Rachel looked flabbergasted, but was momentarily distracted by the ping of her cell phone.

"Great panel," a bearded man in a denim jacket said in passing.

"Thanks!"

"Like herding cats," Rachel muttered. I presumed she wasn't talking to me. Or about me.

A tall, rangy figure in jeans and a black T-shirt with Cloak and Dagger bookstore's logo, appeared in my peripheral. I turned quickly, smiling into arresting green eyes in a tanned, tough face.

Phineas—Finn to his readers—Scott.

He was a lean six foot two, with long, muscular legs and broad, powerful shoulders. His hair was a rumpled strawberry-blond, which he kept short and neat. Well, short anyway. He was handsome in a rugged baby-I-don't-care way, but handsome wasn't the first thought that came to mind. He looked like a guy who could handle anything—and as far as I knew, that had always been the case. Whether working homicide for five years or navigating the fame and fortune that came with the bestseller status most authors can only dream of, Finn handled himself with good-humored capability.

The crowd parted before him, murmuring recognition.

"You made it," I greeted him. I was so happy—and even a little relieved, which was weird because there'd never been any question of his making it. This was his job. Just as it was my job.

"*Hey.*" Finn squeezed my upper arm. "I caught the last half. That was great." He grinned, maybe remembering some of the funnier moments on the panel—or maybe he was as glad to see me as I was to see him.

"When did you get in?" I was still smiling, still gazing into eyes the color of Montana sapphires.

"Just after two." Finn was already backing up, hooking a thumb over his shoulder. "I just wanted to say hi. I've got to meet someone."

"*Oh.* Right. Are we on for dinner?" I took it for granted we were—it was practically tradition by now, but to my surprise he grimaced in regret.

"I've already got plans. How about tomorrow night?"

It took a second to process. I said automatically, "Tomorrow night's the publisher's banquet with Wheaton & Woodhouse."

Finn looked blank, but then said quickly, "Maybe drinks afterwards?"

"Uh…yeah. Of course!" It came out brightly with a pre-programmed smile. I was—surprised. A little confused. Disappointed for sure.

Of course, there was no reason Finn *couldn't,* shouldn't make other plans for dinner the night he arrived. He might be dining with his agent. There'd be plenty of opportunity for meals together over the next few days.

Opportunity for other things, too, presumably.

Hopefully.

No reason to feel…anything, really.

Except.

Except Finn hadn't been—hadn't seemed like—he'd seemed like meeting for drinks was plenty. All he required of me.

No. I was reading way too much into a ninety-second exchange. We were both in the middle of stuff, and he was—

*Not interested in seeing me tonight.*

I listened to the echo of that thought and understood why my stomach was tying itself into double and triple knots, as if there was something wrong. Because something *was* wrong. Finn wasn't interested in making plans for *after* dinner, either.

And that was another disquieting first.

Usually, we spent pretty much every free minute of every conference together—not that there were so many free minutes because attending a conference was not the same as going on vacation. Though spending our down time together made them feel a little less like work.

*Down time.* There was a euphemism.

I realized Rachel had finished checking her phone and was talking to me.

"I missed that," I said.

"Hm? Oh. I said, I'm supposed to be having dinner with Adrien. He was right here a minute ago." She scanned the large conference room, which had nearly emptied out by then.

"Try the bar," I suggested. "I think he and Christopher were headed in that direction."

"Of course they were." Rachel sighed. "You're headed over there as well, I suppose?"

I had been, but suddenly, unexpectedly, I didn't have the energy, the heart, for it. For any of it. The bright laughter and loud chatter. The crush of people. The pressure of all that...emotion.

I wasn't ready to run into Finn, knowing what I now knew.

*Jesus. Enough with the dramatics.*

He made other plans for dinner. What was the big deal?

*You know what the big deal is.*

And yeah, I did. Knew it instantly and instinctively. No words needed.

But it wasn't as if I'd imagined it was going to last forever, our...friendship.

*Didn't you?*

Anyway, we were still friends. Still...partners in crime, as it were. Until Lila and Vaughn decided otherwise.

But I was going to need...

A few minutes to myself would be helpful.

Hell, was there a reason I couldn't order room service and stay in tonight? It was the only night I had free.

"I'm pretty jet-lagged," I told Rachel. "I might make it an early night."

*"You?"*

Given Rachel's astonishment, you'd think I was known for being the life of the party. But maybe that was just one workaholic judging another.

I joked—tried to joke, "I'm not as young as I used to be." No lie, right now I was feeling every one of my forty years like boulders piled on a 17th Century crushing board.

"I wouldn't say that aloud," Rachel said darkly.

I laughed without humor. She had a point. The publishing world was subject to ageism just like the rest of the entertainment industry.

We parted ways outside the conference room and I headed toward the bank of elevators, nodding or smiling briefly as I passed familiar faces moving in the opposite direction down the long marble hallway.

It was still early enough in the conference that the elevator arrived in a couple of minutes. The doors slid open, I stepped inside, leaning wearily back against the mirrored wall, then snapping back to attention as a slim brown-haired man slipped in right before the doors closed.

I smiled automatically, then recognized Kyle Bari.

Kyle was one of mine. One of my authors, that is. He was young—barely thirty—and prolific. Thankfully, as talented as he was prolific. Which isn't always the case.

"Hello, again," I said.

He smiled back, but said nothing. I recalled that it was his first conference—and that, despite the fact that Noir at the Shore was in driving distance of home, he'd had to be coaxed into attending.

"You did a great job on the panel," I told him, which was true.

Kyle had appeared on the Stranger Than Fiction panel with Adrien English, Christopher Holmes, and Grace Hollister. He'd been a little quiet, but engaging and self-deprecating. The audience had warmed to him right away.

He nodded in thanks, not agreement. He was eyeing the binder I held. "*I Know What You Did?*"

"Effective, if not original."

"Do people really try to give you their manuscripts to read at these things?"

"Occasionally." I grinned. "I think agents probably have to deal with it more than editors."

Neither of us said anything for a moment. Then he smiled ruefully. "Do you think it's weird so many of your authors have real-life experience solving homicides?"

"Yeah. I sure do." We both laughed. I added, "But it's only you four, and Christopher isn't even officially mine yet. I've got eighteen authors. The other fourteen leave the detecting to the professionals."

I'd proposed moderating a panel featuring mystery authors who find themselves involved in real-life homicides, and the event organizers had jumped at it. The Stranger Than Fiction panel had been very well attended, given that it was the first panel of the conference and late in the day. Most of the big-name attendees hadn't even arrived yet.

Kyle pointed out, "Finn Scott is one of yours. He was a homicide cop."

My throat unexpectedly closed for a moment at the mention of Finn. Not mine after all, as it turned out.

I said lightly, "Finn was a professional detective, so that doesn't count. You four are all writers. The sleuthing is just a hobby."

He smiled faintly, and I realized I could have phrased that more tactfully. Kyle's sleuthing had involved solving the disappearance of his father, the artist Cosmo Bari.

"This is me," I said as the elevator lurched to a stop at the fifth floor. This was the top floor of the hotel. Kyle didn't move, so… Had he missed his floor while we were chatting? Maybe he was headed for the rooftop deck?

I got out, glanced back.

Something about the way he stood there, so quiet and thoughtful and self-contained, gave me pause. Did he want to speak to me in private?

He said nothing. Made no move.

"Are you on your way to dinner?" I asked.

"Maybe." Kyle made a little face. "It didn't occur to me that everybody would already have plans."

Hell. New Kid on the Block syndrome.

"I was just heading out to grab a bite," I lied. "Why don't you come with me?"

His hazel eyes lit, but he was a polite kid—well, not a kid, but younger than me, for sure—and he hesitated. "I don't want to impose…"

The door started to close. I reached out to block the sensors. "You're not imposing. I'd like some company."

He said, "Well, if you're sure—"

"I'm sure. I'll meet you downstairs in—?" I looked at him in inquiry.

"Half an hour?" he said tentatively.

"I'll see you in half an hour," I said, and let the doors close.

# Chapter Two

I was swearing softly under my breath as I let myself into the Grand Bay Suite.

But really, how was it helpful to sit around feeling sorry for myself all night? This was a much better use of my time and energy.

I tossed the binder to the desk in the little alcove off the living room.

At seventeen hundred square feet, the suite was ridiculously large for one person. I'd booked it with Finn in mind of course, but also, I planned on hosting cocktails for my authors on Sunday evening to address their questions and concerns with the merger.

Dragging the conference neck lanyard over my head, I left it draped with my blazer on the back of the sofa that formed part of the seating arrangement around the marble fireplace. I walked into the private bedroom, which had another, smaller, fireplace, a king-sized bed with wood parquet headboard, a few pieces of tasteful coastal art—starfish sculptures and watercolors of old Monterey—and a fresh flower arrangement.

As I undressed, I stared blankly out the large windows at the blue dazzle of the bay.

The sunlight was fading. Soon the fog would roll in. Normal for May on the coast, but a little gloomy. The California sunshine was one of the things I'd been most looking forward to on this trip.

One of the things.

I did not let myself think about how much I'd imagined Finn would enjoy this room, this view, this giant bed…

Not useful. Not productive.

I strode into the oversized bathroom with its double sink vanity, soaking tub, separate shower, and yes, more breathtaking views of blue water and silver edged clouds. I popped my contacts out, splashed cold water on my face, and considered my dripping reflection bleakly. I decided I didn't give a fuck about the five o'clock shadow. I dried my face, took a swig of Listerine, swished it violently around my mouth, spat, and returned to the bedroom to dress in jeans and a Knicks sweatshirt. As far as I was concerned, I was off-duty tonight.

And after tonight, I'd be too busy to think about anything but work, so…just get through tonight.

I transferred my wallet from my trousers, slid my glasses on, and threw myself a cursory look in the mirror hanging on the far side of the bed. A tall, lanky dark-haired man with colorless eyes and a blank white face stared back at me.

"You're fine," I told him.

I didn't wait for his answer. I grabbed my phone and went downstairs to meet Kyle.

Kyle stood in the lobby talking to Finn and a small, slight, blond person.

My heart sank. *Really?* Was I going to spend this conference running into Finn every thirty minutes?

The three of them were talking and laughing, oblivious to my approach. Finn and the blond waif appeared to be on their way out—the blond wore a heavy turtleneck Aran sweater and Finn wore his favorite brown suede racer jacket.

But, I mean, how did I know if it was his favorite jacket? He wore it at the conferences we'd attended together, and that amounted to less than a fraction of both our lives. The truth was, I knew as little about Finn as he knew about me. So, let's not pretend this had ever been anything more than a semi-regular hookup.

Finn glanced away from Kyle, spotted me and just for a second his expression was unreadable. He was still smiling, though, so maybe I was looking for subtext where there was none.

I lifted the corners of my mouth, crinkled the corners of my eyes as I joined their little circle.

The blond, who was indeed male and older than he'd looked from afar (which was about thirteen) nodded coolly. He had fierce blue eyes behind wood square glasses. His thick hair was platinum blond, cut in a trendy men's fringe haircut that I couldn't help thinking made him look a bit like Howl Jenkins Pendragon.

Finn was saying, "Keiran, do you know Hayes?"

I was pretty sure I'd seen Hayes's photo in *Publisher's Weekly*, but I couldn't quite place him. Edgy-crime-writer-wunderkind-prone-to-violent-excess would have been my first guess.

I said, "I'm not sure…"

"No." Hayes cut across the polite tergiversating. His voice was flat.

Kyle, who I suspected lived a sheltered life, looked taken aback.

I quirked a brow at Finn, said lightly, "No."

There was a flicker of amusement in Finn's gaze. He made the introductions—he was a social and civil guy—which you don't really expect from cops or even ex-cops. Although, Joseph Wambaugh was about as nice a guy as you could hope to meet.

"Keir, this is Hayes Hartman. Hayes, Keiran Chandler is senior editor at Millbrook House."

"I know," Hayes said, still cool, still flat. "He's your editor."

I almost said, *out of curiosity, which of your manuscripts did I turn down?* But that would have been bitchy, and there were plenty of other reasons Hartman might have taken a dislike to me. Like the one he was currently brushing shoulders with.

Well, in the interests of accuracy, his head only reached Finn's shoulder.

I shifted my gaze from them. We were positioned right across from the lobby bar, and I spotted Rachel. She'd successfully tracked down Adrien English, but instead of hauling him off to dinner, she'd joined the group that now included Christopher Holmes, J.X. Moriarity, and Mindy Newburgh. Their laughter floated across the lobby.

Finn said, "Hayes is up for an Edgar. Best First Novel by An American Author."

"Excellent!" I said.

Hartman curled his lip.

What was with this kid? Was he teething?

I said, "Kyle's up for Best Paperback Original."

There was a little twinkle in Finn's eyes. "I know." Finn was also up for Best Paperback Original. He added to Kyle, "My money's on you."

Kyle spluttered a laugh of protest.

"Are you attending the banquet?" Hartman asked him.

"No." Kyle said, and I sighed, which brought that humorous glint to Finn's eyes again. That easy sense of humor was one of the things that had attracted me to Finn's writing. It was one of the things that had attracted me to Finn.

"Me neither," Hartman said. "I can't stand the whole obsession with bullshit celebrity PR. If I win, I'm going to return the statue with a rejection letter."

"Who's your publisher?" I couldn't help asking.

"Black Fig Editions."

Ah, yes. I knew the name if not the catalog. Their advertising tagline was: *Decadent. Disruptive. Noir.*

Because, of *course* it was.

Finn's cell buzzed as a black sedan pulled up outside the lobby glass door. Finn checked his phone, said to Hartman, "That's us." To Kyle and me, he said, "Where are you headed? Did you want to share an Uber?"

Nothing on earth could have persuaded me to climb into a car with Finn and Tiny the Terrible. Besides, I like to walk and I didn't have a place in mind. I figured we'd decide while we strolled around Cannery Row.

However, I said to Kyle, "Up to you."

"I like walking," he said, to my relief.

"Right," Finn said. "We'll catch you later in the bar." He turned to follow Hartman, who was already stalking out the glass doors.

"Later," I agreed, though I knew I would not be there.

Nor would I be missed. Clearly.

I smiled at Kyle. "What are you in the mood for?"

He smiled back. "Really, anything."

"I love Monterey. I haven't been here in a long time. I'm thinking seafood."

Although he lived just a few miles up the coast and was probably looking forward to Mexican for a change, he said easily, "I love seafood."

We walked out through the glass doors, stepping out of the hotel's warm golden glow into the cool-toned hush of early evening. The air was salty and cold. I drew a deep breath and felt immediately better, centered.

"He seems genuinely nice," Kyle commented, and I had no doubt as to which *he*, he meant.

"Yep. Finn's both genuine and nice."

The light had faded to a lovely shade of steampunk lavender, but I could feel the warmth of the sunbaked sidewalk beneath the soles of my trainers. Flecks of mica glittered on the damp pavement.

Neither of us said anything for a minute or two. As the moist breath of the Pacific curled around our feet, I was wondering if I should have brought a jacket. Spring evenings by the ocean could be chilly. Streetlights flickered halos in the thickening dusk, and the distant clang of a buoy bell sounded muted and otherworldly through the fog rolling in off the bay.

"When was the last time you were back in Steeple Hill?" Kyle asked.

The question startled me, until I remembered I'd mentioned having grown up in Steeple Hill the first time we spoke on the phone.

"Two months ago," I said. "I came back for my father's funeral."

"Oh, I'm sorry," Kyle said quickly.

"It's all right. We weren't close. In fact, that was the first trip back in over twenty years."

"Right." His tone was neutral, but I knew what he was thinking. Twenty years didn't sound like *we weren't close.* It sounded like estrangement. Which was what it was.

Our footsteps whispered softly against the damp pavement. The air smelled of seaweed and distant woodsmoke. Very different from New York. But everything about California was different.

The old-fashioned shops along Cannery Row were dark and quiet. In the apartments above, windows glowed cozily behind drawn curtains. The streets were surprisingly empty, but most conference attendees would be eating inside the hotel tonight.

"Is your mother...?" Kyle began tentatively.

"No. My mother died when I was four."

"I'm so sorry..."

I could see he was wishing he'd never brought up what he'd surely imagined was the innocuous subject of my ties to the area. I gave a short laugh. "It's all right. It was a long time ago."

After a moment, Kyle said, "My mother died when I was three."

I hadn't known that about him. But I didn't, in general, know a lot about the personal lives and histories of my authors unless it was relevant to their work—or made the evening news.

"That must have been difficult," I said. "I'm sorry."

He shrugged. "Like you said, it was a long time ago."

This was getting depressing. I changed the subject. "Tell me about your next project."

That's a question guaranteed to stimulate *at least* an hour's worth of conversation from any writer. To my surprise, Kyle hesitated.

I glanced his way, and his expression was uncharacteristically somber.

"Are you taking a break?" It wasn't great timing, but it wasn't the end of the world, either. Better a break than burnout.

"No. No, I have a project in mind. I want to do a standalone."

I said briskly, "A standalone is a great idea. A standalone could be the breakout book we're all expecting. Have you started it?"

"Yes. I'm about halfway through."

"Okay. Well, when you're ready to send it over—"

"Keiran," he interrupted. "We've worked together for a few years and I feel like if I ask you to be honest, you'll... be honest."

I blinked, said, "I've never not been honest with you. I will never not be honest with you."

"My agent is thinking this merger with W&W isn't going to be good for me. In fact, he thinks it won't be good for you. He said you probably won't stay on."

It came out of the blue, but maybe it shouldn't have. Of course there was going to be concern, skepticism, and maybe even a couple of full-on *abandon ships!* I wasn't expecting to be confronted so quickly—or from this quarter—and it took me a couple of seconds to sort through the whirl of emotions, largely panic. Who the fuck was his agent again? I was blanking. Did Kyle's agent know something I didn't? Was there a rumor circulating that I was on the chopping block? *Was* I on the chopping block?

Kyle finished with, "He thinks we should pitch it some-where else. Maybe Theodore Mansfield. I guess Wheaton & Woodhouse's contracts are close to predatory?"

*The P word.*

I pulled myself together, stopped walking and faced him. "I'm not going to tell you where to pitch your next project. That's your agent's job, and it sounds like he's got your best interests at heart. I can tell you that he's right, W&W's contracts are not as favorable as Millbrook's were. But one of the things I've been working on with Lila Pen-derak, my counterpart at W&W, is coming up with-with contractual compromises in order to retain our most valu-able authors."

"Yeah, but that's not me."

"What? It sure as hell *is*. The third book in the Outfit series outsold the first. That's almost unheard of. That's the trajectory every publisher loves to see. As far as I'm concerned, you're absolutely one of the authors we need to make an effort to retain."

"Is W&W going to see it that way? Why would they?"

"W&W has a strongly vested interest in retaining top talent. For a lot of purely practical reasons. I'm planning to go through this in more detail with you and the others on Sunday evening."

"Okay, but if you're not going to be around for much longer…"

I tamped down my alarm, stated firmly, "Unless your agent knows something I don't, I have every intention of being around for the next twenty or so years."

He stared at me gravely in the hazy light, and then shook his head. "Okay."

There was a mixed message. The head was saying one thing, the heart another.

It had to be asked. "Are you unhappy with our working relationship?"

"Huh?" Kyle sounded startled. "No. Hell, no."

"That's a relief." No lie. "Listen, I'm going to do everything possible to make sure this merger works out for all of us." How the hell I'd manage that; I had no idea. But I smiled. "So, tell me about this breakout book."

We resumed walking, and Kyle told me about his book, which did sound like maybe this would be the one.

Eventually, I spotted a painted restaurant sign swaying gently in the damp breeze—a laughing seagull with what appeared to be a surprisingly cheerful shrimp in his beak.

By then, I was cold, tired, and more than ready for a drink. I rested my hand on Kyle's shoulder, guiding him toward the restaurant door, heading for that warm pool of light, just beyond the shadows.

"How about this?"

"Sure—"

I opened the door and scooted him in.

A cheerful looking girl wearing a sailor's cap came to greet us. "Two for dinner?"

We nodded, and she led the way through the half-empty dining room to a table next to the windows overlooking the water.

We settled at the table and the waitress chirped, "I'll be back with the drinks menu!"

"Perfect," I shook out my napkin, picked up the dining menu.

Kyle turned his head to gaze out the window. I glanced past him, past a blond bob at the table right behind him, and stared into Finn's candlelit eyes.

# Chapter Three

Had I done something wrong in a previous life?

Right. Rhetorical question.

Finn raised his brows in silent acknowledgement. I nodded politely.

No fear of being asked to join them. Every author understands that editor-author or agent-author tête-à-têtes are sacrosanct. Granted, this wasn't that meeting, but they couldn't know that.

I stared down at the list of entrees. Hartman was in full discourse, and I could understand why Finn wouldn't want to interrupt that flow of brilliance.

"The problem," Hartman's clear, carrying voice drifted over to our table, "is that so many of the legacy crime writers are still shackled to this rigid idea of plot over character. They treat motive like a checklist item—method, opportunity, motive—and forget that real crime, *real* human darkness, is messy and inconsistent. I mean, how many times can we read about a jealous spouse or a spurned lover before we all collectively roll our eyes? The genre has to evolve beyond formula if it wants to stay relevant. That's why readers are gravitating to fresh voices—writers who understand that ambiguity is more powerful than resolution."

Was he practicing for his panel or having a conversation? Surely, Finn had heard all this before?

I bit my lip, focused all my strength of will on the dinner options before me.

Grilled sole.

Grilled salmon.

Blackened swordfish.

Actually, grilled salmon sounded perfect. I closed the menu.

"And don't get me started on the pacing issues. These so-called modern masters of crime fiction drag us through fifty pages of setup before anything actually happens. They're writing for an era of patient readers who no longer exist. I think part of the reason my work resonates is that I'm writing for now—the streaming generation, the swipe generation. You have to grab them by the throat in the first scene and never let go. The days of slow burn are over. Readers won't wait for you to get to the point."

Finn murmured something noncommittal.

Adorable. Did he imagine input from him was needed to feed the engine? That was a self-propelled motor if ever there was one.

Maybe we could move tables?

Or would that be too pointed?

Across from me, Kyle woke from the trance of watching moonlight flickering on the water. His wide eyes met mine. His lips parted. I winked.

The waitress returned with the cocktail menu.

"Should we start with appetizers?" I asked Kyle.

"Oh." Kyle smiled. "Sure."

It's not about the appetizers. I learned long ago that the point of the appetizers isn't the food itself (though I like crab cake as much as anyone) it's the demonstration that you are willing to spend money on frivolous food for your author.

I left Kyle to choose our starters, scanned the cocktail menu, and ordered a double Hochstadter's Rock and Rye.

"It's not that I'm trying to dismiss the contributions of the older generation—they had their time, and I'm sure they did the best they could within the constraints of their era. But audiences are more sophisticated now. They don't need to be spoon-fed motives or have every plot thread tied off in a neat little bow." Hartman paused to take a sip of his drink.

Again, *who* was he talking to in that lecturing tone? Finn was right across the table. No need to project to the back row.

I couldn't help glancing over. Finn was listening attentively. I knew him well enough to recognize that look of amused tolerance. He got that same look with me sometimes, when I was venting *my* take on writing and publishing.

In the midst of my reflections, Finn's gaze moved from Hartman to me. His eyes were shadowy in the soft light, but it was a steady, serious, appraisal, and my heart picked up speed as though I'd unconsciously recognized some looming threat.

But I'd already identified the threat, so no adrenaline rush required. I'd been judged and found wanting. For whatever reason, Finn had changed his mind. About me. About pursuing anything further with me. Or apparently even spending an extra minute in my company.

Not to make a production out of it. Things changed.

But we wouldn't have had to pursue anything more than what we already had. I would have been fine with that. I could have been content with that. I didn't understand why that no longer worked for him, unless it had to do with the Boy Wonder pontificating at the next table.

"Fried calamari?" Kyle suggested.

I said automatically, "Sounds great."

"I think what I'm doing—what my readers respond to—is respecting their intelligence. I don't write puzzles. I write *experiences*."

*Right, kid. Because you've had so many at your age?*

Okay. Not fair. Experience in all its variety—and brutality—struck whom and when it chose. As I knew very well.

Kyle added to the waitress, "And a glass of the Kendall Jackson chardonnay."

I said a little abruptly, "Actually, I think we're ready to order?" I glanced in inquiry at Kyle.

"*Yes*." He sounded a little vehement, and my mouth twitched.

"Cool!" the waitress said, and took down our entrée orders.

Hartman concluded, "Of course, that's not something everyone can do. *You* do it naturally, instinctually. That's a rarity in my experience. You have to be willing to challenge the conventions, and frankly, not everyone has the courage for that. But I think my numbers speak for themselves."

Not unless 1,000 units was considered midlist at Black Fig Editions.

Finn murmured something too quietly for me to hear.

Hartman suddenly laughed; a relaxed, boyish laugh that seemed to come from another person entirely. "Maybe," he admitted. And his cheerful admission that he was (I surmised) maybe full of shit was unexpected.

So, yeah, I got it. The charm of something new. Something—someone—young and fresh. Someone full of Big Ideas and with maybe a little case of hero worship?

A wave of weariness washed through me.

Maybe it showed. "How many of these do you do a year?" Kyle asked.

It took me a moment to think. "It varies. Typically, seven or eight—and then there's the London Book Fair."

He looked taken aback. "I didn't realize you were living out of your suitcase."

I smiled, but yes. I did just that during the spring circuit. I'd actually looked forward to those trips because Finn was traveling the same circuit.

I was going to have to figure out a new reason to enjoy... anything.

Suddenly, I was out of things to say.

Luckily our sailor girl shipped in with our drinks.

The alcohol helped—by the second round, Kyle and I were chatting like old friends (about what, I have no idea). The food was better than expected, and I was relieved because this very long day was coming to a close, and very soon I'd be able to escape to the quiet and privacy of my hotel room.

Unfortunately, my timing was off. In my rush to get us out of the restaurant, I'd forgotten Finn liked to take his time over meals. Even though they'd probably arrived half an hour before us, we ended up leaving the restaurant at the same time.

This time when Finn suggested we share an Uber, Kyle shrugged and looked to me for the deciding vote.

Of course, I wasn't going to insist on our hoofing it back to the hotel. It was later, colder, and we both had long and busy tomorrow ahead of us.

"Thanks, that would be great," I told Finn, and the four of us crowded into the green Toyota Camry idling impatiently in front of the restaurant. I assumed Finn would take the front, but nope. Hartman announced he was prone to claustrophobia and slid in beside the driver.

Somehow, I ended up nested between Kyle and Finn in the backseat. Three adult males—wide shoulders and long legs—were definitely a crowd in this mid-sized space, and God help us if we had to make an emergency exit. I half-angled my shoulder to Finn, but it really didn't help. I was pressed against his chest, in a way that felt unnervingly familiar. He got his arm free and reached across the back of the seat, resting against my shoulders. Because I was tired and had had too much to drink, it—his warmth and nearness, his familiarity—was unexpectedly overwhelming. The mingled scent of warm suede, Yamazaki 12, and an aftershave that reminded me of sea breezes, sunlit cypress, and driftwood. Tom Ford Costa Azzurra. I had a bottle sitting in my bathroom back in New York. He'd forgotten it when he'd stayed with me.

My eyes prickled unexpectedly and I imagined what would happen if I gave in to jetlag and depression, if I let emotion swamp me; imagined the reaction if I started crying in the back of this fake-pine-scented Uber winding its way through the foggy streets...

I laughed.

Kyle glanced at me questioningly. Finn's breath was warm against the back of my neck. "Something funny?"

I shook my head, not turning, but yes, there was a certain dark humor to the moment.

We probably weren't in the car more than five minutes before we reached the hotel.

Hartman hopped out, waiting on the sidewalk while Finn and I arm-wrestled over the fare. Figuratively. Though nearly literally.

"It's already paid for," Finn said as I tried to thrust a handful of bills at him.

"But we're sharing, so—"

"So, it's my treat."

"But sharing means splitting—"

Kyle joked, "Don't make me break you two up."

"Too late," I muttered.

Finn didn't move a muscle.

"It was a three-minute drive," Hartman bleated from outside the car. "I'm so *done* with all the macho posturing *bullshit*."

Inside the car, there was an astonished silence.

I withdrew my cash, retorted, "Droll, isn't he?"

Finn spluttered an unwilling laugh, and we all crawled ungracefully out of the car, which departed in a cloud of exasperated exhaust.

Hartman led the way through the glass doors. The lobby was much more crowded now, much noisier. Check-in was a mile long, but everyone was in good spirits as attendees greeted old friends and favorite authors. The lobby bar was packed, standing room only, which was how it would be for most of the conference.

"Should we try for a table?" Finn asked our group at large.

"Let's go to the restaurant. Schooners," Hartman said.

Kyle said to me, "I promised Adam I'd phone."

I nodded, said to Finn and Hartman, "I've got a mountain of work to get through tonight."

"Aww, gee," Hartman said.

I met his gaze. Behind the glasses, his eyes were like ice chips.

Definitely not my imagination. He was not a fan.

Finn said to me, "See you tomorrow."

"I'll be here all week," I said as brightly as the piano guy in a cocktail lounge, signing off for the evening.

Kyle and I crowded into the waiting elevator packed to capacity with luggage and conference attendees.

"Thanks for dinner," he murmured. "I really enjoyed it."

"You're very welcome. I enjoyed it, too."

A young woman with red hair and a T-shirt that read I READ BANNED BOOKS, leaned over, and said, "Are you Kyle Bari?"

Kyle confessed he was the author in question, the young woman proceeded to tell him how much she loved his books, and I was able to relax and tune out.

Kyle and almost everyone else got off on the third floor. The red-haired woman fell silent, staring straight ahead. She stepped out onto the fourth floor with the remaining passengers.

The doors swished closed, I let out a long sigh. A few seconds later the elevator reached the luxuriously hushed fifth floor.

There was no sign of anyone in the foyer. No sign of anyone in the hallway.

I unlocked the door to my suite and stepped inside. I'd left the lights on when I'd gone down to dinner, and it was a little like walking out onto a stage. The wall of dark windows reflected my entrance.

Only someone out on a boat or across the bay with a telescope—or maybe the fish in the sea—would have been able to see me, but I still felt a little like something in an exhibit. Uneasy. Exposed.

Which was funny because I'd never been nervous on my own. When you *weren't* alone... That was the time to be on guard. Another lesson from long ago.

I drew the long cream-colored drapes, turned out a few lamps.

It was true about having a mountain of work to get through. My email was jammed with queries, proposals, and actual submissions—and that was the stuff that had already been vetted by Cherry, my PA. I had cover designs to approve, marketing copy to approve, PR strategies to approve, oh, and manuscripts to edit.

But tonight was not the time to tackle anything that required me to be objective and open-minded.

I weighed my options: sleeping pills or another drink?

It was just after nine o'clock. Midnight ECT. So maybe another drink and then bed. I was tired; physically and emotionally drained, so another drink ought to do it.

What I did not want to do, could not afford to do, was lie awake all night, thinking.

I wandered into the bedroom, kicked off my shoes and undressed, trading jeans for blue silk pajama bottoms. I hadn't drawn the bedroom drapes yet, and for a moment I stood motionless, gazing past my reflection into the darkness.

Despite the partying that would be happening four floors down, the suite was silent but for the distant, rhythmic hush of waves rushing against the pilings below. The lights were low— just a soft glow from a sconce by the balcony door and the faint blue haze of the city drifting in from across the bay.

I opened the glass door to the balcony, and the crash of the waves was magnified; the salt-heavy air whispered against my face. I closed my eyes, breathed in deeply.

I loved the ocean. Missed living by the sea.

Leaving the door open, I padded barefoot across the plush carpet into the living room, crossed to the minibar, the cabinet humming softly beneath the polished wood counter of the long sideboard. The little brass handle clicked as I opened it, revealing a neat row of tiny glass bottles of Rock and Rye, gleaming under the LED strip light like potions in an alchemist's shop. Not that I'd ever been in an alchemist's shop, outside of a book.

Judging by spec fiction novels, alchemy was a booming part of our economy.

I took out a bottle, dropped a couple of ice cubes from the metal ice bucket into a short tumbler. You had to love turn-down service in a high-end hotel. The ice crackled as I poured my ready-made old fashioned.

I took a long swallow, savored the burn.

*It'll be okay. You've survived a lot worse than this.*

*You should be glad it ended when it did. Before you let yourself get anymore invested in a fantasy.*

Yep. Very glad about that. Could not have been gladder. In fact, I was the fucking Man from Glad.

I blinked back another burn, this time in the back of my eyes. My gaze landed on the small table in the alcove, caught the glint of lamplight on plastic. Lying next to a half empty bottle of sparkling water and an untouched plate of chocolate-covered almonds was the manuscript I'd been handed at the Stranger Than Fiction panel.

*I Know What You Did.*

I snorted.

Here was the solution to that Finn-sized hole in my evening. I was willing to bet money this would send me speeding off to Dreamland on a bullet train.

I picked up the manuscript, strolled over to the long cream-colored sofa in front of the fireplace, and settled on its comfortable length. I propped a throw cushion behind my head, opened the binder, adjusted my glasses, and began to read.

## Chapter One

It was a full moon that night.

Two boys stood over the body.

"What do we do now?" the younger boy asked. He was seventeen. He was tall and skinny with curly black hair and gray eyes in a bony face like a skull.

I raised my brows and took another swallow of my drink. Was this AI? It had an artificial intelligence feel to it. Granted, a lot of first-time human authors had that basic generic writing style.

"I don't know. Why did you have to kill him?" The other boy was crying. He was eighteen. He was blond and muscular and handsome. Not as handsome as the dead boy. The dead boy looked like a young Greek god had fallen from the sky and died on the rocks. One of the rocks Keiran had used to bash his head in.

# Chapter Four

I jack-knifed up, the glass dropping from my nerveless fingers, liquid sloshing onto me, onto the sofa, onto the carpet as I scrambled to my feet.

I stared down at the discarded manuscript.

*I Know What You Did.*

My heart thundered in my ears. Black spots floated in front of my eyes.

*This isn't real.*

I stared wildly around the softly lit suite, half-expecting... What? Someone to step out of the shadows?

*This can't be happening.*

Was I dreaming?

I waited for a few moments, waited for some revelation, waited to wake up.

From down the hall I heard the distant *ding* of the elevator. I strode to the suite door, peered out the tiny peephole. I had a distorted view of the empty hallway.

I started to open the door, but stopped.

Was that caution or paranoia running rampant? What—who—did I imagine would be out there?

I turned. The manuscript lay where I'd left it. The room looked absolutely normal, but that in itself felt frighteningly wrong.

"What is *happening*?"

My protest, jarringly loud in the silent room, snapped me back to reality.

I walked slowly back to the sofa, picked up the fallen tumbler and set it on the glass coffee table. I picked up the manuscript, studying the contact details at the upper left of the title page.

```
U.N. Owen
```

My lip curled. Someone knew their Christie.

I read the address.

```
U.N. Owen
1926 Old Stage Road
Steeple Hill, California
iknowwhatyoudid@pm.me
(650) 699-5033
```

Steeple Hill.

My legs felt shaky. I sat down abruptly on the sofa.

Okay, but that made sense. That would follow, wouldn't it? Only someone from Steeple Hill could possibly know—

But, no, it *didn't* follow, because the only two people in Steeple Hill who knew anything about the night Dom died were me and Milo. And Milo…

That had not been Milo today.

I couldn't quite visualize the man who'd shoved the manuscript into my hands. I'd barely had a look at him, and maybe that had been deliberate on his part. I had changed. Milo would have changed. But despite the silver hair, U.N. Owen was too young to be Milo. Too young to be a contemporary of ours. That much, I'd noticed.

I stared down at the pristine printed pages.

*This* was not Milo.

For one thing, Milo knew what had actually happened.

But so did U.N. Owen.

Sort of.

Enough.

Enough to paralyze me.

*How?*

Had Milo told someone?

Impossible.

And why would someone wait twenty-three years to come forward?

*Come forward*? Was that what this was?

Following that first flight or fight response, my heart began to calm. My hands were almost steady as I began to flip through the manuscript. I was still afraid. Still completely bewildered. But my brain had kicked in. I had questions. Many questions.

Questions that mounted as I speed-read my way to the first blank page.

I turned to the next page. Blank.

After the first chapter, it was all blank pages.

"What in the hell?" I murmured.

Just a partial manuscript. No note. No cover letter. No explanation. No actual threat, beyond the very existence of this "book."

This was not a serious book proposal. So, what was it? Blackmail? What did U.N. Owen want?

I stared at the phone number.

Why not ask him what he wanted?

Because one thing for damn sure. I was too old for games, mind games or any other kind. Too old to live in uncertainty and doubt and fear. Better to know the worst up front—and plan accordingly.

I thumbed in the numbers on my cell's key pad.

*1926 Old Stage Road...*

Was it even a real address? If I was remembering correctly, Old Stage Road was about a block from "downtown" Steeple Hill. In the old days that area had been surrounded by ranch-land, open spaces, farms, state parks, and beaches.

The phone on the other end jangled loudly.

Once.

Just once, and then I realized what I was doing, the mistake I was making. My heart stuttered in alarm. The phone nearly slipped from my suddenly perspiring hands as I jammed the red disconnect button so hard, the screen flexed.

Stupid. Stupid. *Stupid.*

Even now, even though no one had picked up, it was possible the call could be traced. My number might show as a missed call or turn up logged on Caller ID.

*Jesus.* What was the matter with me? I made my living editing crime novels, and yet my first move was to slip up on something elementary.

I hastily opened the Recents list, tapped and deleted the outgoing call to U.N. Owen, removing it from my call history.

I expelled a breath. There. *Gone.*

But not entirely. Not if someone really wanted to find it. Knew how to find it. Had the authority to access phone carrier records.

Better to make the call from the hotel lobby.

No. Better to call from a payphone somewhere well away from the hotel.

No. Better not to phone at all. Better to go in person and find out exactly what the score was.

Yes.

I needed to look U.N. Owen in the eyes when I asked them what they wanted. When I asked them what they intended to do.

No phone calls. No emails.

And speaking of emails, what the hell with the demand for the private message? Who the hell *was* this person?

Safe to say, I would not have the answer tonight.

Tomorrow…

I mentally reviewed my schedule. Steeple Hill was about a ninety-minute drive one way. Losing three hours out of the first day of the conference would be tricky to manage. But if I left immediately after Finn's Q&A with Rudolph Dunst, I *should* be able to make it back just in time for the Wheaton & Woodhouse banquet.

I could not imagine the conversation with U.N. Owen would take long.

I stared down at the manuscript.

I needed to read the entire thing again, of course. Slowly. Thoroughly. I needed to understand how much U.N. Owen really knew. How much they'd gotten right. How much they'd gotten wrong. How much was guesswork? How much was genuine knowledge?

But abruptly I was all out of…everything. The merger, Finn, and now whatever the hell this was? Whatever emotional currency I'd had left was spent. I was down to pocket lint. I felt sick, shaken to my core.

I had a plan of action and, for now, that would have to do.

Stick to the plan.

In the meantime...

I carried the manuscript into the dark bedroom, stepped out onto the balcony, and shoved the binder down between the large stone urn and the smaller pot containing the little windmill palm. I'd spent enough time in hotel rooms to know that the staff doesn't bother to water the plants while the room is booked.

For a moment, I stood there, hands braced on the iron railing, breathing in the cold sea air, gazing out at the scattered lights glittering beyond the black water, the stars glistening overhead.

"You're fine," I said, as I'd been telling myself for the last twenty-three years.

But for the first time in a very long while, I knew I was not.

Finn was a runner.

I was not.

At conferences, rain or shine, he'd be up at the crack of dawn, pounding the pavement for an hour or so while I headed to the hotel pool.

Which was how he knew where to find me on Thursday morning. In the rooftop pool on the horizon deck, working out all my nervous tension and alarm in the pleasantly heated water.

The rooftop pool wasn't large, but it didn't need to be. Sleek and slate-edged, it stretched like a lap of poured glass toward the far edge of the terrace, where the Pacific fell away into fog and sunrise. Low glass panels lined the perimeter, keeping the wind at bay without interrupting the view.

I had the entire deck to myself until Finn appeared. Even without my contacts in, I recognized the approaching blur in faded jeans and a black T-shirt. I knew his outline, tall and straight and confident. I knew his stride, easy and assured. Like there was nothing he wasn't prepared for or couldn't handle. It's an underrated but very attractive quality: competency.

I didn't think he was smiling until he reached the edge of the pool and gazed down at me. Then I saw the white curve of his smile in his tanned face. He was wearing sunglasses, although the morning was gray and cool and damp.

Late night drinking with the boys? Boy. Almost literally.

He said, "I thought I'd find you here."

I smiled up at him. "And here I am."

He hesitated, glanced behind himself, and sat down on the black mesh foot of the nearest lounge chair. "We missed you last night."

I managed not to roll my eyes, but couldn't help a dry, "Did you?"

I didn't need glasses or contacts to feel the directness of his look.

"Keir—"

"No need." I said lightly, "All good things come to an end, no?"

"Yes." His tone was odd, almost self-mocking. "That's exactly what I thought you'd say."

I made a face. "I'm getting predictable in my old age."

He moved his head in negation, polite and automatic.

With everything else going on, you'd think I wouldn't have the nervous energy for anything but the latest and most pressing catastrophe, but you'd be wrong, because as I stared up at him, my mind was roiling.

*But why? I don't understand why now. Because, after the last time, I thought we were moving toward...*

*Going to try...*

*Not that pretentious kid, surely? He* can't *be the reason.*

I had a million questions, of course. A million objections. But pride held me silent—also the fear that I wouldn't be able to hang onto my composure if he started detailing the whys.

After a moment, he said with uncharacteristic somberness, "That's not the only thing I need to talk to you about."

I took a couple of strokes to the side of the pool. I could smell his freshly showered scent over the pool smells. "No? Okay. If you're concerned with the merger—"

Finn cut me off. "No. I'm not concerned with the merger. I had a meeting with Lila yesterday when I got in."

"*Lila*?" I repeated, like there were so many Lilas, I wasn't sure which one he meant.

"She wanted to know if I was happy working with you, whether I felt my interests were a priority for you, whether, given how long we've worked together, I felt you were still pushing me, still challenging me."

I was so stunned I couldn't speak. Stunned and, yes, alarmed, because if W&W—if Lila—was, in essence, asking my authors for a performance evaluation, then my future with the company was definitely undetermined.

When I didn't—couldn't—speak, Finn said, "I know I owe my success to you, and that's what I told her. Her point was only that it's very common, even healthy, for authors to shift editorial relationships over time."

I found my voice, said harshly, "No, you don't. You don't owe your success to anyone or anything but your own talent and effort. Am I proud of the work we've done together? Hell, yes. But you don't owe me anything."

It was probably more heated than necessary.

Even if I'd had my contacts in, it would probably have been impossible to read his expression behind the dark Ray-Bans. After a couple of heartbeats, he said unemotionally, "Right. Well, to that point, Lila asked if I'd be willing to consider working with another editor. Just to see what might evolve, creatively." He shrugged. "Someone with a new perspective, a different set of experiences, could bring something fresh to the partnership."

I stared at him, stared and realized what his expression meant. I sucked in a breath, a sound so naked, so raw, there was no hiding it.

Finn's face changed. For a perceptive guy—well, we all have our blind spots.

"You said yes." The words came out shocked and breathless.

There wasn't any pretending; it was obvious how I felt, and Finn sounded a little winded too as he said, "I thought it might be easier for both of us."

I couldn't say anything. I stared at him. My heart was pounding so hard I thought I might be having a heart attack. I could barely find the strength to keep treading water.

But as he stared back at me, something flickered in his face. His mouth curved into another of those odd, sardonic smiles.

"Losing the books hurts. Not the other," he observed.

"It *all* hurts," I flung at him. "I can survive losing…the other. Losing the books, losing you off my list, means my *job*."

He looked shocked, but then protested, "Come on. You have plenty of authors making good money for Millbrook—"

*"They're trying to get rid of me!"*

And if that didn't sound totally paranoid, I don't know what would. In my defense, I was dealing with a lot that morning.

Finn was trying to be reasonable in the face of my borderline hysteria. "Come on, Keir. What sense would that make? Lila spoke very highly of you during our meeting."

I dunked below the water, counted to five, surfaced, shaking the water and tears from my eyes. "I've had a meeting, too. With Lila and Vaughn. Where they discussed dividing my list between Lila and myself. They already think I'm overpaid—I currently earn more than Lila, per Lila—and that I've been running my little kingdom without any oversight for way too long."

Finn's expression hardened. The line of his mouth was grim and straight. "Okay. I didn't know that. I'll tell her no. I'll tell her the truth. I'm good where I am."

But now I was almost beside myself with hurt and anger and bitterness.

"No. You know what, Phineas, you're right. It *will* be easier on both of us. And it probably *is* time for you to spread your fucking wings. We've been working together so long I'm probably not challenging you enough, probably not pushing for your…your *creative evolution* the way I should." I had to stop for breath. "And if Lila gets *you*, maybe she'll leave me and the rest of my list alone."

He was stone-still, as if he was seeing me for the first time. As if he was seeing a stranger.

But no. He was seeing the real me. In all my fucked-up glory.

After a second or two he snapped out of his trance and rose.

"You got it," he said, and walked away.

# Chapter Five

I was shivering when I climbed out of the pool.

The truth was, it was too cold for swimming. But it wasn't the gray skies or wind off the ocean that had me shaking as I clumsily toweled off. I fumbled into my jeans, nearly over-balancing, dragged on my sweatshirt, slid my glasses on. They immediately fogged up.

Business is business. You can't fall apart every time something doesn't go your way. What Lila told Finn was true. Most authors don't stay with their first editor throughout the entire course of their career. Some do. When you're lucky enough to find right combination of personalities and creative vision— It takes *time* to develop that partnership.

But fair enough. If Finn believed someone else could help him reach The Next Level—whatever he imagined that might be, because he'd already reached a level of success most authors fantasized about—that was that. I sure as hell didn't want him feeling he had to stick with me out of loyalty if he no longer thought working together was in his best interests.

And, although I'd believed it in the moment, I didn't know for a fact that anyone wanted to get rid of me. It'd be pretty stupid. I was a good, experienced editor. Did they want to get me under control? Oh, hell yeah. It had been clear in my meeting with Vaughn and Lila they thought I was all but running amuck at Millbrook House.

If there was a funny side to all this—well, there wasn't. But it was ridiculous that I was as upset about Finn as I was over someone trying to blackmail me. Or threaten me. Or whatever it was that U.N. Owen was trying to do.

I'd been awake since three o'clock in the morning trying to figure that out.

I'd tried some Google-Fu, and come across several non-Christie references to U.N. Owen.

According to Wikipedia, "U.N. Owen Was Her?" was a theme song composed by ZUN for the sixth Touhou Project game Embodiment of Scarlet Devil.

No. Me neither.

And according to a wiki Fandom, U.N. Owen was the newly created organization by Ludger Cherish and his brother Hans, created after Ludger destroyed the Red Society and started a Cooperative with the other three organizations (Black Rose Woman, Circus, and Old Kids).

Not ringing any bells.

I did come across a U.N. Owen who had self-published a fantasy novel in 2016. Sadly, that writing career appeared to have ended as the majority of writing careers did. It was hard to watch all that initial hope and excitement—the genuine passion for words and worlds—fade away through his many socials. I hoped he'd love the writing itself because so often that's the only reward for the hard work.

A quick scan of the Read Inside sample on Amazon convinced me that this Owen was a completely different writer from the author of *I Know What You Did*.

And that was pretty much it.

A dead end.

Then I'd tried researching Owen's address in Steeple Hill.

Through the property's sale and tax history, I was able to see that it had been a rental for the last decade. Through Redfin's Homeowner's Tools dashboard, I was able to get a list of names of possible previous owners.

Warren & Sherri McClendon

Blaine R. Adler

Maria E. Campos & Hector S. Ortega

Judith A. Latham

The Devlin Family Trust

None of the names meant anything to me. In any case, I wasn't planning on contacting the owner for the name of their tenant. I'd have that information myself once I drove to Steeple Hill that afternoon.

It was cold inside the hotel—the lobby being climate controlled for 600 conference attendees—and colder inside the elevator. I should have settled for the coffee maker in my room. But it was still early enough—or people had been drinking late enough—that I didn't run into anyone I knew. By the third floor, I was on my own again.

On the fourth floor, we lurched to a stop, the bell dinged as the doors began to open, and Lila stepped inside the car.

She was a short, big-boned woman of about fifty. Her brown eyes were wide set and her wiry black hair had a dramatic, natural streak of silver through it. She still favored red lipstick, chunky jewelry, big scarves, and stylish flats. The uniform of NYC legacy publishing lady editors.

She did not look at me. She was staring down at her phone, frowning.

"Good morning," I said.

She jumped, exclaimed, "Oh! *Keiran*. I've been texting you all morning."

That sounded all too familiar. Before I could respond, she peered at me doubtfully, taking in my wet hair and the damp towel over my shoulders. "Were you *swimming*?"

"Every morning." It was barely eight o'clock, so when had she started texting? I asked pleasantly, "What's up?"

Besides Lila, who, three cups of coffee in—assuming I remembered her work habits correctly—was already bouncing off the elevator ceiling.

"I don't remember you being a fitness nut."

"Just a nut?" I inquired, deadpan.

"*Ha*. That, yes. Listen, I thought we should have breakfast together."

I blinked. That would have been an unappetizing idea even if I'd had a good night's sleep. I could already feel the heartburn.

Not that I disliked Lila. We had never been friends, but we went way back and I respected her. She was smart, hardworking, and very good at her job. Also, very ambitious. She had not been easy to work for, but we got along fine once I was promoted to editor and we became equals. In fact, we were almost friendly during Steven Krass's tenure at Wheaton & Woodhouse. Lila and I were the ones who coined the nickname Satan. We'd hated Krass's guts.

I said regretfully, "I'm meeting someone for breakfast, but we could have coffee afterwards?"

Her scarlet mouth turned down. She looked troubled. "Is it with an author? Because that's really why I wanted to get together."

Was she serious? Of *course* I was having breakfast with an author. That's what meals at conferences were for. Did she think I was so far gone I planned on eating for my own pleasure?

In fairness to Lila, meeting with this particular author was a little problematical, given that Christopher Holmes was not yet, technically, on my editorial roster. However, if I knew Rachel Ving (and I did) that detail would be rectified before the conference ended on Sunday afternoon.

If, in the meantime, a little hand-holding was required, well, that was part of my job description: making authors feel seen and valued—and well-fed.

I said, "You want to get together to discuss having breakfast with authors?"

"Well… Well, yes! I think it's important that we're all working from the same script. There's bound to be anxiety over the merger, and we want to be sure we're delivering the right message. We don't want to worry anyone with the transmission of negative information. We need—it's *imperative*—we retain the right talent."

I said mildly, "That's a lot of corporate-speak to digest before coffee."

Her eyes narrowed. "Same old Keiran."

"They say no one ever really changes." I studied her. "Unless you know something I don't, we're working from the same script. It's as important to me as it is to you that Millbrook retains our top talent."

In fact, it was a hell of a lot more important to me than to her, given that my job security undoubtedly relied on it. I'd already taken one body blow that morning, losing Finn Scott from my list. I couldn't afford any more poaching.

Had she already spoken to Finn? Was that what this was about?

"Right," Lila said, although her tone sounded more like *wrong!* "Yes. *I* know you understand that. However, I feel it would project a more unified picture if we met with your authors together. As a team."

I absorbed that, weighed and considered my immediate response, then considered and weighed my alternative response.

When I thought I could answer without choking, I said mildly, "I see. And are we meeting with your authors together? As a team?"

Her cheeks turned pink. I'd rarely seen Lila miss a beat, but she seemed flustered as she replied, "What! *Why*? What sense does that make?"

The problem was, for all my telling myself that Finn's decision to work with another editor was, for *many* reasons, the right choice and the best thing for both of us, that wasn't how it felt. It hurt like hell on every possible level. I was still too raw, too upset, after our poolside chat, to be as diplomatic as I should've been.

I laughed none too nicely, and said, "I see."

And now, Lila was also upset. She bristled. "I'm not sure what that means. What do you imagine is happening here? This is standard operating procedure, Keiran. It's about projecting a united front. It's about…it's about team building."

Only if getting torn apart in the same arena by the same lions counted as teamwork.

Anyway, we both knew this was all total bullshit. It wasn't about team building. It wasn't about projecting a united front. It wasn't about reassuring authors that everything would be okay in the end, and if it wasn't okay, it wasn't the end. This salvo was strictly about giving Lila an opportunity to introduce herself to my authors, the better to cherry pick my list.

Maybe Vaughn had some vague idea that Lila and I would sit down together, put our egos aside, and try to figure out a way to match authors according to our own strengths and weaknesses. But I was pretty sure Lila's view was that she would decide who was expendable on her list and anyone and everyone on mine was up for grabs. I was pretty sure, because I felt the same way about my list.

I got myself back under control, even managed a tight smile. "I'm all for team building, Lila. And you're right. There's a lot of unease and anxiety about the merger."

"Exactly. We should be thinking of what's best for our *authors*—"

I kept right on talking.

"Just like you, I've spent years building relationships with my authors. They know me. They trust me. What message do you think it sends if I show up to a meeting where they're hoping I'm going to listen to and address their concerns—and I've suddenly got a corporate s-side-kick listening in?"

She said coldly, "I'm not and will never be your side-kick, Keiran."

No. And my first word choice had been *stooge*. That would have gone over even better.

"No, you're not. You're the senior editor with a publishing house they don't know, didn't submit their work to, and maybe haven't heard the best things about."

Her brows formed a straight and forbidding black line across her forehead. "At least *we're* solvent. At least *our* authors will get paid."

I ignored that. Millbrook had never not paid its authors. Some of the staff had been paid late this last year. Not the authors.

"If you don't trust me, then sure. You're welcome to sit in on breakfasts, lunches, and dinners with every single one of my authors." I winked. "Especially, if you're going to pick up our meal tabs."

She was not amused. But then, neither was I.

Lila said, "I had no idea you were so paranoid."

I retorted, "Neither did I."

Neither of us spoke for a moment, but then, as we reached the fifth floor and the bell *dinged*, she finally noticed the elevator was going up not down. She gaped at the floor indicator panel. "Where are we going?" She turned to me. "Did you book a luxury suite? Is Millbrook paying for your *suite*?"

"I paid for my own room." I got off the elevator, glanced back at her tight face. "Paranoia must be catching," I said.

Satisfying in the moment, but stupid. Stupid to antagonize her.

I had enough problems without going out of my way to make enemies.

More enemies.

Soaping my chest and underarms beneath the steaming rainfall spray in the oversized marble walk-in shower, I mentally ran through the day's schedule.

Breakfast with Christopher.

Coffee with Lila? Doubtful.

Cherry, my PA, was arriving around eleven. It was her first conference, so we'd need to go through some things.

Lunch with Connie and Gwen Dove, the sister writing team who did the Bookmobile & Beyond Mysteries. *Greta Merriweather delivers books—and uncovers bodies!* That one would be difficult. W&W felt sales had been soft for the last three books in the series. They'd already decided not to pick up the option on the next book.

Depending on how things went with the ladies, I hoped to catch Scottish crime writer Thomas McGregor's interview. If necessary, I could skip that.

Finn's interview with Rudolph was at three-thirty. That one I could definitely draw a line through, which meant I could leave for Steeple Hill right after the McGregor showcase. Or even after lunch.

The W&W banquet was scheduled to begin at seven—well, cocktails at seven, the dinner itself was eight, which gave me...not a hell of a lot of time to be poking around Steeple Hill before I had to make the drive back to Monterey. But how much time would it take to hear what a potential blackmailer had to say?

The important thing was to stick to the schedule. It was imperative to stay on track. Imperative to do nothing that appeared out-of-character or drew unwanted attention.

I listened to the echo of those thoughts and realized it sounded like I was prepping for the role of villain in *Poker Face* or *Columbo*.

I wasn't the villain of the piece. I had zero intention of doing anyone harm, let alone committing murder. But I also had no idea what I was dealing with. No idea what U.N. Owen wanted. Nothing good, seemed a safe assumption.

Maybe this situation could be resolved through open dialogue.

Probably not. Open dialogue would have likely started with...dialogue. Not a fake book submission.

Blackmail?

Blackmail was the obvious answer. I kept coming back to blackmail.

And, if this was indeed an attempt at extortion?

I wasn't going to be blackmailed. That was for damn sure.

But was I really prepared to go to the police? Confess my part in Dom's death?

The wave of cold nausea that swept over me answered that question.

And if I wasn't willing to go to the police—or give in to blackmail—what were my options?

Limited.

At best.

Had Milo received one of these... Well, he wouldn't have received a book submission. He wouldn't have received anything because how would anyone find him? I'd tried for years without success.

Unless Milo was the one behind U.N. Owen?

No. Once again paranoia was waving hello from the fun house. There was no way Milo could threaten me without putting himself in jeopardy.

No, Milo was not U.N. Owen. If not outright paranoia, the idea was surely wishful thinking.

Because Milo was almost certainly dead.

# Chapter Six

"I should have just stuck with Millbrook when I had the chance," Christopher Holmes was saying.

We were sitting in the comfortable indoor dining room of Wave Street Café. Sunshine glinted off the small forest of potted herbs and succulents lining the sills of high windows. Muted jazz played low beneath the clink of dishes and the hiss of the espresso machine. Tucked off Cannery Row and only about a three-minute walk from the hotel, the café was a cozy, upscale-casual breakfast and brunch spot popular with locals, but undiscovered (so far) by conference attendees.

"Why didn't you?" I'd been curious about that decision for a while.

His world-weary sigh was so heavy it nearly blew the foam cap off his vanilla latte.

"I don't know." He grimaced. "I was convinced either Rachel coerced you into it, or you were offering me a deal for old time's sake."

I put down my fork. "You think I'd offer you a book deal if I didn't actually want the book?"

His brown eyes met my gaze directly. "Yes."

*"Yes?"*

"I think you're sentimental, yes."

I smiled ruefully, "I'm not at all sentimental. I wanted that book. I loved working with you and I love Miss Butter-with. Hell, Miss B. was my first big discovery. I was more than happy to regain control of the series."

"But you wouldn't have regained control of the series because W&W still holds the backlist. And the sales had been soft on the last—"

I cut in, "That's not always the fault of the books or the author. Millbrook was prepared to give Miss B. some actual marketing support."

Christopher brightened. "And that's why I love working with *you*," he said. "You're the only editor I ever knew who was willing to admit that the fault in our stars doesn't always lie with the books." He took a bite of an almond croissant, hastily wiped away all the buttery flakes, and added, a little thickly, "Maybe *sentimental* isn't the right word, but I always thought you were pretty soft-hearted for this business."

I only hoped the Dove sisters agreed after we had our lunch that afternoon.

"I don't think Lila is going to kick too hard about losing you from her list. Most publishing houses will accommodate author preference when and where they can—"

He interrupted, "She's not going to kick at all. The Butterwith books bore her to tears and she *clearly* doesn't expect my standalone to set the world on fire."

I thought he was right, but refrained from comment. Cutting off a bite of my spinach and roasted tomato frittata, I asked, "*Have* you been giving any thought to the standalone?"

"Er...no."

I laughed. Classic Christopher Holmes.

"You know, it's been a busy year!" he pointed out.

"I know." I was still grinning.

"I had to solve *another* murder. And, even more stressful, I got married!"

"I know, and I'm very happy for you on both counts. Marriage becomes you."

As did solving murders.

No lie. I'd known Christopher a very long time. I'd been twenty-four when I'd fished Miss B. and Mr. Pinkerton out of the slush pile. That lady botanist and her clever cat had launched my career right along with Christopher's. The Christopher Holmes who sat before me, with the expensive highlights, tiny and tasteful gold ear piercings, and stylish jeans and white Cloak and Dagger T-shirt beneath a black blazer bore little resemblance to the cute but rumpled Christopher Holmes I'd first met all those years ago. But he was still the same funny, smart, and slightly irascible man.

Knowing we'd be working together again was the first real bright spot in what already felt like another very long day.

"You get used to it," he said casually.

"I'll take your word for it."

He considered me for a moment and then turned his attention once more to his crab eggs Benedict.

On our walk back to the hotel, we mostly chatted about the conference, the weather, and, of course, the next Miss Butterwith novel. By then, more conference goers—ye shall know them by their neck lanyards and Google Maps apps—were out and about, looking for somewhere to have breakfast.

The last trails of early morning fog dissipated as we neared the hotel. The sun shone brightly in the blue sky. It was going to be a beautiful day.

We were walking along the overlook behind the hotel when I glanced down and spotted a solitary figure on the beach below—broad shoulders, wind-ruffled hair, long, familiar stride. Even from this distance—well, I'd probably recognize Finn from outer space.

On impulse, I rested my hand on Christopher's arm. "I just want to have a quick word with someone. You know your way back from here?"

"Yeah, of course." His gaze was curious. "Thanks for breakfast—and for hearing me out."

I smiled. "You're welcome. As for hearing you out, we're on the same page. I'm not in position to make promises, but I'm confident it's going to work out."

"I am, too. If Rachel has anything to say about it."

I nodded distracted agreement, and peeled off to follow the cement walkway past the succulents and windswept cypress. Eventually, I found the shady narrow public path that curved alongside the hotel, and then descended toward San Carlos Beach.

Several yards ahead of me, Finn was still striding across the sand, head down, seeming lost in thought. I picked up my pace, crushed shell and gravel crunching beneath my shoes, all sound swallowed by the steady crash and retreat of the tide.

I didn't give myself time to reflect because if I stopped to think. I'd have turned around and headed back to the hotel. This had nothing to do with the books or anyone's career—his or mine. The simple truth was I didn't want—couldn't—leave things as they'd ended that morning.

The low retaining wall gave way to a short set of concrete stairs, edges slick with damp moss and sea spray. I took the steps quickly.

The smell of salt and kelp hit me as I reached the bottom—other smells as well: wet sand, something metallic and raw carried in off the bay. The air was cooler down here, the breeze sharper. My feet slipped and sank in the course, damp sand, as I picked my way through the scatter of broken shells and tangled strands of kelp.

It was much cooler and breezier down by the water. Sea lions barked from the far rocks, and gulls wheeled overhead, their cries sharp and fleeting.

Finn's back was to me, and as I grew nearer, I saw that he was on his phone. Or had been. The call seemed to have ended.

The waves didn't completely drown out my approach—or, more likely, Finn possessed more situational awareness than most people—and he glanced around.

His wary expression changed infinitesimally, but then he held up his phone and smiled ruefully. "The kiddo," he said, as if our a.m. encounter at the pool had never happened.

*The kiddo* was Finn's son, Byron, who was in his freshman year at UCLA.

I asked automatically, "Everything okay?"

"Yeah. He's a little homesick, I think."

My understanding was UCLA was less than an hour from home, but being homesick is not something I know anything about. I left Steeple Hill the day after I turned eighteen, and I never looked back.

I nodded and said, "Finn, I owe you an apology. You have every right to work with whomever you choose. Lila's an excellent editor. It probably *is* time to work with someone who can look at the series with fresh eyes."

His eyebrows rose. He remarked, "That was interesting, this morning. Outside of discussing books and having sex,

I think that was the first completely unguarded reaction I've ever had from you."

He spoke calmly, but the effect of that almost clinical tone was as cold and hard as if I'd been knocked down by one of those waves pounding the shore.

I was still trying to absorb it, when he added, "But, no. I'm the one who needs to apologize. I blindsided you. I'm sorry, Keir. You didn't deserve that. I should have expressed my concerns two weeks ago."

*Expressed my concerns.* Jesus. That was formal. Maybe he should have filled them out in triplicate while he was at it.

I didn't say that, of course. I took another couple of steps forward, close enough to catch the scent of that herbal aromatic aftershave, close enough to reach out and touch him, though I was pretty sure I'd never touch him again. "Yeah. That might have helped. What *are* your concerns? Because the last time we were together—"

"Why didn't you tell me your father had died?" he interrupted.

It was so far out of left field, my jaw dropped.

"I didn't know you knew him," I shot back.

"Another gut reaction," he observed. "You're offended. And angry."

What the hell? I *was* starting to get angry. "I wasn't close to my father. And that, you *do* know."

"I do know that. Yes. That's the extent of what I know about your family."

I spread my hands in genuine bafflement. What the hell did my family have to do with *anything*?

Finn said, "I'm not sure how to put this without hurting you. More than I already have. And that's the last thing I want to do. I really...*really* care for you. It's not about writing or my career, though yes, I'm grateful. I do feel—will always feel—that I owe you. A lot."

"I don't want gratitude."

"I know." He drew a hard breath. "And that's not what this is. This is about...us."

He stopped again. This time I couldn't think of anything to say.

At least I hadn't imagined that there had been, briefly, *us*.

Finally, Finn said, "You're a good friend. You're intelligent and charming and...insightful. You're generous. I think you're genuinely kind."

*Insightful.*

I said through stiff lips, "That's funny. I thought you were kind, too."

His eyes, green as the waves pounding the sand, flickered. It hit home, I think, but he hardened his jaw. "I like being with you. And I did want—for a long time I hoped maybe there would be more."

My heart was slamming against my ribs in heavy thuds. If I'd been hooked to a cardiac monitor, I think alarm bells would have been going off. I could almost hear the panicked jangle of my emotions, like windchimes caught in a hurricane. I didn't want to hear what he was going to say. I wanted to walk away. But I couldn't move. Couldn't speak.

"But there's something..."

*Wrong with you.*

Those were the words he was looking for.

What he said instead was, "...going on with you. It isn't anything new. I realized it a long time ago. At first, I thought you were just very reserved. Then I thought it was hard for you to trust. That you'd been hurt. I told myself you had a fear of intimacy. But it's more than that, isn't it?"

I said tightly, "You tell me, Dr. Phil."

He didn't bite. "We were together for almost four days and you never once mentioned your father had died the week before. I know you weren't close, but there should have been some reaction."

"How would you know, a week after the fact, what reaction I had?"

"You also didn't mention you'd been in California for his funeral. We'd been talking about seeing more of each other, seeing where this...friendship might lead."

"That trip was *before*," I protested. "Before we talked about any of that."

In fairness, we hadn't even really talked about *that* in any practical sense. We'd just sort of agreed that we both wanted more and that Monterey might be the time to explore some of those possibilities.

"I know." He seemed genuinely apologetic—but also absolutely adamant. "I've been trying to figure out how to put it into words without— What I'm trying to say is, I've known—felt—for a long time that something isn't right. Finding out about your father's death crystallized it for me."

I made a sound of disbelief.

"My instinct is you're...hiding something. And I'm too old to wake up and find myself in a-a *Dateline* special."

I think it was random, a shot in the dark, a little flicker of black humor. Or maybe it really was a cop—former cop's—instinct?

But it hit home, hit the target dead center. *Bullseye.*

I couldn't move a muscle, couldn't breathe for a moment.

No small part of my horror was the belated understanding of what it would have meant to drag someone else—to have dragged Finn—into the mess I found myself in.

I guess I'd gotten away with it for so long, I'd started believing I really had escaped. The risk to someone else hadn't occurred to me until Finn articulated it. But yes. If—and now it was feeling more like *when*—the truth about Dom's death came out, the wrecking ball wouldn't just hit me. It would smash into whoever was sharing my life. I didn't want that. Would never have been okay with that. I would never knowingly have done anything to hurt Finn.

As Finn stared at me, realization slowly dawned on his face. He looked stunned. And then aghast.

He said incredulously, "I was thinking more on the lines of secret wife."

"No, you weren't."

His voice dropped; I couldn't hear it over the crash of waves hitting the shore. But I saw his lips form soundless words, "What the hell, Keiran?"

I had no answer. What could I say? To Finn, of all people.

The idea that *we* were going to build some kind of Happily Ever After? I must have been out of my mind.

I could feel a weird smile forming. It wasn't humor. I don't know what it was aside from an inappropriate response to extreme nervous tension. But I could see Finn's eyes getting darker and bleaker.

"Is this funny to you?" he asked.

I turned and walked away.

# Chapter Seven

It's true. No good deed goes unpunished.

Not that all my deeds had been good ones. Even in the moment, I'd never kidded myself about that. But I sure as hell had never intended to do *bad* deeds. I had never acted out of malice.

Did Finn think I was a sociopath? In addition to the other things he thought about me?

Maybe.

Would I know if I was a sociopath?

Maybe not.

What I did know was that I needed to stay as far away from former San Clemente homicide detective Phineas Scott as humanly possible. No more apologies or explanations or efforts to stay friends. Finn was now a threat to me. A clear and present danger.

But *was* he? Or was that my mounting paranoia kicking in?

He didn't *know* anything. And without having at least a starting point, there was no way of his ever finding out more than he'd already guessed. That I had a past. Secrets. That there were things in my life I preferred keeping to myself.

That was it. That was the extent of what he knew. Okay, *and* I was reserved, I had trust issues, and a fear of intimacy. Oh, and yes, I'd been hurt.

In short, your typical forty-year-old American male.

I mean, talk about trust issues: *Ladies and gentlemen, I give you Finn Scott!*

There was no reason to think he was going to start poking around in my past. He wasn't a cop anymore. There was nothing for him to gain by starting his own personal investigation. I believed him when he said he was grateful to me for the help I'd given throughout his career. He was not going to go out of his way to try to ruin me. He had enough going on in his own life without expending time and energy sifting through the rubble of mine.

All I'd ever wanted was peace and quiet and a life spent safely folded between the pages of books. And I'd had that for two very short decades. And then, foolishly, I'd begun to want more, to think that more was possible.

But it wasn't possible. At this point, I would be beyond lucky to find my way back to the sanctuary of that peaceful, quiet life I'd built for myself.

The bar in the lobby was mostly empty when I arrived back at the hotel. Cool, quiet, and mostly empty was exactly what I needed, and I sat down to browse the small menu card of signature conference cocktails. Today was the first full day of panels, which explained the relative calm on the ground floor.

I spotted Hayes Hartman and several other of the young guns of neo noir huddled in one of the cozy seating arrangements near the huge windows overlooking the bay. They were laughing too much and too loudly, and I surmised they were priming the pump before their panels.

The waitress appeared and I ordered the Red Herring. Vodka, Aperol, blood orange, lemon juice, and a splash of sparkling water—garnished with a twist of orange peel.

Citrus, so...practically breakfast juice. Not that I was a big day drinker. I wasn't a heavy drinker at any time, really, but I had a long afternoon ahead—and there was no point pretending I wasn't shattered after the heart-to-heart with Finn.

Anyway.

I glanced at my watch, tried not to listen to Hayes sharing more literary insights from across the room.

"The thing is," Hayes was saying, his voice perfectly modulated for projection, "neo-noir isn't about shadows and trench coats anymore. That's aesthetic window dressing. What we're really talking about is existential rot in the age of late capitalism. The femme fatale isn't a woman now—she's the algorithm. The detective? He's a ghost. Or a gig worker. If your protagonist isn't actively losing his grip on reality, what are you even doing? That's not noir. That's just... crime fiction in a hat."

Had anyone *asked* him?

Thankfully, my drink arrived to numb the pain.

It was nice. The cocktail, that is. Bright and playful but with a sneaky kick. I was three sips in when a cheerful female voice said from behind me, "Reporting for duty, sir!"

I managed not to jump, pasted on a smile of welcome, turning in my seat.

"Cherry! How was your flight?"

Cherry Bing, my PA, was a small, twenty-something Asian-American woman. She wore black jeans, black T-shirt, black blazer, and black ballet flats. The uniform of the young NYC legacy editor. Her hair was piled on her head in one of those deliberately messy I-ran-my-hand-through-it-while-reading-something-brilliant styles. She'd been working for me for about six months, and I already considered her indispensable. Her excitement and enthusiasm for the business was a daily reminder of why books, why fiction, still mattered in a world dominated by technology.

"It was great! I got to sit with Amelia."

"That's nice." Amelia was our romantic-suspense editor. I'd already heard from Lila that W&W considered RS in decline, and as they already had their own romantic-suspense line, they would have trouble justifying a second.

"She's *so* nice," Cherry agreed.

"Would you like a drink?"

Cherry's eyes widened. "Sure!"

I nodded to the waitress, who came in for another landing. Cherry ordered a Cosmo. I ordered a second Red Herring, as a preventive measure.

Cherry told me all about her flight, and I nodded and murmured encouragement when she paused for breath. In the background I could hear the constant refrain of Hayes.

"And don't get me started on these nostalgic callbacks. Noir isn't a mood—it's a mirror. If your story isn't holding up a cracked reflection of the cultural moment, then you're just dressing up trauma in a leather jacket and calling it edgy."

Good luck getting a word in edgewise to anyone on a panel with Mr. Hartman.

What in the hell did Finn *see* in that guy?

But then again: *insightful.*

What did that even *mean*?

Our drinks arrived. This round, I paced myself.

"I'm a little nervous," Cherry confided, two sips in. "I'm not really sure what I'm supposed to *do*."

"No, no. Don't be nervous. That's for authors. In fact, that's how you need to look at it. You're basically here as a liaison for our authors. I've emailed you a list this morning with every attending author, their assigned panel topic, and when their panel is. It's your job to get in touch with them before the panel and make sure they have what they need—"

Her lips parted. I said, "They'll have what they need, don't worry about that. Well, maybe someone will need a safety pin or a pen or a shot of bourbon."

She giggled. "A *safety pin*?"

"A hat pin?" I winked. "I don't know. Basically, you're just letting them know that we're here to support them. We appreciate them getting out and promoting the books, which is what a conference boils down to. The better they do, the better the books do, the better we do."

"Am I supposed to go to the panels?"

"Yes."

*"Really?"* She looked ridiculously delighted. Had she never been to one of these before?

"Yes. Really."

"What if there are two different—"

"Split the difference. Unless we're talking a top tier author. I won't be able to get to Finn Scott's panel, so you sit in on that one. He's an old hand at this, but check in with him and make sure he's got whatever he needs. He will. Don't worry."

"You're *not* going to Finn's panel?" Cherry looked astonished.

Finn and I had not been nearly as discreet as we should have been.

"No. Another thing, if during the Q&A, our authors aren't getting questions, throw them a couple of softballs. That's probably not going to happen. I think I've seen it once in fourteen years. Oh, and at the end of the panel, remember to go up and tell them they did a great job."

"I can't believe I get paid to go to panels!"

"Well, it's the usual stuff as well. You'll be checking my e—"

"Your email?" She nodded.

"Actually, no. Don't worry about my email this weekend. Don't worry about phone messages. You'll have your hands full coordinating everyone's schedules and meetings."

"But I'm *your* PA"

"This weekend, you're everyone's PA Don't worry. I've been doing this practically as long as you've been alive. I've got it down to a science."

She spluttered another of those cute giggles. "How old do you think I am?"

"Twenty-three."

"Oh."

I laughed. "Any questions, any problems, come to *me*." I checked my phone. "I've got to go. I'm taking the Dove sisters to lunch."

"*Ohhh*." She looked sympathetic. Whether on my behalf or the Dove sisters, I wasn't sure.

I rose. "I'll pay for our drinks at the bar—and I'll see you tonight at the banquet."

She nodded, hesitated, then said suddenly, urgently, "Keiran?"

"Hm?"

"About the merger."

I automatically glanced around the room, said, "What about it?"

"Amelia was saying on the plane that she heard from someone at W&W that they don't have PAs. They have two editorial assistants to fill that role for all their editors and assistant editors."

Having been one of those editorial assistants, I could confirm the grim truth of that. At least back in my day, I'd mostly only had to contend with Lila.

Cherry's voice wobbled a little. "Amelia said I should start looking for something else now. She thinks she's going to be let go, too." She swallowed, said, "I just really... I love my job. I can adapt."

*Be careful what you wish for, kid.*

"Of course you can," I said. "We're all going to have to adapt, one way or the other."

Judging by her expression, that sounded bleaker than I intended.

I said, "It's supposed to be a merger. In theory, we're combining the two businesses and keeping what works best from each house. They make more money. We make better books. I'm going to fight for the things that go into making better books, which includes our people. But I'm not going to win every battle." I admitted, "I can't predict the future. I don't want to lose you. It might not be my choice."

She considered, frowned, then beamed at me and said brightly, "But it *might* be!"

I laughed reluctantly. "It might. I hope so. I'll see you tonight."

That was the beauty of youthful optimism. At twenty-three I, too, had believed things would ultimately turn out the way I wanted. And by then I'd had plenty of evidence to the contrary. But at twenty-three, I'd also had the strength to weather the storms. Now I was older and wiser. Now I knew that the right storm at the wrong moment could wreck me.

Hayes and his crowd had moved on. A crowd of well-groomed middle-aged women in pastel business attire had taken their place. These were the established cozy chick contingent. They'd been successfully writing about twenty-something amateur sleuth bakers and amateur sleuth wedding planners and amateur sleuth florists for the last thirty years.

As they debated, with much giggling, the naughtiness of ordering nibbles with their cocktails so close to lunchtime, I paid the bartender and headed for the elevators.

I needed to change before lunch. The Dove sisters offered a very different dining experience from the Kyle Baris and the Christopher Holmeses. I seemed to recall they'd worn gloves the last time I'd taken them out.

I also needed to remember to have Cherry change my flight home. No point now in spending a couple of extra days in Monterey. Finn and I would not be exploring the possibilities or anything else. I refused to acknowledge the sinking feeling in my chest at yet another reminder of things that weren't going to go as hoped. Yep. It was sad. It was disappointing. Life would go on.

The cure for all of it was to immerse myself in work. The sooner I returned to my busy and comfortable routine, the better.

Rudolph Dunst, editorial director at Theodore Mansfield, stepped into the elevator right before me. He was probably in his seventies by now, forever tall, silver, and vaguely translucent—like the ghost of whoever had edited Edith Wharton's early drafts. The years had been lenient with him, possibly out of professional courtesy.

We nodded cordially, and then I glanced casually back at the man who'd silently followed me into the elevator.

Finn.

I jumped. There was no hiding that alarmed start. Finn gazed at me steadily, silently. Still pissed off to discover he'd been right all along?

"Floors?" Rudolph reached for the control panel.

"Rooftop," I said.

Finn said, "Third."

It was weird to feel so self-conscious and uncomfortable with Finn. A few weeks ago, I'd felt comfortable enough, felt like I knew him well enough to...consider getting to know him better? Because, really, that's all it had come down to in the end.

Still. Weird to feel so strained and awkward with someone you'd had sex with in the shower. Weird to know how someone's hair smelled wet, to know the sounds they made during sex, how their mouth felt when it smiled against your own.

I hoped to God I wasn't going to experience this every time we bumped into each other.

Not that we'd bump into each other so often after this weekend.

Rudolph beamed in belated recognition. "Keiran, my boy! How are you?"

"*Very* well," I replied firmly. The firmness was for Finn's benefit.

He glanced Finn. "*Ah*! And Mr. Scott. I'm looking forward to this afternoon."

Rudolph was conducting Thursday's special guest author interview with Finn. A nice coup for Finn.

"Me, too, sir," Finn answered courteously.

Rudolph chuckled. "*Sir.* You're making me feel old." He turned back to me. "You look tired, Keiran. You need to learn to pace yourself. Not every battle's worth fighting."

"That's for sure," I said more tersely than I'd intended.

Rudolph's silvery brows rose.

I'd known, and admired, him a long time. While he hadn't been a mentor, exactly, he'd been extremely kind and always given me excellent advice. When I'd been a very young editor, I'd aspired to grow up to be Rudolph Dunst.

"How's this merger with Wheaton & Woodhouse coming?" he inquired kindly.

"It's more of a buyout." I was acutely conscious of Finn's listening silence.

"It always is."

"But it's preferable to bankruptcy."

"Unfortunately, Millie doesn't have her grandmother's creative vision or her father's business acumen."

I wasn't about to respond to that, not in front of Lila's newest acquisition, but I agreed one hundred percent.

"The industry's changing," Rudolph remarked. "Just the fact that we now refer to it as an industry."

Really, we'd been referring to it as an industry as long as I'd been in publishing, but I nodded.

"It's *all* changed, of course," Rudolph reflected. "The world itself."

"Yes."

"When I started, publishing was smaller—more insular, certainly, but also slower, more deliberate. You cultivated a list over years, sometimes decades. An editor's name carried weight. Authors knew you were in it with them for the long haul. Now…" He offered a graceful shrug. "There's so much noise. So much urgency. Platforms, data, engagement. The books are still there, of course—good ones, worthy ones—but the pace at which they're expected to prove themselves would make even Hemingway sweat. I don't dislike the evolution, necessarily. But I do miss the quiet."

"Algorithms and AI." My smile was rueful. "Metadata, TikTok reviews and platforms." It was an acknowledgement not a complaint. Things change.

"One must evolve or face extinction," Rudolph said. "Which is why this is my last conference."

*"What?"*

I felt Finn stare at me. Rudolph seemed amused at my reaction. "I'm retiring at the end of the year. I only promised to stay on that long if I didn't have to attend any more damned conferences."

"You're *retiring?*"

He chuckled. "Don't sound so shocked."

"No. It's just… It's like hearing Patience and Fortitude handed in their notice."

Patience and Fortitude were the famed marble lions who stand guard before the entrance of the New York Public Library. Rudolph laughed heartily.

"I'll tell you frankly, I'm looking forward to it. I'll miss the people, of course, but a lot of the people I started with are gone now."

"I'm so sorry about Anna," I said sincerely. "I can only imagine what a shock that must have been."

Anna Hitchcock, the *American Agatha Christie* per Theodore Mansfield's marketing department, had died suddenly the previous winter at the annual writing retreat she hosted at her New England estate. She'd not only been TM's bestselling author, rumor had it she and Rudolph had had a long-standing romantic relationship. If so, they'd been more discreet than me and Finn.

Rudolph said vaguely, "Yes, it's a very different world without Anna. She was...one of a kind."

"Yes."

I'd always wondered at the legendary creative partnership between Anna Hitchcock and Rudolph Dunst. Rudolph was kind and courteous, a throwback to another generation. Anna was extremely talented, very clever, but rather chilly. Even her books...so entertaining, but a little cruel.

The elevator jolted to a stop on the third floor. The doors slid open and revealed a small crowd. Finn nodded politely to the space between Rudolph and me, and stepped off the elevator. The crowd parted for him, the Red Sea making way for Moses. Followed by the usual startled, "Oh, are you going *up*?" before the doors slid shut.

"He's a taciturn fellow, isn't he?" Rudolph remarked, as we continued our ascent. "But then he writes those bleak police procedurals. All that violence and betrayal and corruption." He added with a twinkle, "They're very well edited. I'll give them that."

I chuckled.

We talked about nothing in particular until the elevator reached the fifth floor.

"Would you like to stop by for a drink?" Rudolph asked, as we stepped into the hallway. "I always enjoy our chats."

"I'd love to. I'm taking two authors to lunch. Another time?"

"Absolutely. Tonight's the W&W banquet?"

"Yes."

"That should be interesting. Well, enjoy yourself, my boy. No doubt I'll see you at Saturday night's grand event."

"I look forward to it."

We turned and went our separate ways.

# Chapter Eight

"But the good news is, they—*we*—absolutely want to see what you come up with next," I said to Connie and Gwen.

I was treating the Dove sisters to lunch at Fandango in Pacific Grove, about a ten-minute drive from the hotel. The Uber had let us out in front of a low, golden-stone building draped in ivy, its windows shaded by striped awnings and baskets of trailing geraniums. Inside, the restaurant smelled faintly of butter and wood smoke—a comforting blend of old money and European charm, which I'd guessed the sisters would appreciate.

Judging by the coos of approval from the ladies as the hostess led us to a table by the fireplace, I'd guessed correctly.

Soft classical music played beneath the genteel chime of crystal and the low murmur of conversation, The room was painted in warm ochres and cream, and linen tablecloths draped over polished wood like pressed napkins over a lap. Like the sisters, it was the kind of place that hadn't changed its decor in decades. It had no reason to.

Unlike the sisters.

"But we still had so many more adventures in store for Greta," Connie protested tearfully.

Gwen pleaded, "Things were just heating up with Mike the Magician!"

Yes, mobile librarian Greta Merriweather's romantic interest was a professional magician by the name of Michael Cassillas. How the hell Mike earned a living doing magic tricks out in the middle of the Adirondacks was the greatest mystery of the series.

"I know, and gosh, that would have been fun," I told them. "But maybe what you could do is write a little bonus novella and put it on your website, so that fans of the series can see that Greta and Mike did get their Happy Ever After."

They looked so absolutely blank, I wondered if they even *had* a website.

Truthfully, I'd never been a big fan of Greta Merriweather. I'd inherited Greta and the Dove sisters from Daniel Millbrook, who'd inherited them from his mother, our founder, Ethel Millbrook. Greta was Daniel's idea. The sisters were longtime family friends. They'd been schoolmates of Ethel, and Millbrook had been publishing their brand of cozy mystery for more than fifty years. They didn't have an agent to represent their interests, but until the merger with W&W, it hadn't mattered.

Now it mattered.

Fortunately, our drinks arrived before the tears began to fall. For the ladies, small glasses of chilled Lillet Blanc over ice with a twist of orange. For me, Hochstadter's Rock and Rye.

The ladies sipped cautiously.

"It's very nearly a sherry," Connie said approvingly.

"It's very nearly a cocktail," Gwen muttered.

I said, "It's always hard to say goodbye to old friends, but it's a *little* exciting to start a new chapter, right?"

"*No,*" they cried in unison.

I winced.

"Does Millie know about this?" Gwen demanded.

I was saved from answering by the arrival of our smoked salmon rosettes on cucumber rounds.

The Doves dug in to the hors d'oeuvres, debating with each other as to whether the salmon was indeed Scottish or came from Maine, while our server patiently waited to take their lunch requests. I opted for the Niçoise salad. Eventually, the ladies settled on the quiche of the day—a rich, custardy number with mushrooms and Gruyère—and agreed to share a plate of grilled asparagus with hollandaise. Oh, and the salmon, in their expert opinion, was in fact from New Zealand.

The server raised her brows at me, and departed.

With these pressing matters attended to, I tried to steer the Doves back to business.

"There must be other stories you'd enjoy writing, don't you think? Other worlds you'd like to explore through fiction?"

"We've put our heart and soul into Greta and the people of Sugarcoat Inlet."

"Every character is like one of our own dear neighbors. And Greta and Mike are *family*," Connie said.

"And our readers feel the same," Gwen insisted.

Yes. Their readers did feel the same. The problem was, their readers were dying out faster than the unfortunate visitors to Sugarcoat Inlet. Greta's demo was a small one and shrinking fast.

The modern cozy was funny and snappy and sharp. The characters were diverse, their challenges more real world. The Bookmobile & Beyond Mysteries were none of these things.

I said cautiously, "You know, if you're simply not interested in writing anything else, there's no shame in choosing to retire."

They'd had a good run, and after all, they had to be in their mid-to-late seventies. At least.

"*Retire!*" they chorused in horror.

"We can't afford to *retire!*" Gwen exclaimed.

"It isn't just the money," Connie put in. "Writing is our...our...purpose. It gives our lives meaning."

"Exactly," Gwen said. "It's our *raisin*. Our...*raisin d'ours*."

"Raison d'être," I said automatically.

"*Correct!*" they said.

"Okay. If that's the case, then you're going to have to get serious about coming up with a new proposal for W&W."

Gwen said excitedly, "*Oh*! What if Mike the Magici—"

"No," I said firmly. "Something completely new. New characters. New setting. New premise."

They looked crestfallen. And a little frightened.

I was shepherding the Dove sisters through the glass doors of the hotel when Lila charged out of the now-packed lobby bar to intercept me.

"What did you say to Finn Scott?" she demanded, ignoring the sisters.

I looked past her to the bar, where I saw a table of W&W editors watching us with open curiosity.

I said calmly, "When?"

"Today. Whenever! What did you tell him?"

"About what? Working with you? I said you're an excellent editor. I said I hoped you'd both be very happy together."

Her eyes narrowed. "The hell you did. You either told him he owed you or you played the pity card. Or both. I'm guessing both."

*The pity card?*

My heart sped up in a rush of adrenalin. Lila had a reputation for being brusque and abrasive, but that was actually the first time I'd ever known her to be deliberately, offensively rude. In public. Or maybe it was just the first time I'd been on the receiving end of her full outrage.

However, if there was one thing I knew how to do, it was hide my feelings. I gave her my best blank look.

The Doves, though, gasped, their faces flushing pink beneath the powder.

Connie glared at Lila. Gwen put her hand on my arm and said pointedly, "Thank you for a wonderful lunch, Keiran. *And* your usual kindness and wisdom."

They treated Lila to their pale and icy stares before departing in their little ladylike beige pumps.

Lila watched them go. She said with scornful amusement. "I guess the Snoop Sisters told *me*." She glared. "I don't know what you think you're accomplishing, Keiran, by dragging authors into your private war with us."

I blinked. "As far as I know, I'm one of *us*. And I'm not sure what you think you're accomplishing by bringing this up in the middle of a hotel lobby."

That gave her a moment's pause. But she drew herself up and said coldly, "Maybe you should inform Mr. Scott that the *editorial director* at Wheaton & Woodhouse will have the final say on who he works with moving forward. That is not your decision to make. Nor *his*."

Sure. First of all, Finn's latest was already through co-pyediting and typesetting. We were firmly in production now, and barring some last-minute catastrophe, the book would go to press on schedule. As for his next project? Yes, we'd chatted about it, casually, informally. He had yet to propose it. Meaning, nothing—including Finn—was under contract.

Did Lila imagine Finn's agent wasn't aware that they were free to take that book wherever they liked? Did she imagine that Finn and his agent had no idea how much W&W wanted that book?

I said, "I suggest you bring that up with Mr. Scott's agent. Scott told me this morning he'd decided you were right about changing things up, getting a fresh perspective." I shrugged.

Her eyes narrowed. "Oh please! And you're pretending you were fine with that?"

"No, but I could see it from his viewpoint."

"You're forgetting who you're talking to. I *know* you, Keiran."

I couldn't help laughing. "*Do* you?"

"Yes! You weren't remotely open to the idea of Scott leaving your list. And I think we both know why."

"For a lot of reasons," I agreed. "But it's not my decision, so I'll let Finn fight that battle. Who's the new editorial director at W&W?" Not me, obviously.

She smiled. "You're looking at her."

"Congratulations."

"I'll take that in the spirit I know it was offered."

I sighed, and didn't bother to make it sound any less wearied than I felt.

"This is going to get old, don't you think?"

"It's already old," she said. "I know three things about you, Keiran. You never say what you're really thinking. You like to think of yourself as an old school gentleman like...like Rudolph Dunst, but you're just a thug in nice clothes. And three, you pretend to be *so* kind and charming, but you are absolutely ruthless." Confusingly, she concluded with *Hamlet* Act 1, scene 5, *"That one may smile, and smile, and be a villain!"*

I quoted back doubtfully, *"At least I am sure it may be so in Denmark?"*

"What the hell are you *talking* about?"

I said, "Is this because nine years ago I took the senior editor position at Millhouse?"

"*I* promoted you. *I* trained you. And when you were *finally* of use, you left us and went to the *competition*. Now you think you can waltz back in and take *my* job. I don't think so!"

"Okay, well, that wasn't my plan. And clearly, it's not a worry anymore. So perhaps we can just move on from here and deal with things as they are."

"Do *not* patronize me."

"You should have another chat with Mr. Scott," I said. "I'm pretty sure he'll have changed his mind again in your favor."

She eyed me narrowly.

I said, "If we're done for the moment, I'm going to see if I can catch the last few minutes of the McGregor interview."

"Thomas McGregor? He's not with either of us. He's not with W&W or Millhouse."

"Right. He's with Peregrin Press. I enjoy his books."

"You..."

But, yes. I still read for pleasure, now and again. In fact, I thought it was important for writers and editors to continue to read for pleasure. At the very least, it was a great way to remind yourself why you got into such a precarious business to start with.

I nodded politely at the table of W&W editors, still staring our way, and departed.

It was standing room only in the Cypress Ballroom where Thomas McGregor was being interviewed by Nan Goodwin at Noir Nation. This was the first of the conference's Smoking Gun author interviews—and McGregor's first visit to the U.S.—so the size of the audience was not a surprise.

I had trouble concentrating. McGregor had a thick brogue and spoke softly; when they tried to jack up the mic, it started to feed back.

I'd already missed half the interview by the time I squeezed into the back. Almost immediately I spotted Finn and his sidekick Hayes Hartman sitting in the middle of the audience. It would have been hard to miss them—Finn, anyway—because the people around them kept leaning over to tell him they loved his books. So that didn't help my ability to focus, but the main distraction was my conversation with Lila.

I was surprised by how much it had rattled me.

*A thug?*

*Me?*

That was a first. What in the hell was she talking about?

What thuggish thing had I ever done to her? To anyone?

Also, I was confused as to why Finn had changed his mind about going with Lila after our poolside chat. That was moot now, of course, following our conversation on the beach.

Anyway, Finn was the least of my concerns at the moment.

During the meeting with Vaughn and Lila, Vaughn had discussed the eventual possibility of creating a new position, that of editorial director. But he'd made it sound like that was something to be decided after the merger, after we'd all had a chance to work together, to evaluate our various strengths.

The position itself made sense. And it made sense that Vaughn would tap Lila for the role. But I wasn't happy. Given the increasing strain between myself and Lila— well, let's be honest. I wouldn't have been happy about it even if Lila and I had been getting along like old chums.

They hadn't been wrong. I *was* used to running my own little kingdom. The idea of working under Lila's brand of micromanagement was not appealing.

To say the least.

For the first time I seriously considered leaving Millhouse.

It was a truly depressing thought.

I'd declined to sign the DNC clause Vaughn insisted we all had to agree to in order to continue our employment under the new entity (which increasingly sounded like the same old W&W with a few new faces). That wasn't me striking a pose. It was survival instinct. I'd been in the book biz my entire adult life. I knew no way of earning a living outside of publishing. I couldn't afford to sign a no-compete. Especially once I recognized my tenure at W&W might be more insecure than I'd realized.

My refusal had ruffled a few feathers, but in the end, Vaughn—to Lila's clear disapprobation—had accepted it. But I'd used up a lot of good will with my refusal to sign.

While I had the option to leave, to start over somewhere else, the idea was daunting. At my age? I wasn't a kid. And the idea of rebuilding my author list over the next twenty years was overwhelming.

Worse, I wasn't sure where I'd even go. The industry had changed so much. The old indies were vanishing, eaten up by corporate players or quietly folding under the weight of rising costs and impossible margins. Editors were expected to be marketing machines now—part tastemaker, part influencer. There were fewer houses, fewer opportunities, and more pressure to chase trends and turn viral moments into publishing strategies. I didn't specialize in BookTok sensations or high-concept hook-and-sinkers. My strengths lay in developing voices, shaping series, building careers—but that kind of long game didn't show up in quarterly reports.

Even if someone was hiring, I wasn't exactly the bright young thing anymore—unless, I was being compared to Rudolph Dunst.

The truth was, I wasn't sure I had the stomach to start all over again—with no authors, no backlist, no leverage.

So yes, I could leave. Technically, the door was open. Realistically, there was no telling if there was anything on the other side of the door but air.

Perhaps I could turn freelance, but truthfully, I wasn't much of a risk taker. I liked routine and regular paychecks.

I could retire.

My heart shrank at the idea—much as the Doves had recoiled at the suggestion.

No, I couldn't.

Even if I could afford to—selling my father's property in Steeple Hill would help a little, but not enough—what the hell would I do with myself? I didn't *want* to retire. I loved my work. I felt like what I did was important; that I offered value to the world.

I needed to believe that.

But the world, too, was changing. And maybe the value I added was becoming irrelevant.

Rows of chairs ahead, I watched Hayes lean over to whisper something to Finn. Watched Finn's profile crease in a smile.

Maybe *I* was becoming irrelevant.

# Chapter Nine

Steeple Hill was smaller than I remembered.

Smaller. More self-conscious.

Narrow streets once lined with squat, weathered storefronts and sagging wooden awnings were now home to cute boutiques and quaint coffeehouses. Steeple Hill was a tourist destination now, and it showed. The old general store, windows plastered with sun-faded flyers and yellowing notices from the 1960s, had been replaced by a bright and shiny VONS with a parking lot large enough to accommodate half the town should everyone decide to go shopping at the same time. There was still only one gas station, but Joey's leaning, rust-streaked signpost had been replaced with a towering Valero neon sign that at night could be spotted from the main highway.

I'm not sure what made me turn down Seaside Lane. It had never entered my mind when I'd returned for my father's funeral. After the funeral I'd gone straight to the Realtor's office, told them to dump everything in the house, fix the place up, and put it on the market for as much as they could possibly get. I had been clear about never wanting to see it again.

I was still clear about never wanting to see it again.

And yet I'd brought the key. And here I was, driving down Seaside Lane, for one last look.

It turned out property values had jumped over the last few decades and $1.5 million for three beds, two baths in the heart of Steeple Hill had attracted multiple offers. There was no mortgage on the house, so yes. If W&W decided my services were no longer needed, I'd have a little breathing room. Not much, given the rental price of a loft apartment in Manhattan.

Between the houses and twisted oaks, I caught glimpses of the old cemetery on the hill, marble headstones leaning like recumbent stones on an archeology dig site.

A little chill slithered down my spine. It was a very old burial ground, dating back to the 1800s. Nobody had been buried there in decades. That I knew of.

Anyway, there was another historic cemetery over by the art colony, which was theoretically still in use. Back in the day, people bought family plots, sometimes large enough to accommodate generations. My father, who had made no final plans, was buried in Skylawn Memorial Park in San Mateo, about thirty miles away. It could have been Mars. Either way, I was never going to visit his grave.

A lot of the homes through here were now rentals or Airbnbs. Freshly painted and newly landscaped, their colors glistened bright and clean against the dull, sea-stained clapboard of their neighbors. In fact, I almost missed our house as I rounded the last bend in the road, the once dusty blue siding now painted pristine white, the tall, multipaned windows gleaming like polished crystal. The ragged memory of lawn had been replaced by glittering white stone and some kind of driftwood sculpture. Very beach cottage-y.

I parked on the sandy apron in front of the house, the engine ticking as it cooled. For a few seconds, I just sat there, fingers clenching the key I'd dug out of the back of my desk drawer in New York. My heart was thumping unpleasantly.

After all, I wasn't sure my key would even still work. The locks could have been changed after the renovation.

Which would probably be for the best.

Finally, I got out of the car and went through the gate, walking past the FOR SALE sign in the front yard. Seashell chimes hung from the porch rafters, clinking dully in the warm, still air. Sunlight filtered through the overgrown branches of the neighboring house's trees, casting thin, lacy shadows across the freshly painted wood siding.

The newly sanded and varnished porch steps creaked beneath my weight. Sweat broke out on my forehead as I reached the front door—now painted a bright and cheery sea blue.

What I'd told Kyle was true. I wasn't sentimental. So why was I—

My key slid easily into the lock, the mechanism turning with a flat, metallic click. The door swung inward, the sudden rush of cool, stale air carrying the faint, unmistakable scent of fresh paint and sanded wood.

Unfamiliar. Safe.

I stepped inside, blinking as my eyes adjusted to the dim, echoing space. The walls, once papered in faded floral patterns, were now a stark, antiseptic white. The dark wooden floors, scuffed and scratched with twelve-plus decades of foot traffic—the house had been built in 1900—had been sanded, stained, and varnished.

I moved from room to room, the sound of my rubber soled footsteps ghostly in the hollow emptiness.

The house felt stripped, sanitized; the past scoured away with harsh, industrial cleansers. The tall, multipaned windows that once framed views of wind-battered oaks and the overgrown front garden now offered a stark, lonely view of the gravel drive and a short privacy wall of new plantings to shield this yard from the neighbors. The Jennings back in my day. I wondered who lived next door now.

The kitchen, once cluttered with dusty knickknacks and miscellanea, mismatched pots and pans, now gleamed with cold, impersonal granite and stainless-steel appliances. I ran my fingers over the cool, sharp edges of the counter, the faint chemical tang of cleaning agents lingering in the air.

The small breakfast nook where my father, brooding and hungover, would sit drinking his morning coffee and staring out at the wild, overgrown garden, was gone, the windows replaced, sunlight shining on an empty space.

I turned down the narrow hall to the back of the house, my heart resuming its painful thud as I reached the door of my old bedroom.

My hand hovered over the knob as I remembered things I did not want to remember. The "faggot" books that went into the trash, the little stray cat I'd wanted so desperately to keep, the punches that came out of nowhere when I least expected them, the college acceptance letters I'd found tucked away in his desk.

For long moments I stood there, breathing quietly, softly, struggling with it.

*There's something wrong with you.*

You hear it often enough, you begin to believe it.

When I finally turned the handle, the door swung open smoothly, silently, the hinges freshly oiled. But then I'd had always kept the hinges well-oiled. The room was completely empty, stripped of everything that I remembered, everything that had made it mine. Even the built-in bookshelves were gone.

It was just a clean and tidy white box.

My eyes blurred in hot, unwilling reaction and the late afternoon light slanted through the large windows, distorted in attenuated, skeletal shadows across the freshly painted walls.

I exhaled slowly, shakily, and turned, pulling the door shut behind me with a soft, final click.

"Keiran?"

I was getting into my car when I heard someone call my name.

I looked around in confusion and saw a tall, slim woman in jeans and red T-shirt walking rapidly up the road toward me. She had short salt-and pepper hair and looked to me like she was maybe in her fifties.

"Yes?"

She resembled my Realtor, Betty, but as she reached me, I realized it was Judy Jennings. In my memory she was still a woman in her thirties.

"I thought it was you." Her smile was self-conscious, maybe uncomfortable. "You probably don't remember me. Jared and I live next door." She nodded back toward the green and white two-story on the other side of the new privacy wall.

"Judy," I said. "I remember."

"We saw you at the funeral, but you didn't stay."

No, I hadn't stayed longer than it took to make sure he was well and truly going into the ground.

"I had a flight to catch." Which was true, although the flight had been booked for that evening.

"Of course. You're living in New York now."

It wasn't a secret, but I did wonder how she knew that.

"We—Jared and I—just wanted to tell you…we were sorry." She swallowed, surprising us both. She said, a little randomly, "He was a good neighbor."

I nodded. That was true. He was definitely the guy to call in an emergency—unless he was the emergency.

"But…" Judy stopped, her expression troubled. "When you didn't come back, after the funeral, Jared and I started talking. About the old days."

"The good old days," I murmured. I wasn't mocking her. Maybe myself.

She bit her lip, said quietly, "We should have done something. We knew things…weren't right. But he was the sheriff."

It took me a second or two. I couldn't quite say it was okay. It had not been okay. But I did understand. He had not been a man to cross.

Judy was still talking, still trying to explain. "After he lost his job, we thought about going to Sheriff Rankin, but they were friends. And…you were older and making plans to go to college. We kept waiting—what if we made it worse? And then you were gone. We watched you drive away that morning." She rested her hand on her heart. "It was such a relief."

I honestly didn't know what to say to her. I finally came up with, "It was a long time ago."

"Yes. But you're all right now? You look so-so…" She gestured helplessly. "Polished."

"Thanks."

"I mean… Well, you're all grown up."

"Yes." No denying that.

"You're in New York and you're a-a writer?" She looked so hopeful.

"An editor," I said. "Yes. I'm all right. Everything worked out in the end."

"Thank God." It sounded sincere. "I used to pray that wherever you were, you were okay. You were happy."

It's silly, but I was genuinely touched by the idea that now and then Judy Jennings had prayed for me.

"That was nice of you."

She winced, although I meant it sincerely. She started to say something, hesitated. Finally, she asked, "Did you ever get in contact with your mother?"

I stared at her, not understanding, but then remembered that the Jennings had lived next door for as long as I could remember. They might even have known my mother. So yes, they'd have heard the original story: that my mother had run away. Even after my father started saying she'd died, most people believed he was just saving face.

"No," I said. "That would have been up to my mother."

She bit her lip, looked toward the back of the house. "I don't know…"

She stopped.

A weird crawly feeling came over my scalp.

I started to say—I'm not even sure what. I stopped, too. I couldn't ask. Didn't want to know what she suspected. Didn't want to hear what she and Jared had speculated about over the breakfast table for the last thirty-six years. Could still not acknowledge the thing I had also come to suspect, as I grew older.

After all, he'd said she was dead. He was a lot of things. Liar wasn't one of them.

I said instead, "Maybe you'll get some nice new neighbors, and all you'll have to worry about is their barking dog."

She looked at me quickly, smiled. "That would be nice. I like dogs."

"Me, too," I said, though I liked cats better.

The drive to 1926 Old Stage Road took less than fifteen minutes.

The road narrowed as I left the gentrified homes and gardens of Old Town behind, the asphalt giving way to rough, crumbling pavement, then to packed dirt and loose gravel. Ancient, twisted oaks leaned over the road, their gnarled branches casting long, barbed wire shadows across the windshield as I navigated the tight, overgrown curves.

How the hell could this obstacle course have ever been part of the old stage coach route? The name had to be poetic license.

My fingers tightened on the steering wheel as I passed familiar landmarks—the rusted, bullet-riddled road sign for an abandoned campground, the still crooked, leaning telephone pole Milo had sideswiped twenty years ago, the rocky, weed-choked pull-off where Milo and I had once parked to share a joint and complain about whatever we'd imagined we had to complain about before the night Dom died.

The shadows thickened, and if Siri had not assured me I was on the right track, I might have second-guessed the wisdom of trying to corner U.N. Owen in his lair. Instead, I eased the rental onto the narrow, rutted track that snaked between towering redwoods and dense, tangled underbrush. Dust billowed behind the car as I bumped along the uneven drive, tires crunching over a thick bed of fallen needles and loose gravel.

The house finally loomed into view—a long, low structure with weathered wood siding and a steeply pitched roof, tucked deep into the shadows of the surrounding trees. A rusted mailbox leaned precariously at the entrance to the drive, the name *Colby* stenciled in chipped, faded black paint. Weeds had crept up around the splintered wood post.

Colby. That made sense. U.N. Owen was obviously a pseudonym. Now, I had a name. Assuming Colby was still the current renter. The property didn't exactly look well-maintained.

I parked in the small dirt clearing in front of the house, the sedan tires sinking slightly into the soft, loamy earth. For a second or two, I studied the structure, my fingers drumming uneasily against the steering wheel.

While I hadn't wanted an audience, I hadn't expected the place to be quite so isolated, so cut off from the rest of the world by the thick, shadowed woods that crowded close around the property. There were probably other houses out there, but they were well behind the wall of trees.

An ideal location for a writer.

Belatedly, it occurred to me that U.N. Owen might not react well to an unexpected visit from a suspected murderer. Rural California meant he probably owned a gun or two.

I waited for a dog to start barking or the twitch of a window curtain.

Nothing.

No sign of life.

There was no car in the drive. Maybe he wasn't home.

Was I doing this or not?

Oh, I was doing it. No question.

I climbed out, my shoes sinking a little into the soft soil, leaving clearly defined footprints.

The air was cooler here, damp with the scent of wet bark and moss. The dense tree canopy filtered the sunlight into fractured, wavering beams that danced across the cracked front steps as I approached the house.

The rickety front steps creaked; my footsteps thumped hollowly across the boards. A small, iron bell hung beside the door, its metal surface pitted and flecked with rust. I reached up, gave it a cautious ring, the sharp, metallic clang echoing faintly into the dense forest. Birds in the trees overhead took flight in a startling rush of wings.

I waited, listening, but the only response was the faint rustle of leaves overhead and the distant, rhythmic creak of tree limbs swaying in the breeze.

Okay. He might be wearing headphones. I did when I worked.

I rang the bell again, then knocked, the sound dull and muffled against the weathered wood. I waited again, the silence stretching thinner and thinner, my pulse a quick, steady thud in my ears.

I called, "Hello? Anybody home?"

I knocked again, harder this time, my fist rattling the warped wood against its frame.

Still nothing.

"Fuck," I said softly. What kind of blackmailer didn't sit by the phone or computer waiting for a reply to his—or her—threats?

I stepped back, gaze sweeping the dark windows. The streaked glass reflected the fragmented light of the forest behind my blurred outline. I glanced uneasily over my shoulder, then moved cautiously down the side of the house, tennis shoes sticking in the damp, moss-covered earth as I skirted the overgrown ferns and tangled brush that crowded close against the walls.

I peered through a grimy side window, trying to make something, anything out in the dark and featureless interior.

Was that a desktop on a table or the world's ugliest sculpture?

Circling around to the back, I found a narrow, covered porch, its railing sagging under the weight of years of damp and neglect. An old, rusting water pump stood to one side, its handle streaked with a thin, greenish patina of algae. A battered, metal trash can leaned drunkenly against the back wall, its lid askew, a faint, sour odor of spoiled food wafting up from within.

So, someone was living here. Had been living here.

They didn't seem to be home now.

The canopy of trees diluted the light to such an extent that at this time of day, anyone inside that bungalow would have surely turned on a lamp or two.

Unless they were blind.

Or unconscious.

Or dead?

I considered this final option. Blackmail was a risky business. Not everyone would be willing to talk first and decide what to do later.

Had someone decided to murder U.N. Owen?

Or, more likely, was I a guy who had spent the last twenty years reading *way* too many mystery novels?

Probably the latter. But just because I'd read thousands of mystery novels, didn't mean I couldn't stumble into a real-life homicide. As I knew better than anyone.

In fact, suspecting foul play, wasn't it my duty to see if I could be of help to the potential victim?

Yeah, right. Try explaining that one to the local authorities—without having to explain what I was doing there in the first place.

Who said I had to go to the authorities?

My mind continued to race through possibilities.

Could this be a trap of some kind?

Or an incredible opportunity?

If I could get inside, I'd almost certainly be able to identify who U.N. Owen really was. I might find something to use against them. I might even uncover what they thought they had on me.

I hesitated at the back door, my hand hovering over the tarnished brass knob. The door itself looked swollen with moisture, the paint blistered and peeling, the frame warped and splintered.

It wouldn't take much…

For a brief, reckless moment, I considered forcing it open, fingers tightening reflexively around the knob. But then I heard it—the faint, rhythmic crunch of footsteps coming down the gravel drive. I caught a whiff of pipe tobacco.

Hastily, heart thumping, I wiped the door knob with the bottom of my T-shirt, and stepped quickly back into the shadows. My pulse kept up a sharp, staccato beat in my ears as the sound of approaching footsteps drew closer. A male figure emerged from the trees, moving slowly, cautiously, head turning left and right as he looked around.

"Hello?" he called.

I shrank back against the wall, breath held tight in my throat, every nerve stretched to the breaking point.

*My rental car was parked in the drive.*

There was no hiding. He'd already seen my car. I had to brazen this out.

I stepped into plain view, calling cheerfully, "Hey, there!"

He started and turned. Middle-aged, short, stocky, white beard, and yes, smoking a pipe.

He kept a little distance between us, calling, "I heard your car coming up the road. We don't get a lot of visitors up here."

I could tell he was slightly suspicious, but mostly curious. I was a white, refined-looking adult male driving a nice car. I did not fit anyone's stereotypical criminal profile.

"That was me," I agreed. I hooked a thumb over my shoulder, pointing back at the house. "I was looking for... Colby, is it?"

"Troy Colby, yeah."

"He submitted a manuscript to the publishing house I work for. Since I'm in town for a conference, I thought I'd stop by and—"

"You're going to publish *him*?" Colby's neighbor seemed astounded.

"Well, we'll see. I definitely want to talk to him."

"You mean he really did write a book? Is it any *good*?"

"It certainly caught my attention."

"Here, I thought it was all bullshit. He's always claiming he's working on this book or that book. I thought he was making it up."

"Is he around? I knocked but no answer."

Colby's neighbor burst out laughing. "Well, here's a funny thing. He's at a writing conference in Monterey. I bet it's the same damned conference you're in town for!"

# Chapter Ten

Why the hell had it never—*not once*—occurred to me that U.N. Owen might be attending the Noir at the Shore conference?

What. The. Hell.

I knew perfectly well only conference attendees could get into the panels.

No. In the interests of accuracy, local residents and random hotel guests did occasionally crash conference bookrooms and panels. Not often.

But the guy had submitted a blackmail threat in the form of a manuscript. Why hadn't I considered the possibility that he was a genuine fan of the genre? *Jesus.* He was using the nom de plume U.N. Owen. How had that not been my first clue?

On the other hand, how would I have located him at the conference when I didn't have his actual name and could barely recall what he looked like?

*You could have messaged him.*

Yes. I could have messaged him. But if I messaged him, I was admitting…too much. I'd be leaving cyber footprints, cyber fingerprints. I'd wanted to see for myself what I was dealing with. I wanted to look him in the eyes.

Well, instead, I'd got to look his neighbor in the eyes.

Great.

And for good measure I'd treated myself to the pleasure of dropping by the old family homestead so I could dredge up a lot of terrible memories that I'd spent years trying to flush. Not useful. Not productive. Not conducive to my mental or emotional health.

I took a couple of deep breaths as I drove slowly back to the main road.

Focus on the positives. I now had a name. Troy Colby.

And I knew a couple of things about Colby. He was living lean to the bone. He wanted to be a writer. A published author.

Maybe the way out of this mess was simpler than I thought.

Maybe Colby was looking for a publishing contract.

Maybe I could find out exactly what Colby knew—and how he knew it—in exchange for a book deal. Not for *I Know What You Did*, obviously. A real book. A genuine work of fiction.

If there was one thing I knew how to do, it was take a mess of a manuscript and turn it into a publishable work.

Did I want to give in to blackmail? No. Did I think it was wise? No. You didn't have to be an editor of crime fiction to know that once you submitted to extortion, you were opening a vein to your bank account.

But I didn't have a lot of options. I couldn't go to the police. Even if there had been someone left to corroborate my version of events, I was still culpable. I'd be ruined. I'd go to prison.

My knuckles whitened on the steering wheel. I was not someone who would do well in prison. Hell, I was not someone who did well outside of Manhattan.

There had to be another way. And maybe this was it. Maybe I could buy my way out of this nightmare. Or at least the part of the nightmare where I was completely and totally ruined. Maybe this was the price.

Maybe I *deserved* to pay this price for the part I'd played in Dom's death.

On my way out of Steeple Hill, I stopped at the Valero to fill up the rental's gas tank, use the facilities, and buy a cup of coffee for the trip back to Monterey.

I was very tired. I hadn't slept much the night before and the day had been...long.

Very long. A million years long.

Which was how long the drive back to Monterey felt. If it hadn't been imperative I get back for that godawful banquet, I'd have considered getting a room for the night.

Not in Steeple Hill. That went without saying. I'd be overjoyed to never see this town again. But in some safe, anonymous motel down the highway.

Irrelevant. I had to get back. I had to attend the dinner. I had to be up bright and early the next morning for breakfast with Grace Hollister and coffee with...whomever.

It was all starting to blur together.

As the cashier rang up the gas and coffee, I checked my phone for messages. My heart sank at the long list of Recents.

It was already after five. I'd lost time stopping by the house on Seaside Lane. I could spend half an hour going through my messages or I could get back in time for the cocktails before the banquet. It was already going to be close.

I opted to start driving. Not least because I wasn't sure I could handle one more piece of bad news.

As I walked out of the Quick Mart, I happened to notice the car that had followed me into the station was still idling just beyond the reach of the Valero's buzzing sodium lights.

A vintage Cadillac DeVille.

I hadn't seen one of those in decades.

I glanced back at the long, low-slung frame half-hidden in the shadow of a rusted dumpster. The midnight-black paint absorbed what little light reached it. The engine, a deep, rumbling V8, settled into a steady, predatory purr. Through the windshield I could just make out the faint orange glow of a cigarette tip on the driver's side.

I smiled faintly. The scene was almost comically cliché film noir. Hayes Hartman would have strongly disapproved.

I finished filling up the tank, screwed the gas cap in, and got back in the car.

As I pulled out of the gas station, I automatically looked in the rearview. The Cadillac DeVille remained in the shadows, unmoving, as I turned toward the Highway 1 on-ramp.

It had been a beautiful scenic drive in the daylight.

Each turn of the winding road revealed fleeting glimpses of the churning Pacific to the left and steep, shadowed cliffs to the right. Dense patches of coastal fog had clung to the cliffs, swirling around the stands of wind-bent cypress and knotty, low-slung Monterey pines.

But as daylight drained from the sky, it was a different story.

The state highway dwindled to a serpentine, deeply shadowed two lanes. Guardrails were random, and the long gaps between revealed sudden, sheer drops to jagged rocks where waves crashed violently, sending plumes of silver spray skyward.

I was a competent driver, but I didn't drive a lot anymore—I especially didn't drive a lot of narrow coastal roads—and my night vision wasn't great.

The lane dipped and twisted, coiled and uncoiled, the rental's headlights swinging through the darkness of each blind curve, and I found myself tensing each time a car approached, headlights flaring blindingly before whipping past and vanishing into the void.

I couldn't help watching the rearview mirror, waiting for the next car more familiar with the road to speed up behind me, lights flashing for me to move over.

There were not a lot of turnoffs.

Eventually, I did spot a pair of headlights far behind me, but the driver didn't seem to be in a hurry, maybe also unfamiliar with the road, and I was able to relax a little.

It was dark and the moon was rising when the highway finally veered away from the ocean, unrolling into a shady, forested stretch.

I flicked on my high beams, and now and again white light illuminated a pair of glowing eyes in the underbrush or the outline of a deer standing motionless by the side of the road.

It was a relief to have trees and solid ground on either side as opposed to a sheer cliff and open sky. I accelerated a bit, the car lunged forward and we raced on as the trees closed in, redwoods blotting out the stars.

And then—*bang*. I sucked in a breath as the sedan jerked, shuddered, and the steering wheel yanked right.

*Was that a gunshot?*

I hung onto the wheel, let off the gas as the car began to jog. Slowly, slowly I straightened out the wheel. I could hear a loud and alarming hiss coming from beneath the vehicle.

My heart thundered as the car thudded over something solid—with the way my luck was going, I'd probably hit a boulder—or a stray hiker—followed by the heavy and heart-sinking unmistakable *flop-flop-flop*.

The sound of a blown tire slapping against the wheel well.

A blow out.

I began to swear quietly and bitterly.

No. Not great. But better than a gunshot. Right?

Why had I leaped to the idea of a gunshot?

My nerves really were in pieces.

I bumped the car onto a dirt turnout, gravel and sand crunching beneath the tires as I rolled to a stop and turned off the engine.

It was very dark. Very quiet. In fact, the only sound in all the universe was the final oozy trickle of air from the blown tire.

After a shaken second or two, I gathered myself, and opened the driver door, stepping out into the pine-scented night. The air felt chilly and damp against my perspiring skin. I flicked on my cellphone flashlight, the bright beam cutting through the gloom.

The good news was this hadn't happened on a blind curve or on the cliffs overlooking the ocean. The bad news was I was miles from help. The road here was bordered by thick stands of ferns and towering redwoods. No street lamps. No call boxes. Not a lot of traffic. Probably no cell phone service.

Not a lot of anything but trees and shadows

It was the sort of place where a scream for help might echo for miles without ever reaching another human ear.

*Oh-kay.*

Now was not the time to be thinking like an over-wrought mystery author.

Although, actually, the moon, the trees, the lonely winding road—it would make a terrific image for key art in a thriller cover composition.

Yeah, also not the time to be thinking like a frazzled workaholic mystery editor.

Did this car have a spare? Emergency flares? Did I re-member how to change a tire?

Circling the sedan, I aimed my phone's flashlight at the flat tire. It was hard to tell at this angle, but I'd have expect-ed a clean puncture, not a jagged tear.

I frowned. Was I really thinking...well, what *was* I thinking? Sabotage?

No. I had to have hit something.

What?

The faint sound of an engine in the distance snapped me to attention. I straightened, the hair on my nape prickling. I listened uneasily and thought I recognized the muted growl of a V8 engine driving slowly up the road.

Right. Because I was such a car guy, I could recognize a V8 from a large diesel?

Now I was really letting my imagination run away with me.

Headlights flickered across the trees a few yards down. My pulse spiked. I clicked off my phone, instinctively backing into the shadows, and then stepping still farther back, slipping deep into the trees.

*You're losing it, Chandler.*

Probably. Almost certainly. And yet, I dived behind the nearest trunk, and crouched down. I peered cautiously through the ferns, the cool fronds tickling my face. My gaze fixed on the road, waiting...

A second or two later, a car—large, dark, with a long hood and classic, sweeping lines—glided into view.

A vintage Cadillac DeVille.

My heart stopped.

Not my imagination.

Not losing it after all.

"What the hell..." I whispered. But yes, what the hell? What the hell was going on?

The Cadillac slowed as it neared my rental, high beams illuminating the empty interior, the lopsided front.

To my horror, the Cadillac suddenly pulled in behind the rental, red exhaust furling into the night air. The driver's door opened and a man got out.

He was built like a bull. Large and broad-shouldered. He had a face like a bull, too. Long, blunt features, rough-hewn like something carved out of wood. His hair was silver, but he didn't move like an elderly person.

I didn't recognize him.

Or did I?

No. But... There *was* something vaguely familiar about him. Or maybe he was just a type. The archetypal movie villain type.

I didn't move, didn't dare take a breath as he stood silhouetted in the glow of the headlights.

*What the fuck do you want?*

He stared at the tree line and my heart stopped.

He turned back to the rental, peering inside. He tried the door handle.

The rental chirped and its car lights blinked.

*Shit.* My breath caught. The key fob was in my pocket. Had the car just unlocked? Was I still close enough to trigger the system?

Instinctively, I felt for my back pocket, and nearly overbalanced into the damp earth. It was already too late. The car was either unlocked or not.

The man tugged on the sedan door again, slapped the roof of the car, and stepped into the middle of the road, his head turning slowly, scanning the darkness.

Seeming to reach a decision, the burly figure turned back to the Cadillac, his shadow looming grotesquely against the tree trunks. He ducked into the driver's seat, pulled the door shut. The car's engine revved once, then it rolled forward, tires crunching stone and dirt, bouncing back onto the highway, picking up speed.

The red taillights vanished into the mist.

For a second or two I remained crouched and stricken as darkness reclaimed the road. The only sounds were the rustle of leaves and my own shaky breaths.

But there was no time to waste. He'd find out soon enough that I wasn't walking along the road hoping for a ride or trying for a cellphone signal.

I hopped up, sprinted back to the rental, fumbling open the lid to the trunk. To my relief, there was a spare in the back. A jack and lug wrench were nestled in the wheel well.

Hands shaking, I hauled the spare tire out.

*Hurry. For God's sake, hurry.*

I struggled to fit the jack beneath the car. Struggled to remember how this worked.

*Is this right?*

The jack was heavier than I remembered. Awkward and unwieldy. I pinched my hand as I worked to fit it beneath the frame, tore fingernails. I cursed softly, fervently as I pumped the handle.

All the while, I was thinking, *This can't be happening.*

But it *was* happening, and with every passing minute I was running out of time.

It was just hard to understand what had just happened. What was still happening. What did that guy want with me? What would have happened if I'd waited by the car?

If that blowout had happened on the coast road...

I could have had an accident.

I could have been killed.

I listened numbly to the echo of that thought. *I could have been killed.*

The car creaked and groaned as I slowly jacked it up and off the ground, each pump of the jack handle sending a sharp, metallic click echoing into the dense, breathless quiet of the woods.

My pulse raced, my breath coming in short, ragged gulps as I yanked the lug wrench from the tire well, fingers clumsy as I fumbled it into position. The darkness seemed to press closer with every second.

My ears strained for the sound of a returning engine as I knelt, breath misting in the cool, damp air, and began loosening the lug nuts. They resisted at first, the metal creaking under my weight as I leaned into the wrench. I could feel the strain in my shoulder muscles. My cell phone, positioned unhelpfully on the dirt, threw my distorted silhouette against the wall of trees.

*How long before he realizes the truth? How long before he swings the Cadillac around and heads back?*

"Focus," I panted.

Sweat trickled down my temple, stinging my eyes. My fingers kept slipping on the cold metal as I worked. Finally, finally, I cracked the last lug nut loose, the sudden, satisfying give of the metal momentarily breaking the oppressive silence.

Silence? The night was not silent. It was alive with alarming and alien sounds. Rustling leaves. Insects. The eerie cry of an owl hunting.

Somewhere in the distance, beyond the dense line of redwoods, came the muffled pound of the surf, the sound carried up the coastal cliffs on the cold, salt-tinged wind, mingling with the sharp rustle of dry leaves and the slow, creaking sway of the trees. Occasionally, a sharper crack echoed through the darkness as a branch snapped, the sound sending my heart skittering against my ribs in terror.

"Come *on*...."

I yanked the ruined tire free, the shredded rubber sagging in my grip like dead flesh. I stared at it. Even in the uncertain moonlight I could see that the sidewall was clearly, unmistakably slashed—a long, deliberate gash that curved like a scythe blade.

Since this was the very thing I suspected, I'm not sure why it was such a shock.

Maybe because it made no sense.

When had it happened? At the gas station? When I'd gone inside.

This *couldn't* have anything to do with U.N. Owen. It was not good business practice to injure or kill your blackmail victims.

But nothing else made sense, either. How could this be a coincidence?

It couldn't.

Somehow, this was all connected.

I dropped the tire, struggled to fit the spare into place. It had been years, decades, since I'd had to change a tire—and never with the speed of an Indy 500 pit crew.

I fumbled the first lug nut, the small metal disc slipping from my damp, unsteady fingers and clinking sharply against the gravel. My swear was half sob, and I stopped again to listen, every nerve straining, for the telltale crunch of gravel, the guttural rumble of an approaching engine.

*Hurry*, the wind whispered in the tall grass. *Hurry...*

I turned my cell's flashlight beam toward the ground, found the fallen lug nut, and dropped it in my pocket. I forced the spare into place, threading the lug nuts on with shaking fingers, my breath coming in harsh, shallow gasps as I tightened each one in turn. I cranked the jack handle furiously, the car groaning as it settled back onto its wheels with a shuddering thump.

I jumped up, tossed the ruined tire and tools into the trunk, slammed the lid shut, and stumbled back to the driver's seat, half collapsing behind the wheel. I triggered the ignition, and the engine roared to life, headlights flaring against the trees, sweeping giant, monstrous shadows as I peeled out, jerking the car back onto the road.

The speedometer needle climbed steadily as I accelerated, flying down the vast, empty stretch of road back toward the lights and safety of civilization, back to Monterey.

# Chapter Eleven

It was seven-thirty-five when I walked through the door of the Monterey Plaza Hotel, and the first person I saw was Finn. He was balancing several drinks on his way from the hotel lobby toward the banquet room.

He spotted me, frowned—nothing new there—and started to say something, but I nodded curtly and kept moving. It was all I could do not to break into a run.

I didn't bother with the elevators. I went straight for the stairs and arrived on the fifth floor out of breath and drenched in sweat. I unlocked my suite, kicking off my shoes, hopping as I pulled off my socks, shedding my jeans, boxers, tearing off my shirt... I flung myself into the giant shower, breathing in the eucalyptus-scented steam as water streamed down my head and shoulders.

I lathered up, shaved, rinsed off, stepped out of the shower, grabbing for a towel. I brushed my teeth, slapped on moisturizer, aftershave, hair gel...

Finn used to tease me about being overly organized, and yes, I did like everything to be just right. But it was a handy trait to have when you were moving so fast you didn't have time to think.

When I walked out of my suite eleven minutes later, my shoes were polished, my bow tie was straight, and my cufflinks fastened. Sure, my heart was going sixty miles an hour and there were ominous wavy lines at the edges of my vision, but no one was going to be able to accuse me of blowing off this damned banquet.

I did not—could not allow—myself to think about anything but getting through the next four hours.

I strolled into the banquet room just as everyone was finding their table. I got a few curious looks, a few smiles and nods hello, but mostly no one seemed to notice me at all. At conferences, authors, rightly, are the stars of the show. No one cares if an editor does or doesn't show up for an event. Unless the event is delivering feedback to an author in a one-on-one session.

Moving around the large round tables, I greeted authors, asking if they were having a good time, asking if anyone needed a drink, the usual stuff.

"Actually, *you* look like you could use a drink." Adrien English came up beside me and pushed a drink into my hand. He was smiling faintly.

That was thoughtful—and unusual. I think the first author who ever bought me a drink was Finn.

My, "How did you know?" was only half-kidding. I downed three-quarters of the liquid in a large swallow. An old-fashioned. He was an observant guy.

"The number of times Lila Pendergast asked if we'd seen you."

I nearly choked, but managed not to spray the nearest table with whisky and bitters.

Adrien nodded to another table where Christopher Holmes, J.X. Moriarity, Kyle Bari, and a tall, lean man with dark, curly hair were all watching me with unnerving interest.

I wanted to ask—well, I'm not sure what, but was forestalled when Cherry bounced up, her expression apologetic. She looked adorable in a short red silk dress. Her eyes were shining and there were sparkly red butterflies in her hair.

"Sorry for all the phone calls! You were right to ignore me. I figured it out."

I said, just as if I knew what she was talking about, "I knew you would."

"I suddenly remembered what you told me, and I offered her a shot of bourbon."

My lips parted, but sometimes it's better not to know.

"Uh oh," Adrien murmured. He was looking past me.

I followed his gaze and spotted Mindy Newburgh, incoming. Wise child that she was, Cherry departed post haste for her table in the nether regions where supporting staff were relegated.

As Mindy reached me, she demanded, "Keiran, are we still on for coffee tomorrow?"

I didn't quite understand the reason for the narrow eyes or tight expression. I'd accepted her invitation mostly out of curiosity. She wasn't one of my authors, although I'd worked with her back when I'd first been with Wheaton & Woodhouse.

"Of course."

She looked skeptical, but then she glanced behind me, offered a chilly smile, and backed away. Adrien, too, faded out with graceful but strategic haste, and I knew, with a sinking feeling, exactly who was aimed my way.

I rearranged my features into cordial interest, and turned to greet Lila, resplendent in emerald-green. Before I could say anything, she got right up in my face and hissed, "*Why* are you ignoring my phone calls? *Who* do you think you are?"

That was more aggressive than I'd anticipated.

"I-I wasn't ignoring you, Lila. I'm sorry. I didn't have cell service a lot of the day."

"Why would you not have cell service?" Her expression was one of open disbelief. "Where did you disappear to? Where *were* you? I must have phoned you five times."

I said quietly, "I went to visit my father's grave. We weren't on good terms when he died, and since he's buried in San Mateo, I felt like it was something I should do."

Did I feel guilty lying? Of course. Especially about that. But what was I going to say? *I went to confront the man I believe is trying to blackmail me for my involvement in a murder that happened twenty years ago.*

Lila's expression changed. She said a little defensively, "Why didn't—I didn't realize. I mean, I knew your father passed recently. I didn't know you'd lived locally." Her tone was significantly less abrasive.

"Yes. In fact, I put the house on the market when I was here for the funeral. There are a couple of offers on it, so when I left San Mateo, I stopped by to have one last look."

"Yes. That's... I see."

"Unfortunately, a lot of the coastal area has spotty reception. I didn't realize you were trying to reach me. To be honest, my thoughts weren't on work."

That at least was the truth.

She looked uncomfortable. "No. Of course not. You could have told me. Frankly, I was shocked when you didn't show up for Finn's interview with Rudolph Dunst. Given the fuss you've been making over him."

Good old Lila. A breath of fresh air.

"No more fuss." I said lightly, "He's all yours now."

"Mm." It was a noncommittal sound. She struggled with herself and managed a reluctant, "I'm sorry I jumped down your throat, Keiran. Sorry for your loss." She added doubtfully, "I never thought of you as sentimental."

"I'm not. But…"

"He was your father. Yes, I get it."

"Don't worry. I'll be fully present and engaged for the rest of the conference."

She nodded, frowning faintly, and turned away. I watched her make her way to the central table where Vaughn sat talking with Finn. As Lila reached the table, Vaughn looked up and asked her something. Lila shrugged and took her seat.

Finn was studying Lila. He glanced at me. Our gazes locked.

He turned back to Vaughn.

All at once, I was exhausted, drained. The overhead lights were blindingly bright; the volume of voices all talking at once, deafening. An ominous tightness crawled over the base of my skull. The shimmering at the edge of my vision was turning into wavy lines.

Fan-fucking-tantastic. A migraine. *Really*?

I decided to focus on finding my seat. Water would help. I was probably dehydrated. Food. A couple of OTC pain relievers. I could do this.

I located my name placard and took my seat next to Millie—Millicent Millbrook-Abernathy—the granddaughter of our founder, Ethel Millbrook. W&W's VP of sales and their art director were also seated with us, so the good news was I still rated a place at one of the leadership tables. That was reassuring.

Millie was in her thirties. A charming, stately-looking blonde who, sadly, had the business acumen of a Palamino.

She smiled and greeted me with the news that W&W were in negotiation to sign Thomas McGregor.

"That's... Unexpected." Unexpectedly great news. I was pretty amazed because I hadn't got even an inkling from Lila.

"I know. I was surprised, too," Millie said. "Apparently, he was just about to sign with Theodore Mansfield when W&W swooped in at the last minute and made him an offer he couldn't refuse."

"Great for us. Pretty lousy for TM. Who represents him?"

"He does. He doesn't have an agent."

"That's bold."

Here was someone who'd give Finn a run for his money.

I sipped from my water glass, fished the packet of Nuvicare out of my jacket pocket, tore it open, and swallowed two tablets. Hopefully, that would be enough.

W&W's art director, Ariel Newsome, grimaced in sympathy. "These things always give me a headache, too."

I smiled, sipped more water.

Honestly, I don't remember much about the dinner. Vaughn gave a welcome speech, talked about exciting new beginnings, and the dishes began to arrive. I think the main entrée was prime rib and whatever went with that. I didn't eat much and I avoided having a second drink.

Millie also wasn't eating much, though she was drinking enough for both of us. Eventually, she leaned over and said a little shakily, "I feel like I shouldn't even be here. I feel like everyone hates me."

I regarded her, made a noncommittal, "Mm." I didn't see the point in lying. She *wasn't* very popular at the moment.

I could feel her staring at my profile. "Keiran, couldn't you... Talk to people? Couldn't you help them see things from my point of view? Everyone likes you. They respect your opinion."

My surprise had to have shown. But why was *this* the hard part for her? She'd gotten everything she wanted out of the deal with W&W. Tonight would probably be our last public appearance as the publishing company formerly known as Millbrook House. Yes, every Millbrook employee in the room, myself included, had mixed emotions regarding her, but it was very likely the last time she'd see most of us.

Usually, I'd have felt obliged to come up with something polite and neutral. Maybe I was too tired, too shaken by the events of the last twenty-four hours, maybe it was the ominous pulse behind my right eye. The best I could do was offer another of those neutral nods.

Her voice wobbled. "Everyone is acting like I-I sold us out. And I *didn't*! You know I didn't. You know how difficult that decision was. I had to make the right choice for all of us—and for the preservation of Millbrook's legacy."

I smiled faintly. "You did sell us out."

*"What?"*

"Of course you did."

She stammered, *"Keiran.* Y-you of all people know I didn't want to sell. You know how hard it was for me."

"Yes. I know you didn't want to sell. I know it wasn't an easy decision."

"But you still think..." She seemed genuinely shocked.

"You could have chosen to accept our buyout offer," I pointed out. "At the least, you could have waited to find out what our final offer was going to be."

It was a terrible idea to have this conversation now. I should have shut her down immediately.

She said softly, indignantly, "For God's sake, this company is all I have. Once it's sold, that's it. *Game over.* The choices I had to make regarding Millbrook determined my entire financial future. You couldn't *begin* to match W&W's offer."

It's fascinating, the stories people tell themselves. I ought to know.

I said calmly, "In other words, you sold us to the highest bidder. Believe it or not, I understand your reasoning. But don't pretend that it was anything other than that. Don't talk about preserving legacy and making tough choices for the good of all, because it's bullshit and everyone at Millbrook knows it."

*Bullshit?* I was more tired than I'd realized.

Millicent lost all color in her face, so that her carefully applied bronzer stood out like camo paint.

For a few moments she didn't seem to have an answer. But as each second passed, she got angrier and angrier.

She whispered, "How *dare* you talk to me like this, Keiran. You're not a W&W employee yet. You still work for *me*." Her voice shook.

The pulse behind my eye was now a throb. I could feel pain sparking through the net of nerves at the back of my skull.

I said calmly, "If you didn't want to hear the truth, Millicent, you shouldn't have started this conversation. You asked me for a favor. I'm explaining to you why my answer is no. For years you refused to listen to your leadership team and eventually you ran the company into the ground. Then, when we offered an employee buyout—which would have actually preserved the jobs of people you claim to care about, *as well as* protected Millbrook's legacy—you promised to consider our offer, but not twenty-four hours later went ahead and accepted Vaughn's."

Across the table, the members of the W&W leadership team watched us with riveted expressions. Talk about a floor show.

Danny Nguyen, Millbrook's soon-to-be-unemployed art director, said quietly, "Keiran's right, Millie."

Millicent threw him an angry look, whispered hotly, "I-I needed to make a decision. You couldn't have matched that offer! You know that."

I said, "And now, when people are upset about your decision—because it affects *their* financial future—you want me to advocate for you, you want me to persuade everyone that black is actually white. It's not. And I'm not going to pretend it is."

She dipped her head and whispered fiercely, "I could fire you right now. I could *end* your career in publishing."

"There are worse things."

I caught the flicker in her eyes. Oh, right. Until the "merger" was fait accompli, I was still an asset. I was reasonably well liked, reasonably well respected. No doubt there was a perception that if I was going along with the amalgamation of our two companies, it wasn't the worst move in the world. At this moment in time, firing me was not in anyone's best interest—particularly Millie's.

I smiled faintly and sipped my water.

Millicent turned her back toward me and tried to engage Whitney Brown, one of our soon-to-be-unemployed editors in conversation. Whitney was not feeling chatty, and had no hesitation about showing it.

Eventually, our plates were swept away and dessert began to be served.

Danny asked if I wanted another drink. I declined and pressed my fingertips to my right temple.

Was this dinner from hell never going to be over?

Danny's brows drew together. "Are you feeling alright?"

"Not...entirely."

Not at all, in fact. The argument with Millie had been the final straw.

"Excuse me," I murmured and pushed my chair back.

The restroom was empty, thank God.

Spots floated before my eyes as I shoved into the last stall, barely managing to lock the door before I dropped to my knees and retched violently into the toilet.

Perfect. Perfect end to a perfect day.

Except the day wasn't over.

Dry heaves followed—painful, utterly unproductive. I gasped for breath between spasms. By the time it was over, my throat was raw, my eyes stinging with tears, my body drenched with cold sweat. The pounding behind my right eye felt like pain was trying to tunnel its way out of my skull.

Monthly injections of a CGRP inhibitor usually kept my migraines at bay, but now and again, one broke through. The stress boiling in my gut, the long harrowing drive with headlights in my eyes, the blow out, the...the...so many disasters in one day I was losing count. *Oh*. Right. The fact that someone was maybe—probably?—trying to *kill* me?

The last twenty-four hours had provided the recipe for disaster—and this evening was delivering the pièce de resistance.

The scent of perspiration, roasted beef, and expensive cologne still clung to my jacket, and it turned my stomach all over again.

When it was over, I was shaking so hard I nearly over-balanced. I sat back on my heels, breathing slowly, carefully, deliberately. In through my nose. Out through my mouth. Repeat. And again.

It was a well-maintained hotel restroom, but yeah. The combined smell of bleach and lavender air freshener sent another of those full-body shudders rippling through me.

Somehow, I had to pull myself together and get back out there.

I couldn't picture it, though. Couldn't visualize shaking my hair out of my eyes, straightening my tie, and retaking my seat next to Millicent. Couldn't imagine chit-chatting about the book biz for another couple of hours while my head throbbed and white lights flashed behind my eyes like the aliens were landing.

There was no alternative. I'd already been in here too long.

I braced my hands on the cold porcelain, pushed up to my feet, and staggered out of the stall and over to the sink. I hung onto the counter edge, and turned the faucet with shaking fingers. Cold water blasted out. I cupped my hands and splashed my face a couple of times. I rinsed my mouth. Blinked at the mirror.

My dripping reflection stared back—pale, sweat-slick, jaw clenched tight, eyes red. A vein pulsed in my forehead. My pupils were uneven.

"You're fine," I said.

Well, no. I wasn't. But it wasn't the first time I'd had to work through a migraine attack. It wasn't pleasant. It wouldn't be pretty. But I could do this.

*Could I?*

The door opened behind me on a whoosh of voices and laughter floating from the banquet room.

Through the fleet of blind spots floating in front of my eyes, I could make out Finn's reflection framed in the doorway.

# Chapter Twelve

I closed my eyes. Willed him to go away.

"You okay?"

I opened my eyes. "Great. How are you?"

Finn's footsteps echoed on the tile as he came up behind me. "It's your head?"

Right. Because Finn had been through this with me before. And I truly couldn't bear to think about *that* Finn while I dealt with this Finn.

"I'm fine. I just need to take something."

His brows, dark in contrast to his hair, drew together. "I thought you *were* taking something? I thought you took monthly injections."

"And yet you say I never tell you anything." That was sheer bravado because I had to close my eyes and swallow another wave of nausea. I gripped the counter tightly, dipping my head and locking my jaw. My entire mission in life was reduced to not throwing up in front of Phineas Scott.

His hand landed lightly on my back, warm through my damp jacket. "What do you need, Keir? Talk to me."

A shaky laugh escaped me.

"You need to lie down. Let me help you upstairs."

I opened my eyes, stared at him in disbelief. "I can't *leave*. How's that going to look?"

His expression was one of complete non-comprehension. "It's going to look like you're not feeling well. Which ought to be obvious to anyone who sees you. Your face is grayer than your eyes."

"Thank you for noticing..." I closed my eyes again, hung my head. He was right. I desperately wanted—needed—to lie down.

"Keiran." Finn's voice was still kind, but I recognized the *This is the law speaking!* note. "You're done for tonight. No one's going to think less of you because you're ill."

"*I'll* think less of me." Besides, people wouldn't think I was ill. It was a conference. People would assume I was drunk. If there was any justice in the world, I *would* be drunk.

To my shock, he leaned in, his whisky-scented breath warm against my ear. "You care about appearances. Picture this: you, in your beautifully tailored tuxedo, passed out cold in the banquet room."

I raised my head to glare at him.

Finn's gaze was steady, serious, kind. The kindness was the reason, against my better judgment, I'd let myself start to care.

In the midst of these jumbled reflections, the wet counter seemed to give way, the room tilted sideways.

"Whoa..." Finn caught my arm, saying under his breath, "Okay. Going up." He said it like an old-fashioned elevator operator.

This time I didn't—couldn't—argue. My eyes rolled back and I was vaguely aware of Finn sort of ducking down, so that my arm fell across his shoulders. He locked his hard, muscular arm around my waist, and straightened.

After a confused stumble, my feet found the floor, and I woozily allowed myself to be steered out of the restroom.

Finn held me up with a kind of impersonal efficiency that made it easy to detach myself from the proceedings and simply follow his lead. One foot after the other. The floor was still seeming to dip beneath me, and I had to hang on tight.

We must have taken a service hallway because we awkwardly navigated a corner and suddenly it was quiet and the lights were dim. No one around to witness me stumbling along like a drunk on his last legs. Beneath my lashes, I could see the carpet heaving up and down and two pairs of dress shoes narrowly avoiding colliding with each other. My vision tunneled, but I had the impression that Finn spoke to someone and then we got on a...service elevator?

Where the hell *were* we? Flickering fluorescent light... steel walls...the faint hum of machinery...and, distressingly, the smell of detergent and distant kitchen grease.

My knees buckled. Finn's grip tightened. "Hang on," he coaxed. "Just another minute."

I closed my eyes, turned my face into his shoulder, and the feel of his arm around me, the lingering scent of his shower and aftershave were familiar and comforting. Tears stung my eyes, and I told myself it was the migraine, but it was also that I missed him so much, that I wanted so much more than kindness, that I wanted time to rewind to that sunny afternoon in my loft apartment when I had stupidly, foolishly believed my dreams were coming true.

The giant box of elevator lurched to a hard stop, and I gasped as nausea rose once more.

Finn squeezed me. "Just about there," he promised.

The door rolled up and we stepped out into another quiet service hallway. It felt like we'd been wandering through a maze for hours. But then we rounded a corner into another empty hallway and the door to Grand Bay Suite was right there.

It seemed like a miracle.

"Thank you. I'm okay now…" I let go of Finn, feebly pawing my pockets for my room key.

For a terrified moment I thought I'd dropped it downstairs, but Finn, still keeping his arm around my waist, reached into the front pocket of my trousers with casual familiarity and withdrew the plastic key card.

He tapped the key card to the door lock, the sensor turned green, and he shouldered open the door, helping me inside.

I winced at the wall of bright light.

The living room lights were blazing and my gaze fell on a trail of discarded shoes…socks…jeans…sweater…T-shirt…boxers leading from the entryway to the bedroom.

"If publishing doesn't work out you could always try out for quick change artist," Finn remarked.

Hand up to shield my eyes from the light, I reeled away from him, heading straight for the little guest bathroom off the entry hall, slamming the door behind me.

A dreadful couple of minutes passed while I tried to cough up the pain—there was nothing left to offer to the porcelain god—just more shaking and sweating and heaving. The harsh glare of the overhead light made it a special kind of hell. For a weird second, I felt out-of- body, like I was standing over myself watching that shuddering, sick misery.

*"God oh god oh god…"*

I was praying that Finn had gone while the going was good, but when I wobbled out of the bathroom, I could just make out his shadow moving around the suite, drawing the drapes. The lamps were all out. There was only a sliver of moonlight to light the way.

I said huskily, "Thanks, Phineas. I really am okay now. I just need to—I need to sleep."

His shadow walked up to me and wrapped warm arms around me, folding me in, and I let go. I leaned against him and started to cry.

I didn't want to. He was the last person to whom I wanted to show weakness.

It wasn't—obviously, I felt terrible, but this wasn't even the worst migraine I'd had. That particular honor belonged to the Frankfurt Book Fair, 2016. This—this was a contender, for sure, the experience made more richly mortifying by Finn being there to witness it all. But really, it was just the cumulative effect of…everything. Finn on the beach that morning. The day's revelations compounded by the previous day's revelations and the stress of the merger-that-was-really-a-buyout and someone wanting to blackmail me or maybe kill me, no, probably kill me…being in Steeple Hill again, in that house again…

*There's something wrong with you.*

And no wonder.

Finn's arms tightened and he whispered, "Keiran, Keir, don't. *Shhh.* Keir. *Shhh.* Let me help you."

I pulled myself together, drew back, wiped my face. "I…I just miss my cats," I got out.

No. Well, yes. I did. But no. That was not what this was. Pain makes you crazy. That's the truth.

His face was a white blur, but I felt his astonishment. "You…"

But there *was* a certain truth in it. In a hard to explain way, my two rescue Siamese, Wing Ding and Sing Song, symbolized everything good in my life. The comfortable, civilized life I'd worked so hard to build—in some ways, to build out of thin air.

The life I'd had two days ago before the universe started to unravel.

"Well, you'll see the cats in a couple of days, right?" Finn's tone was reasonable, just as if this conversation hadn't gone completely off the rails. His hands moved reassuringly on my back, smoothing the dampness of my shirt

I wiped my face again. "Yeah."

"And they're with the sitter. They're safe."

"Yes." I pressed the heels of hands to my forehead as if I could push the pain back into the box.

"After you have a sleep, you can call the sitter and ask them to take a...a proof of life pic so that you can see the cats are fine."

I knew he was teasing me. But his tone was kindly, like he was reasoning with a small child. He was also coming up with practical solutions for someone in distress, and I could appreciate that.

"Yeah. Thanks. I'm sorry I'm being an ass." I sucked in a breath. "Everything's okay now. You should get back."

"Yep. On my way. Let me just help you get settled."

I didn't have the energy to argue, so I nodded, blinked the tears from my eyes, and we headed for the bedroom, Finn guiding me around the obstacle course of the small dining area.

Outside the glass doors the moon hung low over the bay, half-shrouded in fog, its light threading through the mist like bullet holes between weathered slats. The building seemed to sway gently as the waves below rushed rhythmically against the pilings beneath the balcony. As I stared, a single gull wheeled past, a gray ghost in the gloom, like a silent-winged omen of—

Finn pulled the drapes across the glass doors with a single sweep.

The suite plunged into a soothing dusk. The vibration of the city beyond the windows faded to nothing.

I sank onto the edge of the bed and began to pluck at my bow tie with stiff fingers. It seemed an unreasonably complicated operation when all I wanted was to curl up in a ball. My skull felt like it was being crushed in a vise.

"Here." Finn was back at my side, brushing my hands aside, picking expertly at the knot. "Let me."

I let my hands fall to my lap. Finn worked quickly, silently, loosening the tie, unfastening the first few buttons of my shirt. He helped me shrug clumsily out of my jacket, slipping it from my shoulders and tossing it to the chair by the window. He unclipped my cufflinks, setting them with a soft clink on the nightstand. It was faster, easier to let him take care of this, so I sat silent and acquiescent. I didn't understand why he was being so kind, given the things he'd said that morning.

He knelt to remove my shoes, and I stared down at the pale gleam of his head.

"You're a good person," I said.

He gave a funny half-laugh, half-snort. "Thanks."

I managed the slacks on my own, barely, and then climbed onto the covers in my undershirt and boxers. I turned onto my side and curled slightly, one hand tucked under the pillow, the other pressing my temple like I could pin the pain in place.

But the pain seeped out from beneath my fingers, expanded. I could feel the angry pound of blood beneath my skin.

Finn bent over me. I could smell his cologne—Costa Azzurra—oceanic, cool, faintly herbal. The scent was weirdly grounding.

"Medication?"

I blinked, considering. "I don't think I can keep it down yet."

"Okay. So, then the stuff you take so you can keep the meds down?"

It was beyond me to explain. "It's all in my rescue bag on the dresser." I closed my eyes, surrendered to the monster. I wondered if Finn could see my head pounding from across the room.

He retrieved the bag, disappeared into the master bath, and returned with a glass of water and a pill. "Anti-nausea first."

I shoved up on elbow and he pressed the pill, warm from his hand, into my fingers. I put the pill under my tongue. "It'll dissolve. I don't need the water." My stomach quivered at the very idea and dropped back to the pillows.

"Okay, once that kicks in, you can take your pain meds. What else?"

I swallowed dryly, praying the Zofran wasn't coming right back up. "Nothing. Really. Thank you. You should get back. You'll be missed."

His tall shadow stood over me, motionless as he thought. "You want to get under the blankets?"

I did. I was cold. But the logistics of completely undressing were impossible.

"No. I have to take my contacts out." I added wearily, "As soon as I can sit without throwing up."

Finn turned without a word and disappeared into the master bath again. The light came on through the partially open door. I heard his washing up. He returned with a bottle of saline, a clean contact case from my travel kit, and tissues.

I pushed up again, wearily. "It's a full-service rescue mission."

"This is what we train for."

I took saline and tissues with shaking hands.

He must have felt the tremor, because he said, "Did you want some help?"

That woke me a little. "*Help*? No offense, but—"

"Byron's worn contacts since he was eight, so I actually do have some experience here. I have to turn the light back on, though."

"I'm relieved that you recognize that fact."

He breathed a quiet laugh, the mattress dipped as he sat beside me on the bed. "I'm turning the lamp on now."

He reached over, the click was loud between us, golden radiance spilled into the gloom. I grimaced, closed my eyes.

"Sorry. It's just for a sec." His breath was light and cool on my face, his fingers warm as he tilted my chin up, palm steady beneath my jaw, guiding me toward him.

He said, and there was the faintest thread of humor in his voice. "You have to open your eyes."

I lifted my lashes. Our gazes were level. There were tiny gold flecks around the irises of his eyes. I'd never noticed before.

"Look straight ahead."

It was hard not to flinch—that's the instinct when someone's reaching toward your eye.

I swallowed hard, held very still. My head shook a little.

"You're okay," he murmured.

"That's not what you said this morning."

He didn't move and then his thumb very gently brushed my lower lid down, coaxing the lens out with a rinse of saline and edge of folded tissue. It helped that the tears were back. Jesus. It was like I was melting from the inside out. Wet drizzled silently down my cheeks.

Left eye. Then right.

"Got them," he murmured. He looked away as I hastily brushed my damp face. He sealed the case and clicked the lamp back off. Darkness fell like the softest of blankets.

I said in an ordinary voice, "Thank you. That was above and beyond."

And very weird. But what the hell was one more weirdness in this alternate universe I now lived in?

Finn's shadow rose, returned to the bathroom. That light went out, too.

I reached for the Rizatriptan, and he said from overhead, "Wait. You're supposed to give the other stuff twenty minutes."

"Hasn't it been?"

"It's been maybe five."

I let out a groan that was largely frustration, kicked my way between the sheets and pulled the covers over my head.

From outside my cocoon, I heard, "Would you like some ice?"

I asked tersely, "Are we having drinks?"

"Ice in a towel. Would that help?"

Yes. Probably. I said nothing.

After a few heartbeats, I realized he'd finally left.

It should have been a relief.

It wasn't.

# Chapter Thirteen

I started out of my uncomfortable doze at the softness of a towel, cool ice beneath the plush folds, pressed gently to the back of my neck.

Finn said quietly, "Just me. Rest."

I didn't have the energy for anything else. I closed my eyes, drifted, but I was still aware of the pain. Still aware of Finn, sitting on the edge of the bed, holding his makeshift ice pack to the back of my neck.

After several years, my stomach settled a little, which was a huge improvement, despite the unrelenting pain in my head.

I said, "I'm sorry about this morning. I really did mean that to be an apology."

For a second or two he didn't answer. Then he said, "I know. I'm sorry about this morning, too. That wasn't the way…"

He didn't finish it and I said nothing. I'd started it, but it was a conversation I didn't want to have.

"It's been thirty minutes. You want to try the first dose of rizatriptan?"

I opened my eyes, surprised to find, despite the pain, I'd actually dozed off. "Yeah." I sat up cautiously and took the pill from him. I popped it into my mouth. Took the water glass, swallowed a small mouthful, and washed the pill down.

I handed back the glass and lay back down. I couldn't help the shudder that followed, but I said firmly, "You really should get back. I'll be fine in thirty minutes." That was wishful thinking bordering on delusional, but the pain would almost certainly be down to a manageable level.

"Thanks." His tone was acerbic. "I've had all the schmoozing with Vaughn and Lila I can take in one day."

I wondered about that, but said nothing.

Finn shifted beside me, one hand settling lightly on my temple. "Is it the right side?" His fingertips lightly threaded through my hair, brushing across my scalp.

Tiny chills of pleasure rippled over my skin. I assented. He'd massaged my head the other time this had happened. It was the sweetest thing any guy had ever done for me.

"Yeah," he murmured. "That vein pops out right over that little scar above your eyebrow."

"My father hit me with his flashlight when I was ten."

I hadn't meant to say it aloud. I felt the stillness wash through him.

My heart began to pound—he could probably feel that vein pulsing in response—but to my relief he didn't reply, didn't say anything, simply continued to massage my head with that delicate, instinctive touch, and some of the tension drained from my neck and shoulders.

"Have you always had headaches?"

"Off and on. They were so bad in my early thirties, I was sure I had a brain tumor." I could even smile about it now. "I had a million tests. MRIs, CT scans. So really, a chronic migraine diagnosis was good news."

His touch was very gentle. "I bet."

"I almost never get these breakthrough migraines anymore."

"You're stressed and tired." It wasn't a question. Actually, it was an understatement.

Finn's fingers drifted down, circling just above my cheekbone, then gliding up into my hair. He worked in slow, deliberate motions—along the temple, down behind the ear, and finally to the base of my skull. There, he found that knot of tension and used the pads of his thumbs to ease it loose with steady, deliberate pressure.

I breathed slowly, consciously, and for the first time in hours, the pain felt survivable. The incredible relief made me emotional all over again.

I tipped my head back, trying to sound calm and reasonable, "Finn. I don't understand what's happening. I appreciate your help. You did your good deed for the day. You don't have to stay. I'm okay. It's just a headache. I've been through it a million times. You can go with a...a clean conscience."

He stroked my hair back. "I'm not worried about my conscience."

"No, you're worried about mine, apparently."

"Would you like to talk about it?" The carefulness, the kindness was terrifying.

*"Now?"*

"When you're feeling better."

"Since *when*?" I put my hands over my face, pulled them down and sat up, facing him. "I don't understand you at all. You ended it. Today. Just a few hours ago. But now you want to talk? *Now?* You think I'm...I don't know *what* you think I am. A love rat? A serial killer? A love rat serial killer?"

"Keiran." He didn't move back. In fact, he tried to cover my hands with his own.

"It doesn't matter." My throat closed and I had to squeeze out the words. "You were right. It's easier if it's over."

He was quiet for a moment. "Yeah, that's what I thought. But it's not. Every single time I see you, I want—"

Yes. Me, too. Desperately. But he was the one who'd outlined why it wasn't possible. And he'd been perfectly right.

Finn was still stumbling through whatever this was— maybe just a mistimed apology for the way he'd ended things? Because a heads up would have been nice. I'd been entitled to a heads up.

"I know what I said, but I can't reconcile the you I know with..."

*A 'Dateline' special? His entire fucking literary oeuvre?*

"Everyone is a moon, and has a dark side which he never shows to anybody." One of my favorite quotes by Mark Twain.

"It doesn't seem to matter what I tell myself. Or what I tell you. I watched you this evening. I could see you getting quiet, getting paler and paler. I know that little move, where you rest your fingers on your temple."

He spent years in law enforcement, so yes, he was observant. He was a writer, so yes, he was observant. I wanted to say, *Is there a point to this*? But sadly, I wanted to hear it. I wanted to think he really did care on some level. I wanted to think he regretted ending things at least half as much as I regretted his ending things.

He said quietly, "I can't take the idea that you're hurt or in pain."

I moved my head in negation. Not that I disbelieved him. Of course he didn't enjoy watching someone, even someone he was angry with, in pain. He wasn't a psychopath. But I didn't want him to pretend that it was more than kindness. It meant too much to me.

Finn was still explaining in that painstaking way, "And I realized that, as much as I don't want the silence, the secrets—I even more don't want it to be over. Eight years we've—I've— We got so close and now... It's tearing me apart."

Dismay gave me the energy to get off the bed, to move away. "No. I can't take the back and forth. You didn't have any doubts this morning. You can't tell me you think something's wrong with me and then turn around and say you still care. And then tomorrow—what? It's back to me being *America's Most Wanted*?"

"Keir—"

"It's not right. I accepted your decision. This is... I've never done anything to you. It's fucking *cruel*."

"Keiran." He got off the bed too, and tried to put his arms around me. I pushed at him, but then had to sit down on the mattress. I put my head in my hands. I wasn't crying, though I probably should have been.

Finn knelt at my feet, rested his warm hands on my bare knees. "Keir, listen. Just listen for a minute. I shouldn't have brought this up now. I know you're not in any state to cope with it. I'm sorry. If you want me to go, I'll go. But I'd like to stay at least until you're feeling better."

I wanted to say, "Go." One little syllable. One little word. But it stuck in my throat.

I didn't want him to go. I wanted him to stay, wanted to rest in his arms one last time,

Finn waited and when I didn't, couldn't speak, said, "You'll be more comfortable in bed."

It was an assertion rather than a question, and there was no point arguing the obvious.

I didn't answer, didn't resist either as Finn rose, pulled back the bedclothes, guiding me as I crawled between the sheets and tried to lie very still.

He stood for a beat at the edge of the bed.

"*Do* you want me to go?" His voice was gruff.

This was probably it. The last night we would ever spend together in any way, shape, or form. And I just couldn't...

"No," I said wearily, without opening my eyes. "Not yet."

There was a pause. Then the soft rustle of Finn removing his shoes, then his jacket. The bed dipped as he sat, then stretched out on top of the covers beside me, close enough to touch, but not intruding.

"I'll stay as long as you need," he whispered.

I shook my head wearily, but it was at myself, not him. When I didn't answer, he edged closer, and I let myself lean against him. Just a little. When, after a time, his hand found mine, his long fingers closing around mine with familiar careful strength, I didn't pull away. No. I held on. Tight.

In the hush of the darkened room, the pound of the surf below us echoing my heartbeat, and Finn breathing softly beside me, I finally let go.

Around midnight, I had the second dose of rizatriptan.

Finn, who'd been sleeping, woke up and started rubbing my head once more.

"Did you ever kill anyone? When you were a cop?" I asked.

I'd been having some weird and unsettling fever dreams or I'd never have asked.

Finn was silent. Then he said, "No. I was involved in two shootings. No one died. Thank God."

"Yes," I agreed. It would be terrible. Terrible for someone who cared about the doing the right thing as much as Finn.

"Why?" he asked.

I moved my head, not answering. He didn't push it, and after a little while I dozed off again beneath that comforting touch.

Usually, I didn't sleep well sharing a bed, but over the years, I'd gotten used to Finn. Used to the sound of his breathing, his tendency to sprawl out and take up three-quarters of the mattress, even used to his inclination to hold and snuggle. I was not a snuggler. I did not like to be touched when I was sleeping, let alone held, but somehow, I'd come to accept it from Finn. It was okay with Finn.

It was okay that night. More than okay. I was grateful for his strength and closeness. I felt...safe.

I slept lightly, but I did sleep, though I was vaguely aware of him pulling the blankets over my shoulders a couple of times, vaguely aware of him lightly resting his fingers beneath my jaw once. When the alarm on my cell went off at five, I felt him reach over me and quickly mute my phone.

He said softly, firmly, "Go back to sleep," and I did.

Light filtered dimly around the edges of the curtains—muted coastal gray, with the faint cry of gulls somewhere beyond the glass.

I stirred, blinking against the residual throb in my skull. The pain had receded to mostly memory, though my limbs felt leaden, my stomach empty and hollow.

I had the bed to myself, but I knew I was not alone. I raised my head. I could make out the blur of Finn, sitting in the chair across from the bed, scrolling through his phone.

I reached for my glasses, slid them on.

"Did you win?" My voice sounded gravelly. "The Edgar."

Finn glanced up; his mouth curved ruefully. "Nope. Kyle won Best Paperback Original. I knew he would. The book's terrific. T. McGregor got Best Novel. And Hayes got Best First Novel by an American Author.

I groaned in anguish and Finn laughed.

"Hayes is okay. Just young. Trying to figure out where he fits in."

"I'll take your word for it." I closed my eyes. "Do you think he'll really refuse the award?"

"No."

"I didn't think so."

Finn made a sound of amusement. "How are you feeling?"

I said, without opening my eyes, "A swim, a hot shower, it'll be all systems go."

"Here's an idea. What if you skip the swim and sleep a little longer?" I opened my eyes a fraction, watching warily as he rose from the chair. The mattress dipped as he sat down next to my feet. Finn said, "It's going to be a long day. You had a rough night."

He didn't know the half of it.

"Typical migraine."

His expression was serious. "Yeah? Because that was a lot worse than the other time. You scared me."

I grimaced at the idea he had been afraid for me. "I'm fine. And even if I wasn't, I can't afford to show weakness. It'll be interpreted as..."

"Weakness?" Finn suggested.

"Yes."

He said thoughtfully, "Is it possible the buyout has you feeling just a little paranoid?"

"Of course it has! With good reason." Abruptly, I remembered. "Why did you tell Lila you wouldn't accept a new editor?"

He raised his brows like it was a silly question. "I've already got their best editor. Why would I change things just to change things? I'm not going to jeopardize my winning streak."

There were many things I could have said to that, including pointing out that he'd just lost the Edgar.

Watching my face, Finn said quietly, "You know why. I made the decision on impulse. It was a bad decision based on incomplete information."

"Was it, though?"

"Yes."

I sat up carefully, settled my back against the stack of pillows. Truthfully, I would have loved nothing more than to roll over and go back to sleep. For a year. Forever.

"Did you want to call your pet sitter?"

I blinked. "Why?"

"To check on the cats."

I was momentarily baffled, then I remembered a bizarre dreamlike sequence of events from the previous night that seemed to have concluded with me sobbing in Finn's arms. My entire body flushed with embarrassment.

I said shortly, "If I didn't trust Angelique, I'd never have left my boys in her care."

Finn's mouth twitched, though his expression remained grave.

"What?"

"That's undoubtedly the gayest thing I've ever heard you say."

I scowled. "Well, guess what?"

He continued to study me, a humorous glint in his eyes.

I sighed.

He asked kindly, "Would you like some coffee?"

I flinched, swallowed hard. "Not...yet. Thanks."

"Do you feel up to talking?"

I met his eyes steadily.

"Okay," Finn said. "I'll talk."

# Chapter Fourteen

It was too easy to forget he'd been a cop.

Finn looked handsome and dissolute sitting there on my bed. The ruffled hair, the shadowy eyes, and the gold glint of beard. His tuxedo shirt was unbuttoned, and I could see the pale swirls of chest hair and the taut lines of his abdomen. Like the hero on an OG romance cover. *My Hump Buddy the Billionaire.*

Of course, we weren't hump buddies. Not anymore. I wasn't sure what we were at this point.

He said, "I learned more about you last night than in all the years we've known each other."

"Take it from me. Stop while you're ahead." I said it lightly, but I wasn't joking.

Nor was Finn smiling as he said, "One of the things I originally liked about our friendship was how emotionally self-contained you were. When we were together, you were passionate and attentive and funny. I enjoyed every single minute of being with you. And when we were apart, I felt like that part of the relationship went back into a box. It was all about the work. You didn't seem to need or want anything else from me." He drew a breath that was partly a laugh. "Honest to God, it was perfect, ideal, for where I was at that point in my life."

"Same."

"I did notice that you rarely spoke about your past. Even direct questions, you seemed to ignore or evade with a joke. Which was interesting, because your affect *is* direct. But actually, you rarely speak without thinking or tempering your response. I originally misread that for tact. And you *are* very tactful." He shrugged. "Either way, it didn't matter to me."

I said nothing.

"Gradually, I began to want more. More from our friendship. More from you. I think you recognized that right away. And it was plain you weren't interested. You remained charming, affectionate, but the no trespassing signs were clearly posted. And I wasn't about to risk what we had. I loved what we had."

I'm not sure why that made my eyes sting. Because everything made my eyes sting now? I said huskily, "Same."

"Anyway. Before I knew it, years had gone by, and you were the only person I was seeing, the only person I wanted. I went from thinking of our friendship to thinking of our relationship. I thought you were starting to see things differently, too. The phone calls would last longer. We spent more time together at conferences. You brought me that carved wood bookmark from Japan. And the sailboat bookends. You stock my favorite whisky in your liquor cabinet. I felt like you were opening up, emotionally for sure, but I still knew almost nothing about you. I knew you went to Columbia, so I assumed for years that you grew up in New York state. You never mentioned your parents. Not a word about family. I assumed..."

He stopped and I said, "Am I responsible for your assumptions?"

His eyes narrowed. "No. Not at all. But I was a cop for a long time. I'm trained to read inconsistencies, even subtle ones. I'm trained to notice when someone habitually redirects, deflects, or omits. And I've learned the hard way to trust my instincts when a story feels 'off'"—even if it's from someone I care about."

I nodded wearily. I knew it had to be something like this.

He added quietly, "And I do care about you. I— A lot."

I swallowed. Said nothing.

"But obviously, I had to wonder, *if he can trust me in bed, why not with this?* What kind of trauma makes someone that good at avoiding the truth?"

I mimicked, "*Is it pain or is it guilt?*"

He said evenly, "That's right, Keiran. Exactly. I don't know what you're keeping from me, but there's something. And it doesn't take a detective to know it has to do with your past, your father, and Steeple Hill."

"And so, you decided you didn't want to be involved with me after all."

After a moment, Finn said quietly, "Yeah."

I was silent, listening to the hard, anxious pound of my heart in my ears. I said finally, "I understand. I don't blame you. You could have told me you'd changed your mind before we got here, that's all." I shrugged.

"That's all? That's it? That's all you have to say?"

Not anger. Sadness. His bright gaze held mine. Never wavered.

I swallowed, and my mouth was so dry, my throat squeaked.

I said, "Okay. The truth is, I *don't* understand, Finn. It feels unjust. Because you knew all that—or knew that you didn't know—when we agreed...when we agreed..." Words were my thing, but it was very hard to get these out.

Finn watched my struggle, admitted, "When I learned your father had died the week before we were together... It's hard to explain, but I had to face the fact that I really *don't* know you. That you don't want me to know you. And that was probably never going to change."

"You don't think it's unfair to judge me by your relationships with your family?"

He frowned.

"You're close to your parents, to your kid. Hell, you're close to your ex. I didn't—don't have those relationships. I was close to my grandparents. But they died a long time ago. It's not like I-I *can't*-can't love someone."

His face twisted as though that hurt him. He said quickly, "I know that. I'm not saying that."

I drew a hard breath. "Yes. You're right. My father was..."

"Abusive."

I stared at Finn. Nodded. "Yes. He was."

Unpredictable. Violent. Sadistic. He'd have denied, disagreed with all of that. He'd have said he had a bad temper. *That* he openly admitted.

*You know I've got a temper. Why do you deliberately push me?*

I'm not sure why it seemed important, but I wanted to know. "How did you find out I came back to California for his funeral?"

"I ran into Mindy Newburgh at the L.A. Times Festival of Books. She mentioned it. I think she'd heard it from Lila."

I said indignantly, "What the hell does Mindy know about it? Why the hell would you be discussing me with her?"

Finn reddened. "I wasn't discussing you. But our friendship isn't a secret. Mindy was venting. I guess Lila had discussed the possibility of moving her to your list once the merger is complete."

"That's news to me." Not great news, either.

"She said you'd worked together in the past and she felt that you didn't understand her. Didn't get her creative vision. Believe me, I didn't encourage her. She did all the talking."

"And based on that, you decided to cut me off. Without a word."

His green eyes darkened with emotion. "You're right. That was gutless. At the time, I figured you wouldn't want to talk about it. It's not like I haven't tried many times to talk to you about how I felt. You're very good at politely shutting down a conversation you don't want to have."

"You didn't think this was different?"

"It was different to me, yeah. But I told myself it just wouldn't matter that much to you. I genuinely believed that. You weren't the one who pushed for more."

He was right. And he was wrong. I said, "Just so you know: I wouldn't have done that to you."

He regarded me, then said slowly, "No, I don't think you would've. I apologize. Sincerely. I let my insecurities get in the way."

Before I could respond, he amended, "Insecurities combined with instinct. I was a cop for a long time. I can tell when something is not right." He waited, his gaze challenging.

I imagined trying to explain to him how very wrong things were. Starting with *I think someone tried to kill me last night.*

I nodded, rubbed my forehead.

To my astonishment, Finn rose again, scooting next to me and wrapping his arms around me. It wasn't—it was such an instinctive, natural gesture of comfort—*comfort*. As he held me, I could feel that he was offering strength, compassion, protection. He said—and I could feel the steady beat of his heart against mine, hear his words whispered against my ear, "Keir, I know you well enough to know something's wrong. And getting worse. I thought you were having a breakdown last night."

I tried to say lightly, "It's just the normal noises in here."

But he was way past the fencing and diversions and evasions. "Please, let me help you."

*Please.*

That had to be the first time in my life anyone had pleaded with me to let them take some of the weight off.

Slowly it came to me that that if I was ever going to trust anyone, that person would be Finn. In fact, I did trust him. My silence wasn't about the lack of trust. It was...

Complicated.

It was about not wanting to drag Finn into this nightmare. But also, it was about not wanting Finn to see who I really was. I dreaded losing his respect almost more than I dreaded losing *him*. And there was more, yes. It was also about having to deal with consequences, because once Finn knew the whole story, he was not going to be okay with it. He was not going to take the attitude of letting sleeping dogs lie.

The truth was, these dogs weren't sleeping. They were hunting me.

Was the real me, the old me, really worse than what Finn imagined? Because he clearly imagined something, someone unsalvageable.

I rested my head on his shoulder. Finn gently squeezed the back of my neck. The fact that he didn't try to urge his point, didn't say anything at all, calmed me, allowed me to consider. For the last thirty-something hours, I'd been in constant motion, reacting emotionally to events rather than thinking rationally.

If anyone *could* help, it was probably Finn. He *wanted* to help.

I drew back—it wasn't easy—and untangled myself from the sheets and blankets, climbing out of bed. "I want to show you something."

I padded over to the sliding glass door.

Finn watched in silence as I pulled back the drapes and opened the glass door, stepping out onto the sunlit balcony. I shivered in the morning breeze skipping off the ocean.

He suddenly moved from the bed, following me out onto the balcony, and I wondered if it had gone through his mind that I might jump. He seemed to believe I was in a precarious state, and maybe I was, but I was made of sterner stuff than that.

I half expected the manuscript to be gone—that's how weird my life had become of late, but no. It was right where I'd left it, wedged down between the cement planter and container. I pulled the binder out, brushed the dirt from the damp pages.

I handed the sheaf to Finn and returned inside, climbing shakily onto the bed.

"*I Know What You Did?*" He watched me huddle back under the blankets. "What is this?"

"I'm not completely sure. I'm pretty confident it's not a submission."

He closed the glass doors and dropped into the chair beside the window. He flipped open the binder and began to read. I watched him for a minute or two, watched his eyes narrow, watched his mouth straighten into a hard line.

He read through to the end, and said finally, "That's it? One chapter?"

"Yes."

"Who's U.N. Owen?"

That wasn't the question I expected. I wasn't sure if I was relieved or not. "I think he's an author by the name of Troy Colby."

"And you know him how?"

"I don't. I don't think I do. He handed me this manuscript after the Stranger Than Fiction panel and kept going. I was talking to Rachel and didn't get a good look at him."

"But you know his name...how?"

"Colby lives at the address on the title page."

Finn didn't have to glance down. "In Steeple Hill?"

"Yes."

"Where you went yesterday." It wasn't a question.

"Yes."

"What did he have to say for himself?"

Again, not the question I expected. "I didn't speak to him."

Finn said nothing.

I said, "According to his neighbor, Colby is here."

"*Here*? At the conference?"

"Yes."

Finn frowned. "But you haven't spoken to him?"

"Until yesterday afternoon, I wouldn't have known who to ask for. By the time I got back last night..."

My words dried up as I remembered the reason for the delay. The funny thing was it was already starting to feel distant. Unreal. A terrifying dream—but a dream.

It wasn't a dream, though. I hadn't imagined it.

"You were running late."

"Yes. I had a…flat on the drive back to Monterey." The habit of keeping things to myself was so deeply ingrained that even now I was stalling telling the complete story. "I don't know why—it never occurred to me that he was still at the conference. I assumed his purpose in showing up was to deliver the manuscript. Apparently, he actually *is* an aspiring writer."

Finn looked thoughtful. "Is it possible you previously rejected one of his manuscripts? Maybe you had a run-in at another conference?"

If so, it seemed like an extreme reaction. "It's possible."

"You don't think so?"

"I don't know. It wouldn't explain how he knows…"

"Right. Given your reaction, I'm taking it for granted this manuscript isn't a prank or a stunt. How much of it is accurate?"

"Someone knows more than I would have thought possible. But it's wrong on key points."

That there was no actual location given, beyond outside at night, was interesting. Some of it could certainly have been guesswork. Or simply the most likely scenario?

His green gaze was serious, steady. "Such as?"

"I didn't kill Dom."

"Okay. So, there really was a Dom."

He seemed weirdly matter-of-fact. Was that a cop thing? The trained reaction of someone used to hearing bizarre and alarming information?

"Dominic Baldwin. Yes."

"Is there a Milo?"

"There was. Yes. Milo Argyros."

"Who killed Dom? Milo?"

It was difficult to reply because I wasn't sure he believed me, and of course this was a big part of what I'd feared all along.

"Yes. It was self-defense."

Finn's expression remained unreadable. "What happened?"

At the time it had all seemed black and white. Now, older and wiser, I understood how much I had assumed, how much I had taken for granted, and how other people were liable to view and judge my decisions.

As I hesitated, Finn said, "Start at the beginning."

"Right. I'm not sure how it started. Dom and Milo were both on the football team. They were friends until senior year. But then Dom found out—or at least suspected—that Milo was gay, and he started to harass him, tried to bully him. It escalated. They got into a couple of fights at school and were nearly kicked off the team, but Dom's father was a judge. The Baldwins were rich and influential."

Nothing from Finn.

"Milo's family wasn't rich or influential, but he was our best player. Well, he and Dom were our two top players, so... Nothing happened. There were warnings. No one really made any effort to sort it out. Maybe there was no sorting it out. It went on like that and then, one night Milo phoned me and said Dom had attacked him and Milo had fought back. He was afraid he'd killed Dom and he was begging for my help."

"Why you? Where did you fit in?" Finn asked.

"Milo and I were— He was my boyfriend."

My first boyfriend. My first love.

Finn nodded slowly. "Got it. So, Milo phones you that he thinks he's killed Dominic. Then what?"

"I went to the graveyard—"

"Wait. What?"

"St. Bibiana's. There's a historic cemetery in Steeple Hill where high school kids used to get high or just fool around. Maybe they still do. Milo would go there to drink. Dom knew that."

"Right. You went to the cemetery and—?"

"Dominic was dead."

"Was he?"

My eyes flashed to Finn's. I stared at him. "*Yes.* I swear to God. He was dead. His head was...smashed in." Even now, the memory shook me. "It wasn't a rock, though. Milo said he had to grab a flower urn. He—Milo was covered in blood, too. There were marks, bruises on his neck where Dom had tried to strangle him. It *was* self-defense. Dom would have killed him."

"That's very possible. You weren't there, though. You didn't see it. This is Milo's account of what happened. Correct?

"I could see that Milo had been fighting for his life. He was in shock. Crying. Shaking."

It remained real and present in my memory, and yet as I related a scene I had replayed in my mind thousands, if not millions, of times, the narrative sounded flat and fake. I sounded like I was reading from a script. I *felt* like I was reading from a script.

There was no deciphering Finn's expression. "What happened next?"

"We didn't know what to do. Because of Judge Baldwin."

"Ah. The rich and influential judge?"

"Yes."

"Neither of you went to your parents? Neither of you contacted law enforcement?" Finn sounded like he'd heard this same depressing story a million times. Stupid, violent kids doing stupid, violent things.

I met his gaze. "At the time my father was sheriff."

"I...see." He expelled a long, controlled breath. "Okay. That... I understand why you didn't have confidence in the system. But if it was actually self-defense, why didn't Milo go to the sheriff's department? Or another agency. Why didn't he talk to a teacher? Why didn't he talk to his parents?"

"I don't know for a fact that he didn't talk to his parents. I never told anyone. Until now. I don't *think* Milo told anyone. The last time we spoke, he hadn't told."

"Why didn't he go to law enforcement?"

"Milo knew about—what my father was like. Even if I'd encouraged him to talk to someone at the sheriff's office..." I shook my head. "There would have had to be a trial. His family wasn't well off. How would they afford a decent lawyer? They'd have had to mortgage their home. And Milo was relying on scholarships for college. If he was arrested, even if he was found not guilty, his future would have been trashed."

Finn heard me out. He said curiously, "That's what you thought back then. Is that what you think now?"

I opened my mouth, but he was right. These were the arguments we'd made at the time. As an adult, I could see, not only the flaws in our teenaged logic, but the troubling ethical gaps in our reasoning.

He didn't wait for my reply. "I interrupted you. What happened after you got to the graveyard and saw that Dominic was dead?"

"Milo was terrified and panicking. He wanted me to help bury Dom in the cemetery. I tried. We tried. But we just couldn't do it. Shoveling a hole deep enough to bury a full-sized human?"

Finn said wryly, "It's extremely difficult. The improper or inadequate disposal of the body is one of the most common ways murderers get nailed. It's a major vulnerability because a corpse is large, heavy, and difficult to transport or destroy without drawing attention. Also, most perps underestimate the forensic evidence a body carries."

Fantastic. I had been reduced to a *perp* in Finn's mind.

I said, "Even if we'd had all the time in the world, I don't think we could have done it. And we didn't have all the time in the world. So, I told Milo I'd take care of it."

Finn's brows drew together. "Which meant what?"

I swallowed hard. My stomach felt very rocky again.

*A five-minute drive that had seemed to take hours. The old pickup's high beams carving narrow, skittish tunnels of light through the fog-shrouded pines. The dead weight of Dominic's lifeless form sliding, settling with a horrible finality when I took corners too fast. The rattle of the shovel in the bed of the truck, clanging like a broken church bell with every pothole. The sweet, metallic taste of blood in my mouth—I'd bitten the inside of my cheek without realizing it.*

I said dully, "We loaded Dom in the bed of my pickup. I told Milo to go home. Then I drove out to Pescadero Marsh Natural Preserve and dumped the body."

# Chapter Fifteen

"He left you to handle that by yourself?"

Finn's voice startled me out of my stricken memories. I looked up. I'd never seen that expression on his face before.

I was reminded that there was a side to him I'd never seen. The side that had first chosen law enforcement as a profession. The side that enabled him to carry a gun. To use a gun. To be willing to die in the course of his duties. To be willing to kill.

"He… He was in shock. Terrified. Horrified."

Finn repeated again without any inflection, "Milo left you to deal with that on your own?"

"I…yes."

"Was the body ever found?"

"No."

"Are you sure?"

"It's something I've kept an eye on."

After what felt like a long time, he said, "How old were you?"

"Seventeen."

"How old was Milo?"

"Just turned eighteen."

He nodded as though this confirmed something. "The fact that you were a minor when this happened is significant. That affects your potential sentencing."

I said nothing. The words *your potential sentencing* paralyzed me.

"That said, off the top of my head we're looking at accessory after the fact, tampering with evidence, abuse of a corpse, conspiracy. That's three felonies and one possible felony-possible misdemeanor."

"I know," I said. "Also, obstruction of justice, misprision of a felony, unauthorized use of a protected area, destruction of wetlands, illegal dumping, water pollution... And if I'm especially unlucky, disturbing a protected species."

Finn's brows shot up. "I hope a jury finds it equally amusing."

I said hotly, "Hell no, it's not amusing. I just told you my father was the sheriff. Do you think I didn't understand we were breaking the law? Do you think I didn't look all this up years ago to see...to find out how many years I might spend in prison?"

"Keiran..."

"I've had more than twenty years to think about what I *should* have done versus what I did do. That night shaped the rest of my life. Including—I mean, do you think it never dawned on me what a terrible, *terrible* idea it was to fall for a cop—ex-cop? I used to lie awake at night wondering if I'd be serving my sentences consecutively or concurrently."

Finn's expression softened slightly. "Most of these charges, except for the murder, likely expired long ago."

I said, "There's no statute of limitations on murder. That includes accessory."

In California, that meant anything from three to fifteen years in state prison. Depending on the circumstances it could mean more. This wasn't an area of expertise for me. I helped writers craft stories about catching killers—not following the killer's journey through the legal system. In most mystery novels, the story ended with the killer's arrest.

Finn said, "Unfortunately, that's correct."

In this particular case, he was sympathetic. That would not have been his usual response.

After a moment, he asked ruefully, reluctantly, "Did you fall for an ex-cop?"

"You were there. You know I did."

He changed the subject, and I couldn't blame him. "I understand why, as a kid, you felt you had no recourse. But why didn't you tell me about this? Why didn't you ask for my help years ago? You knew how I felt."

I said bitterly, "Yep, that's the way to treat someone who cares about you. Drag them into the quagmire, too."

Finn gave me an odd look, started to say something, but then apparently changed his mind. "Regardless, I'm glad you told me the truth now. I'll do whatever I can to help you. It's a fucking mess, though. You're right about that. This is not the kind of thing that fixes itself with time."

"I know."

"That kid's family has had to wonder for twenty years—"

I pressed the heels of my hands against my eyes.

There was a sharp silence.

Finn muttered, "Christ. At least, in your case, there are mitigating circumstances. I know people. I still have contacts. I can—"

I lowered my hands, said quickly, "No. You can't get any more involved. I appreciate that you want to help, and any…any advice you can give me will be... But you have to keep a distance."

"If you think I'm worried about my goddamned writing career—"

"No. You don't understand. It's so much worse than… this."

Finn's eyes narrowed. "What do you mean, it's so much worse than this?"

"About a month after it happened, Milo disappeared."

"*Disappeared*," Finn repeated. "What's that mean?"

"I mean, he left. I guess. Without waiting to graduate. Without a word."

"He left, you *guess*?"

"Yes."

"Without a word to *you* or without a word to anyone?"

"Definitely without a word to me. I think without a word to anyone. His family eventually reported him missing."

Finn prompted impatiently, "And—?"

"I don't know. I left Steeple Hill the day after I turned eighteen. I never spoke to my father or anyone else from there again. With the exception of Kyle."

Finn did a double take. "Kyle? Kyle Bari?"

"He grew up in Steeple Hill."

"Did you know him then?"

That was almost funny. "Kyle? No. He'd have been around seven at the time all this happened. Anyway, the art colony residents stuck mostly to themselves. And probably still do."

After a few seconds of bleak reflection, Finn seemed to relinquish whatever sinister idea had struck him. He asked, "What did you think happened to Milo?"

I shook my head. "I didn't know. I thought his nerve gave out. I thought he ran away. He was terrified we were going to be caught."

"You weren't terrified?"

"Of course I was." Terrified. Guilty. Lonely. Life had been difficult before. After Milo left, it had been all but unbearable. "I couldn't leave, though. I didn't have that option. I had to graduate. My grandparents had taken out a reverse mortgage and put the money into a trust for when I turned eighteen. I needed that money for college. I stuck out the last few months and then I left, too."

I couldn't read Finn's expression at all.

I said, "At the time, I felt betrayed. He'd left me with this horrible thing we'd done. He couldn't even say goodbye? Later, I began to wonder. I tried to find him a few times, but he'd vanished. There was nothing. No trace." I met Finn's gaze. "I even thought about hiring a private detective. But I was afraid that might lead someone back to me. Eventually, I began to suspect he was dead. That maybe he killed himself. Then I wondered if maybe someone else had killed him. And after last night, I'm sure of it."

Finn said slowly, wonderingly, "I feel like I'm in that story about the guy who comes back from a trip and the servant tells him his favorite dog died."

I laughed shakily. "The Climax of Horrors."

"Yeah." He fell silent, thinking. "Locating Milo is a priority. If he can confirm your version of events, that would go a long way toward keeping you out of prison."

"But that's what I'm trying to tell you," I said. "I think he's dead. I believe he must have died that same year."

"Why? Why do you believe that?"

"Because I think someone tried to kill me last night."

Finn slowly sat back in his chair. "Go on."

I said, "I know how it sounds. I swear to you, Finn, I'm not making this up."

He gave a funny laugh. "I think if you were making this up, you'd probably try not to incriminate yourself so thoroughly. Tell me about last night."

I told him. All of it. About going by the old house, about tracking Colby down and talking to his neighbor, about the long, terrible drive home and the blowout in the middle of nowhere. I told him everything with the exception of Judy Jenning's oblique comments. Even if I'd felt ready and able to confront the possibility that my father had killed my mother—and I didn't—wasn't—things were complicated enough already.

Finn heard me without interruption, though his face grew dark and severe.

When I'd trailed into silence, he said, "Where's the rental car now?"

"I left it with the valet when I got back last night."

"And the slashed tire's still in the trunk? You didn't dump it along the way?"

Why on earth would I have dumped it along the way? Oh. Right. To cover up the fact that the tire wasn't slashed. That there had been no flat. That I was making it all up. That was the way Finn's brain worked. Rudolph had been spot-on in the elevator when he'd characterized Finn's writing as *Those bleak police procedurals. All that violence and betrayal and corruption.*

"It's in the trunk. Yes."

I watched doubtfully as he rose, tucking in his shirt, buttoning it. With a businesslike air, he rolled up his sleeves, crisp white cotton against tanned forearms. "Where's the claim ticket? I want to have a look for myself."

"I'm not sure that will prove anything. I could have slashed the tire."

He stopped in the process of slipping on his shoes and surveyed me. With a shade of exasperation, he said, "Keir, stop thinking like an editor of mystery novels for a minute. You were tired, stressed, and spooked last night. Anyone would have been. You're not a mechanic. You might be wrong about what damaged the tire. And you might be reading more into the fact that the driver of the Cadillac stopped to help. Coincidences do happen."

I opened my mouth, but he cut me off. "We can't be guessing. We can't be theorizing. We need to know for sure whether someone really does intend you harm. Because that changes everything."

He was right. I nodded wearily.

Something changed in his expression. He said more patiently, "It's going to take me at least forty-five minutes. You didn't sleep much last night. Why not nap while you can? It's going to be a hell of a long day."

He didn't sound like he was looking forward to it any more than I was. Understandably.

"All right. The claim ticket is in one of my Levis pockets."

He nodded, turned to go, and I said quickly, "Phineas?"

He turned back; his brows raised in inquiry.

"I'm sorry for involving you in this. It's the last thing I intended."

Finn's smile was sardonic. "Now *that* I know is the truth."

I tried to sleep after Finn left.

I stretched out on the bed and closed my eyes, listening to the rumble of the surf beneath the building. I wanted to sleep. I needed to sleep. But I kept seeing Finn's face as I'd poured out the whole sick, sad story. I couldn't not remember how his expression changed from concern and caring to disbelief to professional distance.

He was never going to think of me the same way again. I couldn't blame him. But it was still difficult.

Regardless of how much Finn deplored my actions, he would try to help, though, and I had finally reached the point of being more grateful for the help than afraid of the consequences.

Last night had been the turning point. Crouched down in the mud and mist, believing I might die in the next few minutes, I'd had an epiphany.

I, too, was tired of the silences and secrets.

I did not want to die. That went without saying. But I also did not want to live without companionship and love and intimacy.

I'd built a good life for myself. I was financially comfortable. I had work I enjoyed and found meaningful. I was liked and respected by my colleagues. Mostly. I had friends and an active social life. I had my dear little cats. I had my health. Most of the time.

None of which changed the fact that I was lonely.

Intensely lonely.

And had been for years.

Security. Stability. Safety.

The three tenets of my adult life. Every choice I'd made since leaving Steeple Hill for college had been made with those three goals in mind. And I'd achieved those goals.

And then some. I'd achieved everything I set out to achieve.

And the payoff was that I was lonely.

Secure. Stable. Safe. Lonely.

Ironically, I was about to lose all of it—with the exception of the loneliness.

It was going to be a whole lot lonelier moving forward.

Once again, I saw Finn's expression. The realization. The shock. The withdrawal.

He was one of the good guys, though. He'd help me as much as he could. And once we'd exhausted every possible avenue to delay the inevitable, he'd come and visit me in prison, like he did some of the other felons he felt some affection or responsibility for. He'd speak up at my parole hearings. He'd help me find work when I got out.

Because there was no question I was going to prison. Hopefully, not for fifteen years. Hopefully, I'd get parole. I did not want to try to rebuild my life in my sixties. My fate would depend on a number of things. But we both knew I was going to prison. Which was still better than being dead.

Either way, I was going to lose everything I'd worked for.

Either way, when this was all over, I would be starting from scratch.

Either way, I was going to lose Finn. Maybe not his loyalty. Maybe not his friendship. But any kind of future of together.

Midway through my revelations, I'd watched him fall out of love with me. And that hurt worse than any slap or punch my father had landed.

My cell pinged a notification and I jumped. Grabbing the phone, hoping it was Finn, I scanned the reminder—scanned it again—and swore.

I was supposed to be taking Grace Hollister to breakfast at nine o'clock.

It was eight-twenty now. I closed my eyes, struggled for control.

What was the *point*?

Was there *any* point to this? Given what lie ahead of me?

No. There was not.

And yet, I was already on my feet, striding into the bathroom, turning the shower taps on full blast.

Grace was a very nice woman and she'd made the trip all the way from the English Lake District. Not solely to have breakfast with me, of course, but she'd wanted to discuss...what they all wanted to discuss: their fucking books, their fucking careers, their fucking marketing budgets.

I sucked in a couple of lungsful of steamy eucalyptus, closed my eyes, and concentrated on how good the jets of very hot water felt on my tired body. My thoughts cleared.

*Focus on the here and now. Stay in the moment.*

Of *course* there was a point to this.

W&W was going to do their best to bully Grace into one of their godawful unfavorable contracts, so of course I needed to prepare her.

We'd signed her after she'd written an engaging non-fiction account of her first trip to Britain and subsequent involvement with a former jewel thief (to whom she was still married!) and the hunt for a missing work by Lord Byron.

Oxygen network had even optioned the book.

She was currently working on a well-researched, witty historical mystery series featuring Lord Byron. Unfortunately, W&W felt the historical mystery market was glutted.

So, yes, we absolutely needed to have this breakfast.

I finished shaving, turned off the water, brushed my teeth, liberally applied eye drops, superglued my hair into submission, and hunted for my jeans. Finn had kindly picked my scattered clothes off the floor and tossed them to the sofa. I examined the Levis and realized the knees were caked in mud.

I blinked against the memory of the reason for that, returned to the bedroom, and found a spare pair of jeans. I pulled on a clean white Oxford shirt—classic N.Y. male editor vibe: slightly rumpled Oxford shirt, blazer, worn but expensive desert boots, and beat-up messenger bag. Except I didn't have the energy to lug around even an empty messenger bag.

I put on my glasses and left the room, half-jogging to the elevator. Stepping inside, I pressed the button for the first level. I glanced at my watch. I was probably going to be about five minutes late, given the likelihood that we'd be stopping at every floor.

Impatiently, I leaned forward to press the close-door button and just before the doors slid shut, a man suddenly slipped through the shrinking gap. He must have thought the elevator was empty, because he jumped. Truthfully, we both jumped. I'd half expected Troy Colby to barge in.

Instead, I recognized Thomas McGregor.

Somehow, I managed not to go completely fan boy.

Like Finn, McGregor was a former cop who wrote highly regarded hardboiled police procedurals. His books lacked the black humor and compassion of Finn's. His themes veered more toward the Shakespearean and the prose...the prose was gorgeous, complex, lyrical. Even critics who found his plots silly melted into puddles over his extraordinary mastery of the English language.

"Good morning." I said politely, pretending that I hadn't just recoiled like the heroine in a Lifetime thriller trapped in a high-rise with a mad killer.

Granted, so had McGregor. He looked at me, nodded in polite dismissal and stared straight ahead at the control panel.

I'd been reading him for years, but had never managed to meet him before. His book jacket photos were usually in black and white and, I couldn't help thinking, were a bit out of date. He was now about my age, medium height, and stockier than his author photo would lead one to believe. His hair was brown with reddish glints that I didn't think were completely natural. Why do so many men opt for red when their hair begins to gray? Anyway, his eyes were very bright, very blue. He sported one of those formidable hipster beards and a nicely tailored blue Harris tweed blazer.

"I enjoy your books very much," I offered.

He nodded in acknowledgement but continued to stare straight ahead.

The message was loud and clear: Do Not Bother Me. Or maybe Get Tae Fuck, seeing that he was Scottish. Anyway, I didn't take offense. Not all authors are people persons. In fact, the job practically requires the opposite: creatives who are comfortable living with their own uninterrupted thoughts for hours, days, even months at a time.

Conferences can be especially challenging for that personality type, given that an author's role at a conference fell somewhere between celebrity and rug merchant.

I wasn't exactly bubbling with joie de vivre either, so I was happy to shut up and lean back against the wall.

On the fourth floor, three women and a spindly youth boarded, instantly recognized McGregor, and proceeded to tell him at length how much they loved his work. He did not ignore them, but he seemed stiff and uncomfortable. Maybe he didn't do conferences.

On the third floor, several more people crowded in, clutching their book bags and coffee cups. Cherry, my PA, was among them. She spotted me, and leaned around a short, bearded man to exclaim, "Oh, Keiran! I've been trying to text you!"

"Have you?" I pulled my phone out, checked it, and yes, I'd had two texts from her in the last two minutes.

"Damn," I murmured. "Finn muted my phone this..." I caught her expression, realized what I'd said, and swallowed the rest of it.

Cherry beamed at me. "Oh, *yay*! When you skipped his Smoking Gun interview, I was afraid you two—"

I raised my brows meaningfully and she cut herself off, blushing. "Grace has to cancel," she said quickly.

*"What?"*

It sounded more indignant than I'd intended, and everyone in the elevator stared at me.

"She's not feeling well."

"*She's* not feeling well?"

"Nooo. She was so sorry, but she sounded terrible. She's definitely coming down with *something*."

Our fellow travelers shrank back a couple of centimeters as though *terrible* was catching. Actually, it was.

I processed this new intel, sighed, and said, "Okay. That's all right. I'm sorry she's under the weather."

I was, and I was also definitely going back up to bed.

Cherry nodded but suddenly gave an evil laugh and whispered way too loudly, "Ariel Newsome was telling everybody in the bar last night what you said to Millie."

"Oh, God," I said in alarm.

"No! It was *brilliant.* I wish you'd been there. After the banquet, we all went down to the lobby bar and *our* art department and *W&W's* art department started doing shots in your honor."

I stared at her in horror.

"Really," Cherry insisted. "You're a hero. You're *our* hero."

I widened my eyes at her and made the time-honored gesture for *shut up.* Except *that* gesture is one of zipping the lips and I did a slashing motion across my neck. No wonder she looked confused.

The spindly youth giggled.

We reached the second floor where most of the panels were being held. Everyone scooched over, making way for Thomas McGregor, before piling out in his wake.

"Should we liaison?" Cherry turned back to ask, blocking the doors from closing.

"Huh?"

"Like yesterday. Did you want to get together to go over some things? Is there anything I should know about today?"

"Uh... I'll send you my notes later. Just, you know, carry on."

"Do you need me for your Backstory interview?"

"My— Sure. Bring smelling salts."

She laughed. "And a shot of bourbon?"

"Exactly." I made a little shooing motion, she stepped back, and the doors closed.

I pressed the button for going up again, pressed it desperately, but of course it had to finish its descent into the bowels of hell.

On the first floor, the doors slid open and Hayes Hartman stepped inside.

So, in fact, I really *had* descended to the bowels of hell.

Hayes stared at me with his glittery blue eyes and took his cell phone out.

I didn't have the energy for Mr. Hartman, but I also couldn't get behind the adolescent rudeness of pretending another person wasn't standing three feet away.

I said, "Congratulations on the Edgar."

Hayes gave a short laugh. "Thanks." He continued to stare at his phone.

I said, "Hayes, have I done something to offend you?"

He made a wondering expression and theatrically gasped, "Gosh. What could you have done, Keiran?"

"I honestly don't know. Have we even met before?"

He glared. "You don't remember Bouchercon in New Orleans?"

"I remember Bouchercon in New Orleans."

"But you don't remember me?"

"I—" *No* was clearly the wrong answer. *Did* I remember him? Maybe he'd looked different? People changed. Granted, B'con NO had only been two years ago.

I was still trying to think of a diplomatic way to say *not really*, when he demanded, "You don't remember holding one-on-one feedback sessions?"

I did not. Which is to say, I remembered having one-on-one feedback sessions with about six authors that weekend. Not a lot, compared to how many I'd conducted back in my junior editor days, but multiply that by several events a year multiplied by a decade?

Yes, regrettably, the endless parade of authors and their five-page submissions tended to blur together in my mind.

Hayes said, "That's ironic. Given that the book you trashed just won the Edgar."

I echoed, "The book I *trashed*?"

I was pretty sure I'd never trashed anyone's book. Trashing books is typically performed by rival authors.

His lip curled.

I said, "I'm not infallible. My opinion is informed, but in the end it's just another opinion. I'm glad the book did well for you."

"Sure, you are." He went back to scrolling through his phone.

It was exasperating, to say the least. There had to be more going on here than a forty-five-minute critique *he'd requested* two years ago.

I gave him a look of disbelief, shrugged. What more was there to say?

Hays murmured, "You may have Scottie snowed, but you don't fool me."

*Scottie.*

Okay. Now I got it.

Not as complicated as I'd imagined.

# Chapter Sixteen

The sound of Finn letting himself back inside the suite woke me from the light sleep I'd fallen into when I'd returned upstairs.

I opened my eyes, listening lazily as Finn moved around the main room. I heard the drapes opening, felt the light change in the bedroom, the wash of sea breeze as he opened windows and glass doors in the living room. It felt peaceful.

Despite everything that had happened, I felt strangely calm.

A little while later I heard Finn speaking on the phone, but his voice was low and I couldn't make out the words.

He seemed to be on the phone a while, or maybe he made a couple of different calls. I continued to drift in and out of sleep.

When the floorboard outside the bedroom creaked, I opened my eyes and turned my head.

Finn had returned to his own room since that morning. He wore charcoal trousers and a flatteringly fitted moss-green dress shirt. He'd shaved and his hair was neatly combed. He looked handsome and assured—and unfairly well-rested.

"How are you feeling?" he asked.

"Better than I did." I sat up and rubbed my head briskly. "What time is it? Do you have a panel?"

"Mm-hm. The Thin Blurred Line. With J.X., Pat Robinson, and your very favorite author T. McGregor"

"Ha. I wouldn't say Thomas McGregor is my *favorite* author."

Finn's mouth quirked. "That'll be a disappointment to Lila. She's hoping you'll accept an All-Star trade before the All-Star Game. T. McGregor for me."

"For *you*? Like hell. Are you serious?"

"I sure am. I heard her whole pitch to Vaughn. I think she wanted me to hear it."

I absorbed it and said, "Is that what you want?" I braced myself for his answer.

"I do not. Damn. I forgot my pen. Do you have one? Preferably not red."

"Do I have a *pen*? Is that a serious question? Check my messenger bag. It's by the little desk in the alcove."

Finn moved out of the doorway. I called, "It's all irrelevant, isn't it? I don't think I'll be doing a lot of editorial work in San Quentin. Unless I'm in charge of the prison newsletter."

He must have done a complete 360 because he stepped back into the doorway and said, "That's a little pessimistic."

"Just keeping it real."

Finn's brows drew together. "You're not going to prison if I can help it." He added, "What would your cats do without you?"

I got that he was joking, but I was still a long way from being able to laugh at any of it.

I said carefully, "I appreciate that. But there's only so much you can do."

He tilted his head, considering me. "What's going on?"

"I'm pretty sure you were here for the grand reveal."

"I was. And I'm still here. I plan to be here for the foreseeable future. Until such time as you decide otherwise."

Like that was even a possibility?

"Is it up to me?"

"Hell, yes, it's up to you." He seemed a little perplexed.

I held his gaze. It wasn't easy. "I kind of got the feeling this morning you'd perhaps experienced a-a change of heart."

Finn looked taken aback. "About you?"

"I wouldn't blame you."

"Keiran." He frowned and came over to the bed, putting his arm around my shoulders. "Are you serious? You're in doubt how I feel about you?"

"You were shocked this morning. Rightfully. Nobody expects the... Torquemada."

Finn scoffed, "Is a panicked seventeen-year-old kid supposed to have been the Grand Inquisitor?"

Because Finn wrote bleak and bloody crime fiction and leaned into that jaded ex-cop persona—his author photos were full-color illustrations of rugged masculinity and athletic prowess—it was easy to forget that he'd graduated from USC with a B.A. in Humanities. He was a tough guy—sure as hell he was tougher than me—but he was also educated, perfectly capable of clearly communicating his thoughts and feelings, of listening to others, of laughing at himself, and making love—not just fucking—with skill, delicacy, and tenderness.

I didn't answer, and he said calmly, "One of the things about being a cop is you learn early on that good people sometimes do bad things. Sometimes with the best intentions."

I nodded. That was a common theme in his books.

Finn said, "It's a horrible story and, yes, I was shocked by some of what you told me. But it's not like I didn't know I was going to hear some troubling things. If I didn't care— If I didn't plan on helping you—I wouldn't have pushed for the truth. I'd have let you keep your secrets and I'd have moved on. One way or the other, we're going to work this out. If you do end up doing time, well, you'll serve out your sentence. You'll get through it one day at a time. There are worse things. Right?"

I swallowed. "I don't know. Maybe not for me. I'll be a convicted felon. My career, everything I've worked for..."

A muscle moved in his jaw, but he said briskly, "I think you're a hell of a lot stronger than you give yourself credit for. But. The goal is to keep you *out* of prison. The goal is to avoid destroying your career and the life you've built. We've got some things going for us, including your age at the time and your home life. But I'm not a lawyer. We're going to get advice from actual experts at navigating this side of the system. People who can recognize an extenuating circumstance a mile away."

I nodded.

Finn said firmly, "I'm not going anywhere. Believe it or not, I'm as invested in the outcome here as you are."

Probably not, but I appreciated the thought.

"Okay." I nodded, expelled a long breath. "Thank you. Sorry for the...wobble."

"You're allowed the occasional wobble." I couldn't see his face, but I heard the wry humor in the sound he made before he dropped a quick kiss on my temple and let me go. He rose. "Anyway, you have no idea what a relief it is to know that you're *not* a love rat and that my retirement is still safe."

That wrung a weak laugh out of me.

Finn grinned but was serious again as he said, "Take it easy until I get back. We'll order breakfast and talk. We'll figure out our next steps."

His expression was relaxed, neutral, but I knew him well enough to know what he wasn't telling me.

"The tire was slashed, wasn't it?"

His eyes met mine briefly. "Yep. It was. And Troy Colby *is* staying in this hotel. So, I think it's great idea for you stay here and prep for your Backstory interview."

It's not like a lot of preparation was required to discuss my career in publishing.

"I can't hide out in my hotel room. That's not going to solve anything."

"I'm not suggesting you hide out. I'm saying cool your jets while I do this panel and the signing and then we'll sit down and put together a plan for moving forward."

I truly did not like the idea of sheltering in place; however, I couldn't help wondering what I'd do if I happened to bump into Troy Colby.

Also, if the driver of the Cadillac DeVille was connected to Colby—and it was hard to believe that the slashed tire had nothing to do with U.N. Owen—then he knew exactly where I'd been headed last night. He knew exactly where to find me.

Which, frankly, was an alarming thought. So yes, maybe I could use my down time to do a little online reconnaissance.

"All right. It's not like I don't have plenty of work waiting. I can catch up on some email."

"Exactly. How about you deadbolt the door after I leave?"

"Yes. Okay." I got up and followed him to the entryway. Finn opened the door, leaned back, and kissed my mouth, gently, casually. "I'll see you in a bit."

"Knock¯em dead." I heard the echo of that and winced.

Finn suppressed what sounded like a chuckle and pulled the door shut behind him.

For the record, I did touch base with Angelique, who did send proof-of-life photos of Wing Ding and Sing Song. I smiled like a goof at pics of my little pals getting along perfectly well without me, and then settled down with my laptop in the airy sunlit living room of my suite.

There's a lot to be said for the beneficial properties of fresh air and sunshine. Oh, and getting enough sleep. I felt a thousand percent better than I had even a few hours earlier.

After drinking a couple of glasses of water, I briefly checked email and texts, read the social media posts on the conference. It was all pretty much as expected.

General complaints.

*Why do they schedule the best panels all at the same time??*

*The moderator talked more than the panelists. Again.*

*Why are so many men on the 'Women in Crime Fiction' panel?*

Newbie author anxiety.

*Smiled at someone I thought I knew. They were a total stranger. Now we're apparently having drinks at 5.*

*Someone asked what I'm working on. I panicked and said 'a memoir'*

*Why does every networking event feel like the cafeteria in Squid Games?*

Judging by the live reporting, Noir at the Shore seemed to be going off without a hitch. Or rather, the hitches were all the normal and predictable ones. None of my authors had posted anything offensive or career-harming. Frankly, a little *more* posting would not have come amiss.

I skimmed my email for emergencies and urgencies, and saw nothing that couldn't wait until next Friday. Was I still flying back on Thursday? I had no idea. It seemed unlikely Finn and I would be sightseeing. But maybe we'd be working on my legal defense. Maybe I'd be running for the border.

My heart sank. I'd been so absorbed in work I'd actually forgotten the looming disaster for a few minutes.

"God." I rested my head on the back of the sofa, blinked up, watched the shadows from the ocean flickering on the pristine white ceiling. My cell phone went off. I gave a disbelieving laugh. There really was no rest for the wicked.

I picked up my cell, peered at the caller. Lila.

I swore softly and tried to infuse warmth into my voice as I answered.

"Hi, Lila."

There was a pause and she said, "I didn't expect you to answer."

"Why?"

"Well, you never do."

That was utter bullshit but I let it go.

She said, "Nobody's seen you today. I thought perhaps you were making another pilgrimage."

Wow.

Something had happened to Lila in the years since we'd worked together. Though never what one would call a smooth operator, she hadn't been openly rude or deliberately unkind. In my opinion, this was not the behavior of someone confident of their position or happy in their work. Which was interesting. And not particularly encouraging.

I said mildly, "I don't have anything officially scheduled until two. I thought I'd catch up on some work."

"Vaughn and I were hoping the three of us could have lunch."

I glanced at the clock notification tray on my laptop. Eleven-thirty. Nothing like waiting until the last moment. I wondered what had triggered this sudden need to break bread with me. My conversation with Millie the evening before? It was hard to picture Vaughn being outraged on Millie's behalf.

I said apologetically, "I appreciate the invitation. The thing is, I had to leave the banquet early last night because of a migraine. I'm still a bit under the weather."

Which was one-hundred-percent true.

"A migraine?" Lila sounded disbelieving. But then she said thoughtfully, "Is that what happened? Come to think of it, you did used to get migraines. Frankfurt 2016. I remember. You were a mess."

*Thank you for noticing?*

I said, "As much as I'd like to meet with you and Vaughn, I don't think I'm up to it."

"Oh." She seemed to brighten. "Are you not going to do the Backstory interview this afternoon? I can take your slot if necessary. I've certainly done enough of these in my time."

I said, "That's very kind. I think if I take it easy this morning, I should be okay."

"Are you sure? You want to be at your best. You're representing W&W now."

Not really. The whole point of the Backstory interview series was to highlight the work and careers of individual editors. Very few editors spent their entire careers at one publishing house. I was no exception.

I said, "I'll keep that in mind."

"I can never tell if you're being sarcastic."

I said honestly, "I don't have the energy for sarcasm."

She said, "I'll tell Vaughn you can't make lunch. Maybe he'll want to reschedule. I'll let you know." She added grudgingly, "I'm sorry you're unwell."

"Thank you, Lila. I'll talk to you later." I didn't wait for her reply. I clicked off.


When I finished answering emails, I jotted down a few notes for the Dove sisters.

I'd been thinking the best bet for their next project might be historical, notwithstanding W&W's usual misreading of the market. Nothing so far back in time that the ladies would have to do any serious research. Maybe a series set in the 1950s or ˉ60s when they'd have been active and young. A period they knew well and were comfortable with.

Actually, Lila had sparked the idea with a comment she'd made when the Doves and I returned from our lunch at Fandango.

*Snoop Sisters.*

Perhaps a series along the lines of the 1973 limited series on NBC?

The sisters certainly had the platform.

Having sketched out my general thoughts, I decided to find out whatever I could about Troy Colby—starting with the conference program.

Sure enough, in the attending authors section was a bio and slightly blurry photo that had to have been a selfie.

*Troy Colby is a transgressive neo-noir fabulist whose work interrogates the porous boundaries between fiction, memory, and myth. A self-described "archival provocateur," Colby has been anthologized in numerous limited-edition chapbooks and was a finalist for the 2021 New Veritas Prize for Unclassifiable Literature. In 2019, his experimental short story cycle Papers Without People was long-listed for the Folio/Fragment Award, and his microfiction suite* **A List of Things We Forgot to Bury** *received an Honorable Mention from the Mid-Atlantic Fiction Forum.*

*Though elusive by nature and design, Colby has led private writing salons in Prague, Montreal, and a disused railcar in Northern Vermont. He is the founding editor of Palimpsest Engine, a quarterly zine devoted to post-genre storytelling, and his essays on semiotic absence have been "circulated informally" in graduate writing programs across the U.S.*

*Currently revising his first full-length novel,* **Everything True Is Dangerous***, Colby declines to provide a publication date, citing "the collapse of linear time" as a mitigating factor. He lives off-grid and off-list.*

"What. The. Fuck?" I said, "Prague, Montreal, and my ass. This guy *cannot* be for real."

The photo was for real, though. Mid-thirties. Acid-washed hair. Assorted piercings. The slightly out-of-focus photo matched my slightly out-of-focus memory. Not to mention Colby's slightly out-of-focus bio.

This was no one from my past. He wasn't old enough to be a contemporary. And, at first glance, he didn't seem to have any connection to, well, Planet Earth. I'd spent my adult life in publishing and I had no clue what most of that list of supposed accolades and accomplishments meant. I didn't think there was a verifiable publishing credit in the entire thing.

How could Colby possibly know anything about Milo, myself, or Dominic?

Was it possible Kyle knew him? Knew of him? I had no idea if Kyle participated in Steeple Hill's local writing community, but I'd bet my bottom dollar that Troy Colby was a fixture.

I skimmed the bio again and couldn't help thinking that Colby needed to meet Hayes Hartman. They'd probably get along like a house on fire.

The difference was, Hayes was talented enough to actually win an Edgar. Colby sounded like someone more in love with the idea of being a writer than the actual writing. Actually, he sounded like a complete poseur.

But even that was pure guesswork because there wasn't a damn piece of real information in that bio.

In the midst of my reflections, I heard the electronic lock to the suite click open. I glanced over warily—I hadn't bothered with the deadbolt since I was up and about—and relaxed as Finn opened the door.

He looked preoccupied—and then, when he saw me on the sofa—relieved.

"How did it go?" I asked.

He shrugged, came over to the sofa, and dropped a kiss on my upturned face. "What you'd expect. J.X. was funny and on point when he could get a word in edgewise. If T. McGregor actually spent a day walking the beat, I'm a romance writer. And as usual, Pat Robinson monopolized the airspace."

I nodded distractedly and said, "Will you read something for me?"

He didn't question it. "Sure." Finn joined me on the sofa, his shoulder comfortably pushing mine. I handed him the folded-back program. "Troy Colby."

His brows shot up. "This is the guy?"

"You tell me."

Finn began to read. His brows drew together. He read the three paragraphs again.

When he'd finished reading, he looked at me.

"It's a joke," he said.

# Chapter Seventeen

"Preposterous, right?"

"No," Finn said. "I mean this is a joke. He thinks he's being funny. And he's thumbing his nose at the entire writing establishment."

"Yes. A private joke, sure. But I do think he's hoping no one's really going to question his CV."

"How likely is that?"

"Beginning writers do tend to stuff a lot of meaningless credentials into their bios."

"This isn't a list of obscure Midwestern lit mag awards. This is *a finalist for the 2021 New Veritas Prize for Unclassifiable Literature.*"

I laughed out loud, surprising myself. Finn smiled at me.

"You have to give him credit for a sense of humor," I said. "But I also think some of that is aimed at me. *A List of Things We Forgot to Bury? Everything True Is Dangerous?*"

Finn grunted. "What else did you find out about this clown?"

"Nothing. I'd just started looking when you came in. I slept most of the morning and then went through my email."

"Good. You needed the sleep. How's your head?"

"It's okay." I was still coming out of the postdrome. That "migraine hangover" phase was a lot of why I'd been feeling low and anxious and weepy that morning. Well, some of it, anyway. My head gave the occasional twinge. My shoulders, neck, and abdominals were sore, but the worst of it was past.

Finn rose, moving to the room phone. "You feel like breakfast? I'm starving. I've had too much coffee on an empty stomach."

I still wasn't hungry, but I said, "Sure."

"Cereal, fruit, scrambled eggs?"

That was my usual breakfast, and I nodded.

Finn placed the call to room service. When he returned to the sofa, I said, "I ran into Hayes Hartman in the elevator. He said I trashed his book?"

Finn's brows drew together. "When were you in the elevator?"

"Right after you left to check out the rental car's tire. I'd forgotten I was supposed to take Grace Hollister to breakfast. Anyway, she had to cancel, and on the way back I ran into Hayes."

"I see. Well, that's kind of bullshit on Hayes's part. He incorporated your critiques into his rewrite. And mine as well. And pretty much everyone who gave him feedback. So, I'm not sure why he's singling you out."

"I think he's got a thing for you."

Finn raised a shoulder in dismissal. "To tell the truth, I think he had a thing for *you.*" There was a gleam of amusement in his eyes.

*"Me?"*

"I think so. He had a little bit of an editor crush. I have a feeling he believed you two would be instantly simpatico, you'd recognize his brilliance, offer him a life-changing contract, and become his mentor."

"Oh. Ouch."

Finn smiled faintly. "Don't worry. I looked over those edits. You were your usual tactful self. He was just hoping for something you weren't able to give him." He stretched his arm across the back of the sofa and I moved closer and rested my head on his shoulder. He kissed the side of my head absently. "I know you've got the Backstory interview at two. What do you have after that?"

"Coffee with Mindy Newburgh at four. Dinner with Adrien English at seven."

"Why don't you cancel Mindy. I think we should drive into Steeple Hill."

I sat up straight. "*Why?*"

"I think we should talk to Milo's family. See if Milo eventually turned up. I want to know how much, if anything they know about what happened."

If he knew Milo's family still lived in Steeple Hill, he'd already started investigating. As much as I wanted—needed—his help, I felt a surge of fear. There was no putting this genie back in the bottle. I knew that. But I couldn't help wishing I could put a pillow over the genie's face.

Finn was still talking. "In this case, it makes the most sense for you to take point. You're an old friend passing through town. You're just checking in. It's a natural thing to do. It signals concern, not guilt, and gives you plausible deniability."

"Yes. All right." I forced myself to relax. "I can do that."

Finn's gaze met mine. "But your active involvement in the investigation will end there. Ask the questions anyone would ask. Stick to the script."

I didn't point out that he hadn't given me a script.

Finn glanced automatically at my open laptop. "Don't start playing detective. Don't start poking around. You let me handle the rest."

"Which will entail what?"

"We don't want a formal investigation. Not until we know exactly what we're dealing with. We've got to be strategic and careful and very thorough. I'll start with looking into missing persons databases, search for old school records, driver's license activity, financial traces, etc. I'll check for any legal name changes that might suggest Milo reinvented himself. And I'll look into the actions of Milo's family following Milo's disappearance."

"They reported him missing."

"Well, they would, right? They'd do that whether they helped him disappear or not."

Before I could reply, someone knocked heavily on the door.

"Room service!"

Finn squeezed my shoulder briefly, rose, went to the door. He glanced out and opened the door. The uniformed server wheeled in the cart, Finn thanked him, tipped him, and closed the door behind him.

"You want to eat on the balcony or is the light too bright for you?"

"I'll wear sunglasses. I can use the fresh air."

I went to get my sunglasses while Finn rolled the cart to the glass doors and moved the covered dishes to the small iron table. The light was dazzling, but the cold ocean breeze felt good.

I was not hungry, but it was essential to eat. I took a few sips of chamomile tea, started with the scrambled eggs, eating slowly. Finn was having pancakes, as usual. He insisted he only indulged in pancakes at conferences and book events, but since a good part of his life was spent at conferences and book events, it seemed to me pancakes were a major part of his diet.

I said, as if our conversation hadn't been interrupted, "Since Colby's here in the hotel, what do you think about me speaking to him directly?"

Finn looked up. "Why?"

"It would be helpful to find out how much he really knows, for one thing. For another, maybe it's possible I could offer him a book deal or something."

"Like what something?"

I shook my head.

Finn put down his knife and fork. "Okay, that's a terrible idea. For a number of reasons."

"Such as?" As if I didn't know. But it was frustrating not to be in control. Frustrating to be told I had to sit back and wait for Finn to save me—or not save me.

"Bad optics, bad precedent, bad move."

"Sorry. You're going to have to explain a little further than that. If we could give Colby whatever it is he wants, that could be the end of it."

You don't have to be an editor of crime fiction to know that's not how blackmailers work, but I was clutching at straws.

Finn shook his head. "First of all, he's not alone in this blackmail scheme—assuming that's what it is. We've also got the driver of the Cadillac—unless you think that was Colby?"

"No. It wasn't Colby."

Or had it been? I was starting to doubt my memory. It had been dark. I'd had an impression of size and age, but the driver's hair had been silver. He'd moved easily. Maybe he was younger than I'd realized?

Finn said, "Even if Colby is the only one who actually knows anything, it's too risky. It borders on witness tampering—even if Colby isn't officially a witness yet. It could look like you're trying to buy his silence or intimidate him through the pretense of a professional relationship."

"I *am* trying to buy his silence!"

"The point isn't lost on me," Finn said grimly. "Did you hear me when I said we needed to be strategic and careful? Approaching Colby puts you on record. Any conversation could be recorded, overheard, or twisted. It indicates panic. If Colby's fishing for leverage, approaching him confirms that you believe there's something to hide."

I opened my mouth, but he spoke over me.

"And finally, it makes you look guilty. Even a sincere offer could be read as a bribe, threat, or an attempt at manipulation."

"Extortion is a crime, too."

"It sure is. But so far, he hasn't tried to extort anything from you. He submitted a weird partial manuscript that freaked you out for reasons he might be unaware of."

"You're joking."

"That's what a lawyer would argue. The guilty flee, etc."

I swallowed, nodded once, curtly, and stared out at the choppy white-capped water.

I could feel Finn's gaze as he continued to plow his way through his pancakes. He said finally, "If, depending on what we learn from Milo's family, I think talking to Colby is warranted, I'll talk to him. But it's a risk."

"No." On this point I was adamant. "If one of us has to take that risk, it'll be me."

Finn didn't bother debating. He sat back, sipping his coffee contemplatively. "Tell me about Milo."

"Like what? Why?"

"Victimology," he prompted. "We start the investigation with the victim."

"I know, but Dominic was the victim."

"We know who killed Dominic. The mystery here is what happened to Milo."

He was right. I wasn't sure why I was arguing. "Right. Milo was… He was different. Different from Dominic for sure. Different from everyone else I knew. He wasn't just a jock. He was smart and talented."

"Did you grow up together?"

"I met him in theater."

"*Theater*?" Finn echoed. "You do not strike me as the theater type."

I smiled faintly. "I know. I'm not. But I was an introverted kid. Shy. Self-conscious. Painfully awkward. If I had to get up and speak, I'd break into a cold sweat. So, I decided I would take speech. But speech class was full and so I ended up having to take theater instead. And that's where I met Milo."

"Was Milo a theater type?"

"He had a really good singing voice. He always got a role in the musicals. His acting was so-so. It didn't matter because he was so good-looking. He had that type of personality that draws people in. He could talk to anybody."

Finn's mouth curved. "And he talked to you."

"He did." I smiled, too. Fondly. "Mostly about books and writing. I wanted to be a writer back then."

Finn's brows shot up. "I didn't know that. What happened?"

I laughed. "It turned out I didn't like writing that much."

*"What?"*

"I mean, I loved writing bits and pieces, scenes, vignettes. I loved crafting beautiful sentences. I loved imagining stories and dreaming about the lives of the characters. But the actual *writing*, the prolonged effort of stringing all those sentences together—all the boring transition and filling in of blanks and having to ensure it all made sense— It's hard work if you don't enjoy it. And I didn't. I preferred reading. Ultimately, I preferred editing."

Finn started laughing. "That's the funniest thing I ever heard."

"No, but seriously. It turned out that I was much better at looking at the big picture and explaining why something worked or didn't work. Analysis and advice. Those are my strengths."

"They're a couple of your strengths, for sure."

"*Oh*, I'm also insightful. I get that a lot."

He winced.

I chuckled, sipped my tea.

"Did Milo also want to be a writer?"

"No. His plan was to attend college on football scholarships and then go into acting. Like Mark Harmon. Mark Harmon was his idol."

Finn nodded, swallowed his coffee. He continued to regard me in that meditative way.

I admitted, "I don't know what the attraction was for him because I wasn't—he was super popular and I was... not. It didn't help that my father was the sheriff and so everyone automatically assumed I was a snitch. I was socially backward and—" I made a face "—*had a face like a skull.*"

"The *hell*," Finn said, and he actually sounded angry.

My smile was rueful. "It's okay. I wasn't a cute kid. I was never handsome. I was tall and thin and I had eyes like a tarsier. But I was smart and hard-working. I graduated with honors. I got into my college of choice. I excelled in my chosen career." I shrugged. "I didn't need handsome."

Finn said, "I think you're the most handsome, elegant man I ever met. You have the sexiest mouth and the most beautiful eyes I've ever seen on a human."

It was probably all the meds still floating around in my system, but Finn said it with such fierce sincerity that it made my throat lock, made my face quiver.

I managed to joke, "You should hear what my fellow primates say!"

Finn shook his head, not even entertaining the idea.

That instant if unnecessary defense? It was ridiculously meaningful. We didn't talk to each other like that. We didn't pay each other extravagant compliments or say romantic, flowery things. In fact, I loved how light and breezy our relationship was. We teased each other, joked and bantered, we laughed a lot. I'd known right away that Finn found me attractive and that he preferred spending time with me. And it was the same for me. That we didn't have to say it made it, in my eyes, more special, like we shared a secret language. Like Nick and Nora Charles in the *Thin Man* movies—only gay and with Oxford commas.

(And amiable debates about the number of gun battles one could reasonably have per book.)

Finn growled, "Okay. Tell me more about this asshole who dragged you into his quagmire and then left you to hold the bag."

I blinked at that particular description. "I don't think he did it deliberately."

"Maybe not. What else can you tell me about him?"

"His family was Greek. They owned a little Greek restaurant. Very exotic for Steeple Hill at the time. Everybody in the family worked there. His parents and grandparents were very conservative. Church every Sunday. I think his grandparents went on Saturday as well. Milo's older brother, Geo, went to jail for a couple of months for stealing a car and a decade later the family still whispered any time the subject came up."

"Milo was closeted," Finn deduced from that jumble of information.

I nodded.

"And you were closeted?"

"I was invisible. It didn't matter what I was. The only person who noticed me was Milo. He was the first guy who ever kissed me. The first guy I ever fooled around with."

I had loved him with all my lonely heart. Just the fact that he was willing to talk books with me was enough to make me love him.

Finn said, "What do you think Dominic was doing in the cemetery that night?"

I'm not sure why, in twenty-plus years, that particular question had never occurred to me. But it hadn't.

My lips parted. It took me a moment to admit, "I don't know. I guess he went looking for Milo."

"What time of year was it?"

"Spring. April." Just about the same time of year as now.

"And what time—at what hour—did Milo phone you?"

The questions seemed so random.

I said, "It was after one. I don't remember the exact time. I'd been sound asleep."

"Was it a school night?"

"Yes," I said.

"Was your father home?"

I said dryly, "He was rarely home at night."

"And it took you how long to get to the cemetery?"

"Maybe five minutes? I drove my pickup truck over."

"How carefully did you examine Dominic's body?"

I began to wish I hadn't had those scrambled eggs.

I said shortly, "I didn't conduct a forensic examination."

*He'd been warm.*

That was the first thing.

I hadn't expected it.

The second thing was the weight—not just the heft of Dominic's limbs, but the way they folded and flopped with no resistance, boneless and loose, like something was broken inside. He was limp all over, and that, more than anything else, had made it horrifically real.

*Crouched beside him, my knees digging into the soft grass, two trembling fingers pressed to his neck. Like I'd seen in movies. But I already knew. The skin beneath my fingertips was soft, sticky with blood. There was no beat, no pulse. Just a dreadful unreal silence.*

His blue eyes were open. I dreamed about that for a long time. Not all the way open, not dramatically, just half-slits, unfocused, glassy, gazing somewhere past my shoulder. There was no light left in them, but they hadn't gone dull yet. That came later.

I pulled myself together and said, "He hadn't been dead for long. His skin was warm. But there was no pulse. No breath. I checked. I checked again at the preserve. Before I..."

I quickly talked myself away from the memory. "There was a faint purple blush forming along the side of his neck, and his head lolled, so at first I thought maybe his neck was broken, but later I realized it was the blood settling."

"Lividity," Finn agreed. "Did he have a weapon?"

"Who? Dom?"

Finn assented.

"No. Not that I saw. I didn't go through his pockets or anything. I didn't touch him any more than I had to." Granted, at the preserve it had taken a lot of touching, a lot of dragging and hauling and heaving to get him into the water.

"Were there cuts on his hands? Bruises on his face?"

I swallowed. "I'm not sure."

"Was the injury to his head on the front or the back?"

"It was on the right—no, I was facing him. It was on his left side. The left side of his head."

I didn't appreciate the sudden interrogation. I realized that these were the questions Finn should have—would have—asked earlier, but he'd been rattled. I hadn't recognized it at the time. He, too, was good at hiding his emotions.

Finn circled back, repeated, "Cuts on his hands? Torn fingernails? Bruises on his face? Did he have a bloody nose? Swollen lip?"

"It was a long time ago, Finn," I protested.

"You won't have forgotten what his face looked like," he said with absolute certainty.

He was right. I did remember.

I said, "There was crusted blood beneath his nostrils. His upper lip was cut."

"What about his hands?"

"I don't remember that his knuckles were swollen. I think there were a couple of nicks. Not actual cuts, no obvious bruising."

"What about Milo? Besides the bruising around his throat. What other injuries did he sustain?"

"His knuckles were swollen. I do remember that because it hurt him to flex his hand. He was afraid he'd broken a finger. He had trouble with the shovel. I don't think his face was bruised. But he didn't claim Dom punched him. He said Dom tried to strangle him, and there were dark marks on his throat. I could see the outline of fingers. He didn't lie about that."

"It doesn't sound like it. What do you think Milo was doing in the cemetery? April on the coast is cold and damp. You were home in bed, so he wasn't there fooling around with you."

"He went there to drink sometimes."

Finn nodded, cocked his head, and asked curiously, "How do you think Dominic knew to find Milo in the cemetery that night?"

# Chapter Eighteen

"**F**ourteen years ago, Keiran Chandler, senior editor at the boutique publishing company Millbrook House, began his career in publishing as an intern reading the slush pile at Wheaton & Woodhouse."

The audience laughed at conference organizer Deb Rivera's introduction.

"In addition to founding Millbrook House's prestigious Prime Crime line, Keiran is the architect behind the Inkwell Award, establishing Millbrook House's commitment to nurturing emerging mystery authors. His enviable list includes numerous award-winning and bestselling authors including Finn Scott, Kyle Bari, Danica Dassault, Jo-Jo Bakewell, and Christopher Holmes. Please welcome Keiran Chandler."

I couldn't help wishing Deb hadn't mentioned Christopher Holmes. Since he still wasn't officially on my list, that was liable to be a sore spot with Lila, who was sitting front and center in the first row. But it was a very nice introduction and I got a generous round of applause as I made my way onto the stage and took the armchair opposite Rudolph.

Rudoph smiled with mischievous warmth and winked. I smiled back, adjusted the nearest of the matte black microphones positioned between us.

The ballroom was standing-room only. But interviews and panels with editors were always standing-room only. Even in the era of self-publishing, we were still perceived by many as guardians of the gate, stingily clutching the keys to the magic kingdom. That wasn't entirely untrue, but there were many more kingdoms now. And fewer gates.

"Good afternoon and welcome to this year's install-ment of Backstory," Rudolph began in his smooth cultured voice. "For those of you unfamiliar, this is our nineteenth annual chat with an editor acknowledged by their peers to be a leader within our industry. Today, that someone is my good friend, the esteemed Keiran Chandler."

Murmurs of approval and another round of applause rippled through the room. I gave a wry grin.

"Say hello," Rudolph prompted.

I said, "Good afternoon. I know half of you think I ex-ist to crush your dreams, and the other half think I can magically make them come true. The truth, as always, lies somewhere in between."

Rudolph smiled faintly, and asked, "Keiran, I've been dying to ask—what went wrong in your life that made you want to be an editor?"

This was the same question he started every Backstory interview with, but it never failed to get a round of laugh-ter.

I said gravely, "Sadly, I failed to make it as a violinist. Editing had fewer splinters."

It got a bigger laugh than it deserved.

"Come to think of it, there *is* a lot of violin-playing in publishing." Rudolph mimed playing a tiny violin, and I laughed.

In fact, everyone laughed. Rudolph was rightfully one of the most beloved figures in our industry.

"A bit."

Rudolph leaned in conspiratorially. "But seriously. You've built something rare—authors who adore you, colleagues who respect you, and a near-legendary gift for extracting the gold from the dross."

More applause and a couple of whistles from—I was pretty sure—my stable, who were crowded at the back of the room like the class troublemakers.

"Thank you." I meant it sincerely. After the weekend I was having, any kind words were balm on an open wound.

Rudolph's expression softened. "You've been at Millbrook how long now?"

"Ten years." I added, "Six months, seventeen days, three hours, and two minutes."

"But who's counting, eh? That's longer than most publishing houses stay solvent these days."

That earned another laugh, though this one had more teeth. Now that the merger with W&W was more than rumor, opinions, anecdotes, and unsolicited advice were starting to circulate. Author anxiety was rising fast. It would be fever pitch by Sunday.

Rudolph's next few questions were softballs: What's your greatest strength as an editor—and don't say you care too much! What's your greatest weakness as an editor—and don't say you care too much!"

I did my best to be honest but entertaining. "I think my greatest strength as an editor is my ability to view the work as a skilled objective outsider. My greatest weakness? I'm probably not alone in this, but I like what I like. And the older I get, the more set in my likes and dislikes I am. I don't like gratuitous anything. I don't like emotional pandering. I don't like twist endings that don't make sense.

Oh, and I have a tendency to rant in public about things I don't like."

Rudolph chuckled. "Any regrets about passing on a particular manuscript?"

I couldn't help wondering if Hayes had complained about my trashing his book to every single conference attendee.

"I'm not sure. Maybe not. If I pass on a book, it's not necessarily that I don't believe the book could do well. It's more about what I think I can bring to the equation. Just as every book is not for every reader, every editor is not for every book."

"That's quite good," Rudolph remarked. "Did I say that?"

The audience laughed, of course, and I said, "I'm pretty sure you did."

Rudolph gave me another of those sly winks. Then he snapped his fingers and commanded, "Three author blind spots. Go!"

"Uh...Thinking 'real' equals 'interesting.' Dialogue that sounds like dialogue. Plot that happens simply because the author says so."

"Very good." Rudolph turned to the audience. "He's after my job!"

That got the biggest laugh yet.

I happened to glance at Lila. She was scowling as she scrolled through her phone.

The rest of the interview was mostly old war stories and humorous industry anecdotes.

Finally, Rudolph uncapped a silver water bottle and took a sip. "We have a few minutes left, and I'd be remiss if I didn't turn things over to the crowd. Questions? Comments? Confessions?"

Laughter eddied through the ballroom. A few hands shot up. A volunteer with a wireless mic moved through the sea of chairs.

A tiny blonde in a ponytail and pink sweatshirt featuring a bespectacled rabbit and the slogan I STOP FOR PLOT BUNNIES took the mic.

"Hi, Keiran. I'm an aspiring author, um, an emerging mystery writer and, um, I guess I was wondering—what's the one thing that makes you keep reading a submission past the first page?"

I smiled. "Hi. First and foremost, I'm looking for an authentic voice telling an interesting story. And by authentic, I mean a voice that doesn't sound like everyone else—or AI. I'm looking for clarity, confidence, maybe a little restraint. The best writers don't waste time proving they're clever—they're busy telling a story I can't put down."

I don't remember what the response to that was. I don't remember what the second question was or who asked it, because the third audience member who stood up and took the mic was Troy Colby.

I'd been so sure I wouldn't know him if I saw him, but when a tall, silver-haired man near the side aisle slowly unfolded from his chair, my scalp prickled in alarmed recognition.

He was dressed in dark jeans and dark T-shirt and his conference badge was turned backward. I hadn't noticed any tattoos when he'd handed over *I Know What You Did*, but he was covered in them. As if he wore ink long johns beneath his clothes. Despite the room's soft, low lighting, he wore dark glasses.

Taking the mic, he said in a low, slightly raspy voice, "Keiran, do you think editors have a moral responsibility to their authors? Even after the contracts end? Or is it just business?"

What the heck did that mean? The question was as vague as his bio.

I felt that the obvious answer—*say, what?*—would be walking into a trap, so I took a leaf from Colby's book, leaning forward and letting forth.

"I think editors, good ones, understand that what we're doing isn't just transactional. Books come from deeply personal places. We shepherd them into the world. That doesn't mean we always get it right. But yes, I think we have a responsibility—if not to every author, then to the integrity of the work. And maybe to the people we were when we said yes to it."

Blah. Blah. Blah. Sheer nonsense.

Rudolph tilted his head, as if intrigued. I stared over the sea of heads toward the back of the room where I knew Finn was. Was he getting this? (Whatever it was.) I couldn't think how to signal him.

*Thou art the man!* Like Poe's short story?

"One more question?" Colby suggested.

I looked at Rudolph, who understandably seemed like... *uh, whatever.*

"Keiran, how much of a writer's life belongs in their fiction? If something happened to you but not *only* to you, is it still your story?"

"Your part of it is your story." It was a lame answer. I was terrified he was going to give a specific and career-ending example.

I don't think Colby even heard my reply. He wasn't interested in answers. Asking the questions was the point.

"And do you think an editor's personal history ever colors the way they respond to a manuscript, even if they don't realize it? Like, maybe they reject something that hits too close to home?"

A tide of thoughtful murmurs. On the surface, it was a smart, nuanced question. In reality? *Jesus.*

I adjusted the mic.

"Whether conscious or not, writers draw from their lives all the time. However, the job of the author of fiction is not to write an autobiography. The goal of fiction is to write recognizable truth while making everything up. And as for editors... sure. We're human. We have blind spots. Sensitivities. We also have an instinct for the real thing. Like an art critic, we know it when we see it."

Colby nodded, but didn't smile. He handed back the mic and sat back in his seat.

Rudolph took a beat, waited for someone else to speak up and then finally said, "Friends, regretfully, this will be my final year hosting Backstory."

He paused to let the murmurs of dismay and outright protests play out, before continuing "The time's they are a-changing and we all know it. I've had a good run. It's time to start a new chapter. Time to hand the torch to the next generation. That said, I can't pretend I haven't been wondering about what comes next—for legacy publishers such as Millbrook House, for our wonderful, talented authors, for our gifted, dedicated editors like Keiran Chandler."

He said a few words more, but it was a brief and pithy farewell.

When he was finished, Rudolph reached across the small table and laid his hand briefly over mine. "Thank you, my boy. Good luck to you."

I turned my hand and shook his. "Thank you, Rudolph. Good luck to you."

"Good luck to us all," he said a little cryptically.

"He's getting impatient."

I was not talking about Rudolph. I meant Troy Colby.

Finn and I were in his red convertible Mercedes-AMG CLE53 on our way to Steeple Hill. Finn enjoyed driving. In fact, rather than flying up for the conference, he'd driven from San Clemente to Monterey. He was an excellent driver and I was happy to take shotgun. The trip had felt endless the day before, but with Finn behind the wheel we made excellent time. I could even relax and enjoy the coastal scenery a bit.

The placid sunshine felt good on my face and the salty breeze whipping through my hair was bracing, cleansing.

Finn replied laconically, "Yep."

"Which means he might escalate."

"Maybe. But it also means, he's going to start having doubts. Which is good. We want him to question what he really knows, how strong his position really is."

"He didn't seem doubtful today," I said.

"It's hard to say what he seemed. His questions were pretty vague." Finn reached across and absently squeezed my thigh.

He was a tactile guy, prone to brief, casual touches, but I was getting more reassuring squeezes and strokes than usual, and while I wasn't typically emotionally needy, I did appreciate those silent signs of caring and support.

Eight years was a long time, and I did know a lot about Finn, although most of it was probably pretty trivial. I knew he had sensitive skin and sunburned easily, which was why, beneath that pricy Costa Azzurra, he always smelled faintly of sunscreen. I knew he and a few other crime writers often got together for pickup basketball games at conferences. I knew this beloved red sportscar was the first thing he'd treated himself to when he'd started to earn big money. I knew he played the piano beautifully, classic jazz, but that he mostly listened to Tom Petty and Moon Martin. I knew he was crazy about his kid, liked big dogs, Japanese whisky, and Dylan Thomas.

There was a wealth of stuff I didn't know—because I hadn't wanted to know. The more I'd learned, the more I'd cared, and that was something I just couldn't afford to do.

But now...

When it was maybe too late, I wanted to know everything.

Then again, I already knew—had always instinctively known—the most important things: that he was unshakably honest; that quiet, kind steadiness was his default; that he took care of people without making them feel managed or useless.

He was doing that now.

I glanced at his profile. "Thanks for doing this."

His mouth curved, though his gaze remained on the curving road. "This morning's panel was my last scheduled event. I've got to fill the time somehow."

I shook my head, smiling.

He glanced at me then, said, "Rudolph Dunst thinks a lot of you. He made that clear during that interview."

"He's always been really helpful, very supportive. With everyone. That's just how he is. A true professional. Unfailingly generous with his time and advice. He always took the attitude that we were all in this together. That together we were doing something important, something that really mattered."

"He's the last of a dying breed."

That was a depressing thought.

We drove in silence for another mile or so before I said, "Don't you think it's weird that this all suddenly started up again? For more than twenty years nothing happened. And now..."

"There was a confluence of events," Finn said, "probably starting with your father's passing. He was the former sheriff, so the local paper would have covered it. Would have covered the fact that you showed up for the funeral. There was probably a little information on you, just enough. You put the house on the market, which would have stirred additional interest, raked up some memories."

I said, "Speaking of that. When I told the Realtor to put the house on the market, I told her to dump everything. She didn't feel that was right, so she boxed up whatever legal docs she thought might be needed down the line and shipped it all off to me. The box is still sitting in storage. But I'm wondering if there was something in his possessions that triggered...something."

"Your father was sheriff at the time. Is it possible he knew what happened? Would he have withheld information to protect you?"

"Not a chance. Knowledge of my involvement would have just confirmed his worst suspicions. Anyway, his drinking was out of control by then. I don't think he'd have noticed my complicity—hell, I don't think he'd have noticed a crime in progress if he'd wandered into the graveyard in the middle of Milo hitting Dom over the head."

Finn snorted.

"But maybe there was something in all that junk. Betty, my realtor, sold whatever she could as far as furniture, tools, knickknacks, and then donated the rest."

"It's a small town. Just the act of selling everything off— especially the fact that you handled it long distance—putting the house on the market, would certainly spark speculation, conversation. People talk."

"Yes."

"Then, shortly after, you showed up for a writing conference in Monterey that undoubtedly received some local coverage."

"That's all true. But if anybody actually knew anything, why would they wait for me to resurface? Why wouldn't they have gone to the police twenty years ago?"

"Maybe Colby *doesn't* know anything for sure. You pointed out several inconsistencies in the manuscript. Some of this could be fishing." He seemed to weigh his thoughts before adding, "The truth is, given your friendship with Milo, there was probably a fair amount of speculation about your potential role in Dominic's disappearance. People would talk. They always do. The police would listen. They always do. But you need more than gossip and speculation to file charges. You have to have proof."

"My friendship with Milo wasn't a secret, but I wasn't part of his circle."

"There sure as hell would have been speculation regarding Milo, even before he ducked out. For a lot of people, leaving the way he did would have confirmed their suspicions."

"You're assuming he left voluntarily."

"I am. Yeah."

"Why?"

"No body."

"But…"

"We know why Dominic's body wasn't found—by the way, that's also an assumption on your part. Remains might have been found but not identified. But what would be the reason for hiding Milo's body? And if it was suicide—most suicides don't attempt to conceal their death. They might try to hide that they've committed suicide, but typically people don't want their families to agonize over a mysterious disappearance."

I hadn't considered the situation from that perspective. It seemed my original instinct had been correct. Milo had bailed.

Finn said, "I want to know how much local law enforcement suspects. I need to get my hands on cold case reports, coroners' records, or old sheriff's logs to see if unidentified remains were ever recovered in the Pescadero Marsh area. If no body was ever found, it's harder to prove a crime— even with your confession."

The confession no one had heard but Finn.

# Chapter Nineteen

The Argyroses still lived in the same little house, but they were not only keeping up with the Joneses, they seemed to be doing considerably better. For sure, better than any of them had been doing twenty years ago.

Gone was the patchy lawn, the sagging porch, the sun-bleached plastic geraniums in cheap pots. The stucco was fresh, the trim recently painted a sharp navy blue. A well-maintained silver Camry sat in the driveway. The lawn was green, the flower beds were neat, edged with stone, and the porch had been redone in composite decking.

Maybe the good folks of Steeple Hill had finally developed a taste for Greek food?

I raised my hand to lift the cute brass shell-shaped knocker, then lowered it again and wiped my palms on my jeans. I tried again, knocking briskly on the blue surface.

My heart was hammering as I waited. Seconds passed and then the door suddenly opened.

Mrs. Argyros was smaller and grayer, but I'd have known her anywhere. Not least because she was wearing the same long yellow cardigan and dubious expression.

I opened my mouth, but she put her hands up waving me away. "No thank you! We have everything we need!"

It did look that way.

I said quickly, "Hello, Mrs. Argyros. You probably don't remember me. I'm Keiran Chandler. I was a friend of Milo's in high school."

She stopped waving and squinted at me. I was sure she didn't recognize me. Then her face lit with a flicker of polite surprise.

"Oh! Yes—Milo's friend. Sheriff Chandler's boy. You studied together sometimes, right? Government, was it? Milo had trouble with government. That teacher! Or was it history?"

"English," I said. "And theater. Occasionally."

I had a vivid memory of walking down that little hallway behind her, closing the bedroom door behind us, so we could "run lines."

"I heard your father passed. It was a shame what happened to him," Mrs. Argyros said. "He was a good man. A good sheriff. Such a shame he lost his job like that."

I murmured something vague. But the only shame was that it had taken the powers that be so long to notice that he was drinking on the job.

Mrs. Argyros stepped back and waved me in. "Well, come in, dear. I remember now. You were going to be a writer."

"It didn't quite work out that way."

"No, of course not. It's very hard to be a writer. It takes a special kind of person."

Which I clearly had not been. I smiled faintly, stepping inside.

Inside, the house was warm, clean, and faintly scented with something citrusy and expensive—the kind of candle you didn't find at the grocery store. The carpet had been replaced with polished hardwood, and the kitchen in the background gleamed with brushed steel appliances and a countertop espresso machine that looked like it required a barista's license to operate.

It was a far cry from the cluttered kitchen and hand-me-down furniture I could still recall. The walls were still covered in a gallery of family photos, though. Mostly of Milo. Milo had been the youngest of five, a surprise baby. There were pictures of him with his dog Ditto, Milo in football pads, Milo in detective costume complete with fedora. Photos of Milo right up until the age of eighteen— and then only blank walls.

She indicated a blue sofa near the window and I sat down.

"You have a lovely home, Mrs. Argyros."

She sure did. And that familiar yellow cardigan? This edition was lambswool, not rayon.

She took the chair opposite and looked around the living room. She smiled a well-satisfied smile. "I do. I've been very blessed. I've got eleven grandchildren now."

"Whoa," I said. "*Eleven.*"

She chuckled. "And another on the way. Though I expect it'll be a while before I get to hold that one."

"Congratulations."

"And how are you? You moved back East, didn't you? Went to live with your mother's family while you went to school?"

Was that the story? I'd wondered what my father told people. Assuming he bothered to tell them anything.

Mrs. Argyros was still talking—she'd always used to run on in an almost stream-of-consciousness fashion, and it seemed that hadn't changed. "I would never have recognized you! Such a tall, gangly boy. I told Milo once that you looked like a hungry scarecrow, and he said, '*Ma! Don't you ever say that to him!*' But you were such a sweetheart. Always so polite." She leaned forward and studied me intently. "If I didn't know, I'd think you were French now!"

*Huh?*

"French now?" I asked cautiously. Did she think I'd moved to France?

"You know how French people take such nice care of themselves. Their hair and their hands are always just so. Such nice skin."

I deduced that *French* was a compliment. "Thank you," I said. "How's Mr. Argyros these days?"

Her face fell. "Constantine passed away four years ago. He's in heaven with our grand-baby Andrew now."

In heaven with the grandbaby? Not with Milo? She didn't think Milo went to heaven or she didn't think he was dead? But then, dead would be hard to accept for any mother.

"I'm so sorry to hear that. He was a real force."

Kind of a bull in a china shop, to be honest. He and Milo had argued furiously and constantly.

"Yes. His heart. It was sudden. That's the best way, I think. Now my boy Georgi runs the restaurant with his sisters. Still the only Greek food in Steeple Hill!"

"Certainly, the best Greek food." I smiled.

She gave a merry little laugh. "Yes! We have wonderful food."

I didn't want to waste time talking about the restaurant, given that Finn was already over there checking things out.

I said gently, "Seeing that I was in town, I thought I'd stop by. I was wondering if you'd ever heard from him. From Milo."

Mrs. Argyros's shiny dark gaze fell. Her smile tightened. She reached for a tissue from the square floral box on the living room table and pressed it to the corner of her eyes.

"No," she said softly. "Not since he left. Nothing. Not a word."

I nodded slowly, studying her. She dabbed her eyes again, but I couldn't see any trace of wetness. Her voice didn't waver. Her fingers were steady. The tissue didn't tremble.

Granted, she wasn't crying over Constantine, either. Milo had been gone a couple of decades. Maybe she'd finally made peace with his disappearance?

Could you ever really make peace with something like that?

Maybe she was lying.

"I'm sorry," I said. "I'm always hoping I'm going to hear some good news one day."

She nodded absently, dabbed her dry eyes again. "I have to think wherever he is, he's in a better place."

"That's probably a good way to look at it." I rose. "Well, I don't want to keep you. I know you must have things to do. I just wanted to check in."

She rose immediately—I couldn't help thinking in relief—and led the way back to the front door. "You always had nice manners, Kevin. Your father raised you right."

I caught a glimpse of my expression in the hall mirror and almost laughed.

On the front steps, I said, "Thank you for taking the time to talk to me. Look after yourself."

"Oh, I don't have many worries. My boys take good care of me!" she assured me gaily.

I smiled and headed back to Finn's car. I was not smiling as I climbed behind the steering wheel.

I spotted Finn sitting on the cinderblock wall on the far side of the laundromat parking lot next to Constantine's, and I felt an unexpected surge of...

Hard to explain. Relief, for sure, but also the certainty that here was someone who was not going to lie to me, not try to use me, not attempt to trick or manipulate me. Despite everything, despite his earlier doubts, Finn was on my side. I knew that. Whatever else he had been or would be, he was a true friend. That would not change. It was something—he was someone—I could genuinely count on. Rely on.

Trust.

After leaving that house, driving through these streets that would live forever in my dreams, it meant a lot to have someone in my life I could completely trust.

I pulled neatly between the parking lines and got out, going round to the passenger seat.

"How'd it go?" Finn got into the driver's seat of the convertible.

I shook my head. "I think you might be right."

I could feel his gaze on my face. "You think Milo's alive?"

"I think it's possible." I glanced at him. "Which, if true, I'm obviously relieved about. But."

"But it's a godawful thing to have done to you." His eyes were the shade of wintergreen.

I nodded. Just for a moment, remembering, I couldn't speak.

"I'm so sorry, Keir." Finn rested his hand on my shoulder, his thumb tracing my collarbone.

I nodded again, drew a sharp breath. "I know. Thanks. I mean, I don't know for a fact that he's alive. But his mom slipped at the end and said, '*My boys take good care of me*'. She only ever had two sons. Although maybe she means Geo and her grandsons. I don't have any proof. The absence of tears is not proof. But if Milo *is* alive, I really don't understand what's going on. He *knows* what happened. He's the one who *made* it happen. He can't accuse me without being dragged into it himself. What would he have to gain? He *can't* have anything to do with this. He could be alive and not have anything to do with this, right?"

Finn didn't answer. I realized we hadn't moved from the parking space in front of the laundromat. "Are we waiting for something?"

"There's a vintage Cadillac DeVille sitting in the back of the restaurant parking lot. I'm going to pull around the block so you can take a look at it. I know you didn't get the license plate of the car that stopped after the blowout, but if this one doesn't match your memory, if it's the wrong color or make, it would be helpful to eliminate it."

I stared at him in disbelief, snapped, "Of course, it's the same car! What are the chances that a different Cadillac just happens to be sitting in parking lot behind the Argyros family restaurant? We both know it's the right car. *What the hell is going on*?"

"I don't know," Finn said calmly. "Let's see if we can verify if it's the right car."

I closed my eyes. "Yes. Right. Sorry."

"It's okay. We're going to get to the bottom of this."

I nodded. Finn put the Mercedes into gear and we slowly circled the block. For several long seconds I had a perfect view of a 1969 deep green Cadillac DeVille.

"It's the same car," I said wearily. "Same make. Same model."

"You described the car you saw as black."

"It looked black at night and in the gas station lights. I see now it's dark green." I looked at him. "I know it's the same car, Finn."

Finn said nothing. He turned down the next street and we wound through the town, leisurely making our way back toward the main highway.

He let me deal with it for a couple minutes and then he said, "According to the DMV, that particular Cadillac is registered to the Devlin Family Trust. Do you know what that is?"

"I've heard of it. I'm trying to remember in what context. I don't remember a Devlin family in Steeple Hill."

"Okay, well, I'm going to do a little more digging. Coincidences happen, but it's hard to believe that particular car is sitting in the Argyros family's restaurant parking lot, but it has no connection to the events of the last couple of days."

I said bitterly, "I'll say it's hard to believe."

We didn't talk a lot on the drive back to Monterey.

I couldn't help feeling like I'd traveled lightyears since that morning. Things I had believed to be absolute truth for half my life were now revealed to be something entirely different.

I had made life-altering decisions based on faulty understanding. On lies and deception. I still wasn't sure what was the truth.

The worn road hugged the cliffs, sun-warmed asphalt unwinding south as the afternoon light turned molten gold. To our right, the Pacific stretched wide and glittering blue, the waves catching fire where the sunlight hit them, rolling in slow, endless rhythm against the bronze rocks far below. The salty air held traces of wild fennel and eucalyptus. High overhead, black specks wheeled, their cries lost in the whoosh of wind and the muted growl of the engine.

Finn didn't speak, one hand steady on the wheel, the other resting near—but not quite touching—my knee. I leaned my head back against the seat, eyes half-closed against the glare.

Somewhere inland, the hills rose in soft, sun-drenched folds, the grass turning silver in the breeze. Ahead, the road dipped and curved again, the ocean a constant pulse at the edge of the world. For a moment, it almost felt like a dream—too bright, too beautiful to be real.

*Milo might be alive.*

That wasn't the bright beautiful part, though it would be a relief.

Finally, I shook off my funk, checked my cell, and swore. "*Shit.* I forgot to cancel with Mindy!"

"Uh-oh," Finn said, although he didn't sound particularly excited.

I raked a hand through my hair. "I can't believe it. What the hell is the *matter* with me?"

"You've got a few things on your mind."

"I never do stuff like that!"

"Exactly," he said calmly. "You never do stuff like that. You're allowed the occasional slip."

"Not with her, I'm not. Not right now, I'm not. Vaughn and Lila already wanted to have one of their impromptu get-togethers this afternoon. God knows what that's about."

I listened to the agitated echo of my words in the loud silence that followed.

Finally, Finn said, "Keir, you missed a meeting. Personally, I think it's a meeting you can afford to do without. But if it's going to keep you up tonight, send her flowers and an apology. Send her a box of chocolates or a bottle of wine."

*But for the love of God, shut up about it.*

He didn't say that, of course.

"Am I wearing you out?" I asked wryly.

"Nope. You're wearing yourself out. Which worries me. You don't have to be your best self twenty-four-seven. You don't have to be everything to everyone at every moment."

I opened my mouth to object to that characterization, but Finn kept talking in that calm, untroubled way.

"I know you take a lot of pride in that juggling act, and it's impressive the way you keep all those shiny balls spinning in the air. But the world isn't going to end if you drop the occasional ball. I would rather have an imperfect you around for the next fifty years than a perfect you spontaneously combusting in the next five. I'd like to have you in my life for a long, long time."

I stared at him in surprise.

Finn glanced at me, added, "Since you're asking."

"Hm." I turned my head to stare out my side of the car. After a moment, I realized I was smiling.

# Chapter Twenty

"I brought you a gift." Adrien English slid a plastic-wrapped square across the table to me. "Don't feel like you have to wear it."

By seven on a Friday night, El Cantaro glowed like a lantern in the dusk. Its windows were fogged slightly from the warmth inside, and the scent of cumin, roasted garlic, and lime hit as soon as the door swung open—earthy, sharp, and mouthwatering.

I chuckled, tore open the plastic and shook out the folds of a black Cloak and Dagger Bookstore tee. "Heck yeah, I will. It's what all the cool kids are wearing. Thank you. This is really kind."

Adrien snorted.

We'd found the restaurant by chance, a cute little place on Foam Street.

Inside, the walls were painted the color of ripe mangoes and chilies, hung with folk art, and framed papel picado cutouts that fluttered faintly in the breeze from the open back window. A handwritten specials board leaned near the counter, chalk smudged from many fingers and revisions.

The funny part was El Cantaro was vegan—unlike Adrien and me—but it smelled so incredible when we walked in, we'd decided to stay.

The air was thick with the low clatter of dishes, the sizzle of something being seared in the back, and the occasional hiss of the espresso machine. Conversations overlapped in English and Spanish— not loud, layered—the warm hum of people lingering over mezcal cocktails and mole enchiladas.

The light cast from mismatched pendant lights and flickering votive candles in recycled glass holders was soft, golden, and slightly uneven. Tables were close, but not uncomfortably so, and the floor staff moved with practiced rhythm, slipping in and out of the kitchen with steaming plates and quiet apologies.

"So, are you really going to do a What Not to Write book?" Adrien dipped a tortilla chip in salsa and bit into it with a satisfying crunch.

"*Me?*" I gazed at him in astonishment.

Adrien arched an elegant brow. "That's what you said during the Backstory Q&A."

"*I* said I was planning to write a book?"

He looked amused and curious. "It was the second question. The lady from Milwaukee said she'd been to one of your writing workshops once upon a time, and she wondered if you'd thought of doing a book on writing. You said it was something you'd thought about occasionally, Rudolph Dunst said that was a terrific idea, and you said, *well, that settles it.*"

"I must have been drunk."

He laughed. "I suspect you were joking."

I had zero recollection of that conversation, having short-circuited after realizing Troy Colby was sitting in the audience.

"I think I'll leave the writing to the professionals."

"Too bad. Dunst and the lady from Milwaukee were very enthusiastic at the idea. As am I. You've given a lot of excellent advice over the years." He quoted in a professorial tone, "*Assuming Emotional Impact Without Doing the Work.* Emotion comes from context, character investment, and pacing—not just content."

I murmured, "Feeling isn't earned by naming the feeling."

"Exactly. Useful stuff."

Our waiter arrived to take our orders.

"Are these real fish tacos or Monterey-imposter fish tacos?" Adrien inquired.

The waiter deadpanned, "No fish were harmed in the making of this dish, sir."

Adrien gave me a quizzical look, but ordered tacos made of seasoned seitan, bright cabbage slaw, and creamy chipotle cashew sauce. I went for mushroom enchiladas with mole sauce and ordered another round of margaritas.

"Speaking of writing, what's the final decision on signing the contract?" I asked after the busboy topped up our water glasses.

Adrien flicked me a look under his lashes. "I want to continue working with you, Keiran. You're a great editor. I really mean that. I think, however, it might be wise to wait to see where the chips fall."

That wasn't the news I'd hoped for. "I'm not sure what that means."

"Well," Adrien said briskly, "What it means is W&W's catalog has become formulaic, prioritizing safe, brandable, mass-market crime fiction over interesting or risky voices. Their books are all spine. No heart."

I nearly choked on my tortilla chip.

"You asked," he said.

"I did. Don't hold back."

The truth was, as a successful bookseller, Adrien had a perspective unlike any other author on my list. I was interested in what he had to say, particularly since he'd already articulated one of my greatest fears.

"They treat indie bookstores like a necessary evil. Their reps don't visit, their discount terms are insulting, and they never return emails unless you've sold a thousand copies of their latest airplane novel."

I swallowed. Reached for my margarita.

"They're allergic to queer protagonists unless they're dead, closeted, or were clearly only created for diversity points. And if they do publish something queer, it gets quietly buried under a cover that looks like a parking ticket."

"I won't argue that. But I think that's an arena in which I can have influence."

"Maybe. I have no doubt you'll do your best. Honestly, though, I can't imagine you being happy in that corporate environment. You love books too much. You love writing too much." He said almost sympathetically, "You love your authors too much."

I didn't know what to say to that.

Adrien said, "I think W&W will either burn you out or you'll quit. Maybe both." His expression was apologetic. "I'm not in the same position as a lot of your writers. I don't have to earn a living writing. I write because I love it. But if I never publish again, I'll be fine with that. I can still write for my own enjoyment." He shrugged.

I absorbed it, nodded. "Okay. I appreciate the honesty. Have you thought about where you'll take the next Leland book?"

"I meant what I said. I'm waiting to see where the chips fall. I don't think you'll stay at W&W. I could be wrong. A year from now, Rachel may be pitching *Serpent's Tooth* to you again."

It wasn't easy to hear, but I'd meant what I said. I did appreciate the honesty.

It struck me that four of my favorite authors were technically between contracts. Vaughn and Lila weren't going to lose any sleep over Grace Hollister and Adrien English. But Kyle had just won the Edgar and his book sales were trending up. And Finn... Was Finn Scott.

Finally, Christopher Holmes, also back to winning awards and trending up—though not technically between contracts—was strongly signaling he would not be producing if he could not get his editor of choice.

All of which, theoretically, improved my leverage.

Not that I should *need* to improve my leverage. My track record should have spoken for itself. But somehow, every time I spoke to Lila, I got the feeling she was recalculating my value-added cost.

Anyway, from there, the conversation moved into more pleasant channels. Adrien chatted about the bookstore, his dog, his cat, and the challenges of being married to a P.I. (he made it all sound a bit like a musical comedy). It was nice seeing him looking so healthy and sounding so happy. He had to be in his late thirties by now, but he still looked years younger and ridiculously handsome. Silky black hair, eyes the same color as my Siamese cats', that perfect bone structure—and a smile you felt in the center of your chest. His were the kind of looks that only improved with age.

And the best part was, he seemed utterly unaware of it. He was naturally funny, engagingly self-deprecating, and a genuinely good listener.

"No more amateur sleuthing?" I inquired after we'd ordered chocolate tamales and Mexican coffee for dessert.

"That's a funny thing," he remarked. "There was a time I couldn't stop falling over bodies." His smile was rueful.

"Well, you never know," I said. "One of your suburban neighbors could be up to no good right this minute."

"Oh, I think I know," he replied. "But I keep an open mind."

It wasn't until we were walking back to the hotel, that he said suddenly, "Keiran, you know the blond tattooed guy who asked all those rambling questions during the Backstory Q&A today?"

"Yes?" I hoped I didn't sound as wary as I felt, but there was something in Adrien's tone.

"He's sort of attached himself to our group the last couple of days. He seemed a little odd, but okay. Mostly quiet. But this afternoon, after the Q&A, he started asking questions about you."

I said without any inflection, "What kind of questions?"

"General stuff at first. How long each of us had worked with you. What you were like as an editor. But then he started getting more specific: Did you live alone? Do you have a partner? Where in Manhattan do you live; did anyone have your personal email or personal phone number. Did anyone know your room number? Your floor number. Were you staying on your own or did you have a roommate? The kind of thing that set off alarm bells for everyone at the table."

"I have to admit, I'm not thrilled hearing this," I remarked.

"We blew him off, which I think offended him. I haven't seen him since. That doesn't mean he's not out there."

I glanced at Adrien. His gaze was somber in the lamp-light.

"I'll keep an eye open. Thanks for letting me know."

"Maybe you should alert hotel security," he said. "The guy's name is Troy Colby. He keeps his badge turned over most of the time, but he was drunk the first night and accidentally introduced himself to Christopher."

"I'll think about it. I don't want to make it into a thing if he just wants to pitch his manuscript."

Adrien gave me an odd look, but left it there.

When we reached the hotel, I said, "I was going to join Finn and some other writers on the terrace. Did you want to—?"

He smiled, shook his head. "Jake should be arriving in an hour or so."

"Oh, that's nice."

"It is, yeah. After the conference we're driving up to San Francisco to stay with Christopher and J.X. for a few days."

"You and Christopher have become pretty close these last couple of years." Frankly, it surprised me. They were very different—not counting their propensity for getting themselves into hot water.

Adrien grinned. "I think he enjoys mentoring me."

I chuckled. "Very droll."

"I thought so."

We strolled to the elevators, still chatting. Adrien said goodnight and disembarked on the third floor. I was on my own the rest of the trip.

On the fifth floor, the elevator dinged and I stepped out.

At the sound of the service door down the hall, I glanced back and my heart froze at the sight of a tall, silvery figure coming my way.

My gasp must have carried, because Rudolph called, "Keiran, my boy. Did I startle you?"

Hell, yes, he'd startled me.

After my conversation with Adrien, I'd leaped to a horror movie scenario with Colby, butcher knife in hand, lying in wait, ready to pounce. In fact, it was only Rudolph, damp hair in tufts, wearing a navy hotel robe cinched neatly at the waist. A towel was slung over one shoulder, and he carried a pair of swim goggles.

"I'm getting nervous in my old age," I said lightly.

"Old age!" Rudolph scoffed. "Believe me, your best years are yet to come."

Hopefully, I wouldn't be spending them in a maximum-security facility.

But no. I was not going to give into those thoughts. I was not going to indulge my fears.

"Did you have a nice swim?" I asked.

"Excellent. The view from the pool is magnificent. Like swimming in the stars."

"I've been swimming most mornings." I nodded down the hall. "It's chilly on the terrace tonight. I'm going to grab a jacket."

Rudolph hesitated. "I was just about to fix myself a nightcap. Would you like to stop in for that drink?"

At the moment? No. I wanted to get down to Finn. I wanted to spend every possible minute I could with Finn, seeing that there was some uncertainty as to how many minutes were left.

Plus, I wanted to update him on the new and troubling revelations regarding Colby.

But something about the way Rudolph stood there, composed but a little wistful, silently dripping on the plush carpet, got to me. He must be so lonely at conferences, now that Anna was gone. As nice as being revered by your colleagues must be, it would still feel lonely crawling into an empty bed at night.

I could identify with that only too well.

"Sure," I said. "I'd love to."

His eyes lightened and he smiled. "Excellent! I always enjoy our little chats."

The Presidential Suite occupied the quietest corner of the top floor, and featured wraparound views of the bay. Like all the fifth-floor suites, the interior discreetly whispered old money and refined taste. Hardwood floors gleamed beneath Persian rugs, and the living room was anchored by a curved fireplace of sea stone and copper. Floor-to-ceiling windows framed the ocean like a painting in constant motion, and the furniture—deep leather chairs, carved side tables, and a dining nook set for four—looked less like hotel décor and more like the reading room of a private club.

The lights were dimmed to a mellow golden wash. The balcony doors stood cracked, letting in the scent of brine and fog. Rudolph poured us each a finger of something amber—presumably scotch—no water, no ice.

He handed me a short tumbler. "Cheers."

"Cheers." We clinked glasses and wandered over to the chairs before the fireplace.

"That was an excellent interview today," Rudolph remarked. "It's nice to go out on a high note."

Presumably he meant himself, but these days I couldn't be sure.

"You're a very generous interviewer." I held up my glass. "And this a very good scotch."

He smiled. "Macallan 25." He set his glass on the low glass and iron table, and began to briskly towel his hair. "You're very well-liked within this industry, Keiran. More importantly, you're very well-respected."

"That's very kind. Thank you." I sipped my scotch.

"Just stating facts."

I smiled politely.

"Between us—you have my word it will go no further—how do you really feel about the merger with Wheaton & Woodhouse?"

I sighed, and I think that sigh said it all, because he grimaced.

"It's unfortunate," Rudolph agreed. "I blame Daniel. He should have forced Millie to rise up through the ranks, just as he had to do. Instead, he simply handed the company over to her, and the silly girl ran it right into the ground."

Pretty much. I said nothing.

He finished drying his hair, which looked wilder than ever, and picked up his glass again. Staring into the golden liquid, he said casually, "Have you considered your other options?"

I smiled faintly. "If we're being honest, I'm not sure I have many. I appreciate the kind thought, but I'm forty and ours is an age-biased industry. I don't think most companies would agree that my best years are still ahead of me. Plus, there's a scarcity of equivalent roles. A lot of houses are downsizing or folding editorial departments into publishing teams. I suspect W&W have something like that in mind. It's highly unlikely I'm going to find a position with the same salary, healthcare, and retirement benefits. I'll be lucky to hang onto this one."

"*Ah,*" Rudolph said thoughtfully.

"And it's not as though I can bring my author list with me." I thought of Adrien English. "A few authors would probably follow me. But I wouldn't have the leverage I have now—assuming I still have that leverage."

"Yet, you've always struck me as an optimistic personality."

"Usually. Right now, I'm trying to temper wishful thinking with pragmatism."

He smiled absently. "Did you sign a DNC?"

"No."

"Very wise. However, knowing Vaughn, *were* you to strike out on your own, it's very possible he might try to blackball you."

I hadn't even considered *that* sickening possibility.

Considering the fact that I might be going to prison, maybe I needed to stop worrying about my lack of options and be grateful for my remaining days of full-time employment.

Into my silence, Rudolph said, "Suppose a reputable publishing house *were* looking for an editor of your caliber, someone with your experience and social media cachet? A house that could match your salary, healthcare, and retirement benefits?"

"What house is that?" I asked skeptically. A light bulb went on in the dusty corridors of my brain. "*Theodore Mansfield*?"

Rudolph raised his brows.

I blinked. "Is that even a possibility?"

"As you know, I'm retiring at the end of the year. Thankfully, TM is *not* planning to fold our editorial department into a publishing team." He shuddered, although maybe that had to do with his damp clothes. "They're very wisely planning to fill my position."

"But wouldn't that happen from within house?"

"Dear God, no. Our editors are all bright young things we hired for their fresh perspectives and next-gen voices. We need an actual adult in the room, someone to bridge the gap between the old fogeys on the board of directors and the children in the playpen. You would be the perfect solution."

I can't deny, my heart jumped at the idea—and then plummeted.

Even if I didn't go to prison, didn't have a trial, wasn't arrested…could I contemplate starting from scratch? Editorial director was a big step up—was I really qualified to take that step? If I went to another publishing house, it would be all-out war with W&W, and God knows what that would mean. Also, regardless of what Rudolph believed, a lot of TM's editorial staff, inexperienced or not, would deeply resent that top position going to an outsider. And finally, could I really contemplate abandoning what was left of Millhouse? Abandoning my remaining colleagues? Abandoning my remaining authors? Authors who were going on record in order to remain on my list?

Rudolph watched me for a moment, then said, "You don't have to decide now. I admit I've proposed your name to the board."

"Rudolph…"

"No. I'm not asking for an answer. I don't plan to leave until the end of the year. I'm just reminding you that there are *always* options."

"I don't know what to say."

"Nor do you need to say anything at this point. It's simply something to consider."

"Yes. Thank you for even thinking of me." I finished my scotch and set the glass on the table. "I should probably get going. I'm meeting people for drinks."

"Yes, you should go enjoy yourself." Rudolph waved a languid hand, and then reached for the decanter on the table between us. "I'll tell you this. If I had it all to do over again, I'd have spent more time drinking with friends."

I laughed, but I think he was serious.

# Chapter Twenty-One

I was preoccupied when I walked out of Rudolph's suite, understandably, which was maybe why I didn't immediately notice the man standing a few yards down the hall.

When I finally spotted the tall figure with silver hair and tattoos, hovering in the middle of the hallway, the jolt of recognition felt almost inevitable.

That said, I think my sudden appearance surprised him as much as he surprised me, because he snapped erect and took a couple of steps backwards.

I hadn't forgotten what Finn said about *bad optics, bad precedent, bad move.* I remembered every word.

I also remembered what Adrien English had said less than an hour earlier.

I hadn't approached U.N. Owen AKA Troy Colby. He was not just by chance wandering on the fifth floor. He had come after me, and I instinctively felt my only option was to confront the threat.

"U.N. Owen, I presume?" I called.

He turned and started to walk away.

"I'm not amused."

He faltered and turned back. He scowled. "Are you talking to me?"

Seeing that we were the only two people in the hall, it was a safe bet.

"You handed me a manuscript at the Stranger Than Fiction panel? That's not how submissions happen. But *had* you gone through the proper channels, your manuscript would still be a hard pass. I don't like gimmicks and I don't like games."

He wasn't wearing his dark glasses, and his very pale eyes bugged out of his head as he goggled at me. "W-What?"

"Using my name for a character? No. I don't like cute. I don't care how minor that character is. It's too cute. Yes, you got my attention, But for all the wrong reasons. If you *are* serious about submitting a genuine manuscript, send three chapters of a book you actually intend to finish, along with a synopsis and a cover letter with the name of the editor you're submitting to. However, Millhouse Books does not accept unagented submissions."

*"Are you crazy?"*

"That's it. You can stop pestering my authors. You've got my verdict."

It took every ounce of will I had to turn my back, pull out my key card, and wave it in front of the electronic lock to my room.

Colby stepped toward me, I could feel his breath against the side of my face. My neck muscles locked; my head started to shake with tension. The lock sensor turned green.

I opened the door, gave Colby a forbidding look, and pulled the door shut.

My final glimpse, before the door settled heavily into the frame, was of Colby's open mouth.

I turned the deadbolt, stepped back from the door, and pulled out my cell. My hands were so unsteady I nearly dropped the phone.

It took two tries before Finn answered. I could hear boisterous voices and laughter behind his, "Are you still at dinner?"

"No. I'm upstairs—"

"Come on down. J.X. and Christopher are here. Hayes, Pat Robinson—"

I interrupted, "Colby was up here."

Finn's voice changed. He suddenly sounded a whole lot more sober and a whole lot less cheerful. "What do you mean? In your room?"

"Wandering around in the hall outside."

Finn said sharply, "On my way," and disconnected.

I'm not sure how many times I paced up and down the floor before I heard the electronic lock beep and click over. The door opened and Finn, wearing jeans and a black Aran knit sweater, stepped inside.

"Keiran?" he spotted me by the fireplace. "Are you okay?"

I came to meet him. "Is he still out there?"

"Colby? No. I saw three women headed for the hot tub. Nobody else."

"He was waiting in the hall when I left Rudolph's room."

Finn put his hands on my arms, steadying me. "Okay. Let's start at the beginning. You came back from dinner and—?"

"Even before that, on the walk back from dinner, Adrien was telling me that Colby has been hanging around, trying to find out what floor I'm on, if I'm on my own."

Finn was guiding me to the sofa. I folded onto the cushions, gazing up, trying to gauge his reaction.

He was not happy.

There were lines in Finn's face that hadn't been there when he'd walked into the room.

"He's getting frustrated," Finn said. "We saw that during the Backstory Q&A. You're not reacting as expected."

"Neither is he!"

I didn't resist when Finn joined me on the sofa, taking my hands in his.

"You're okay, Keir. You handled yourself like a pro at the Q&A. Now walk me through what happened up here. Why were you in Rudolph's room?"

Jesus. I hadn't even had time to assimilate the unexpected proposal from Rudolph. Well, not a proposal. *Had* it been a proposal? A suggestion, maybe. I didn't want to pin too much on a casual conversation over 86 proof whisky.

I said, "I thought I'd grab my jacket before I joined you and Hayes—"

"Ha," Finn growled.

"But when I got off the elevator, Rudolph was coming back from the pool and he asked me to have a nightcap. So, I said yes, we had a nightcap..."

"And?"

I swallowed. "When I left Rudolph's, I spotted Colby standing a few feet from the door to this suite. He saw me, turned, and started to walk away, and I—"

"*Please* tell me you didn't speak to him."

"But that's not a normal reaction, Finn," I protested. "To just ignore this weirdo and his libelous manuscript when he's trying to infiltrate my authors and find out my room number? That's not what an innocent person would do."

"You spoke to him." Finn actually dropped his face in his hands, which scared the hell out of me.

"I *had* to. I couldn't pretend I didn't see him, so what's my excuse for not asking the normal questions?"

Finn raised his head and scrutinized me. "What *exactly* did you say to him?"

I related the entire conversation.

Finn heard me out in silence.

"You think I made a mistake," I said.

"Hell, yes! I said don't engage. What part of *don't engage* translates to a hallway dissertation on cover letters and character names?"

"What choice did I have? I couldn't pretend I didn't see him. We looked each other in the eyes."

Finn opened his mouth, but then closed it.

"Finn, he believed me."

Finn's brows drew together.

"I saw it in his face. He believes that *I* think it's all a gimmick. Maybe he won't believe it for long, but he believed it in the moment."

Finn was silent, thinking.

"I went with my instinct," I said. "That's all I had."

He said finally, "*If* it's true that he believed you, that he believes you have no clue about what happened between Dominic and Milo, it gives you a tactical and psychological advantage. That's a big if. Either way, though, it's dangerous because he's liable to double down to clarify the threat."

"But it buys us time. Doesn't it?"

"Maybe," Finn agreed grudgingly. "You managed to avoid confirming anything, you showed no reaction to pressure, you kept your own cards hidden. He still doesn't know what you know—or how rattled you are." He added, "You took a hell of a risk."

"I felt cornered. I had to go with my gut." I offered it as both explanation and apology.

Finn let out a long, controlled breath. "All right. You were there. I wasn't. You're smart. You know the stakes. I'm not going to second guess you." He met my eyes, grimaced, and said, "I mean, I *am*, because the idea that you confronted him on your own scares the shit out of me. We don't know how dangerous this guy is. But you're right, if he bought what you said, he's got to be very confused at this moment."

I leaned forward and rested my forehead on his shoulder. He put his arms around me immediately. "What's this?" he asked gently.

I moved my head in negation.

"You kept your head," he said quietly. "I'm not happy about it, but it was a gutsy move."

I sat up, rubbing my eyes. "I'm just tired." As I gazed around the room, I belatedly noticed Finn's suitcase standing by the dining room table. "Did you move in with me?"

His breath came out in a half-laugh. "Is that all right? I thought it was easier than running back and forth between floors every time I need to brush my teeth."

"Of course. That was the original plan before…"

Before everything had blown up. Before Finn had suspected I was keeping secrets and that getting more deeply involved with me was liable to drag him into a whole lotta trouble.

And now, when he knew for *sure* I'd been keeping secrets, and getting more deeply involved with me had *definitely* dragged him into a *huge* fucking mess, we were closer than ever.

Life was strange.

I said, "The thing is, Colby's too young."

"Too young for what?"

"He can't be a lot older than Kyle. He'd have been a child when everything happened between Milo and Dominic and me."

"He may have grown up listening to speculation and rumor. Or he may simply be an opportunist, and your original idea that he might accept a publishing contract as a blackmail payoff wasn't so far off mark."

"Maybe Colby is just the messenger. Maybe U.N. Owen is someone else. Maybe U.N. Owen is Milo."

"I don't think Milo is U.N. Owen."

It had been difficult for me to accept the idea, but once reconciled to it, I'd felt it was an inevitable conclusion. Milo had the most to gain by pinning Dom's death on me. He was the only person who knew for sure I'd been at the graveyard that night.

So, Finn's grim certainty surprised me. "You don't?"

"No. While you were gallivanting around old Monterey with Adrien English—"

"Droll."

His mouth twitched, but he continued, "I was checking up on a few things."

"Milo *is* dead?"

"I don't think Milo is dead, no. But I also don't think he's behind this attempt to wreck you."

"Wreck me?" I echoed uneasily. "You don't think it's just blackmail?"

"Unfortunately, no. If that tire had blown on the coast road, there's a good chance you'd have been killed. You said it yourself. Killing their victims is not the blackmailer's usual business model."

I digested that unwelcome news.

"You remember I asked you about the Devlin Family Trust?"

I nodded mechanically. Even though the thought had already occurred to me, it's not easy to accept that someone hates you enough to kill you.

Finn said, "A family trust is a legal entity used to hold and manage assets—typically for things like estate planning, tax efficiency, privacy, and control of assets after death."

"Right. The Devlin Family Trust owns the Cadillac DeVille that followed me. I'm still not sure—"

"The Devlin Family Trust also holds the deed to the house Colby rents."

*Hell.* That was where I'd heard the name before. When I'd first tried to find out who U.N. Owen was.

"Not a coincidence, obviously."

"No. The trust was set up in the name of Mary Catherine Devlin-Baldwin."

I stared at Finn. "*Baldwin*? Judge Baldwin?"

"His wife. His late wife, to be exact. There's nothing inherently shady in the trust. Mary Catherine Devlin-Baldwin came from money, and the trust was part of how that money was managed."

I said, "Judge Baldwin *can't* be behind this. He wasn't— yes, he would have used his influence to keep Dominic from being kicked off the football team. But that's not what I meant when I said he was rich and powerful. He's a good man. A sincerely good person. Caring. Generous. Everybody, and I mean *everybody,* in Steeple Hill looked up to him."

Finn looked unimpressed.

I said weakly, "He sent me Christmas presents every year."

Because I was the sheriff's kid, sure, but it had still been a thoughtful gesture. Those had been genuinely nice gifts.

Finn said, "I'm simply telling you where the trail leads."

"But that can't be right."

"You don't think Dominic's father might have some hard feelings toward the people he believes disappeared his son?"

I felt like I'd walked into a meat locker, felt the chill in my bones.

"But how would he know any of this? How would he know we were involved? How would he have found out? And why would he come after *me*? I didn't kill Dominic. Where would he get the idea that *I* killed Dominic? I didn't even *know* Dominic. I don't think he ever spoke directly to me in my entire life."

Finn said, "I think we should ask him."

*"Ask him?* Ask *Judge Baldwin?"*

"I think that's the simplest and best option."

I stammered, "B-but what if we're wrong? We can't talk to him without revealing…revealing way too much. I'd be implicating myself to a judge."

"Retired judge. But yes, I think we should be completely candid. Don't forget. He's also in legal jeopardy. If Baldwin orchestrated or knowingly participated in a plan to harm, blackmail, or discredit you—or worse—"

"But maybe he didn't!"

Finn didn't seem to entertain that possibility, because he kept right on. "That's conspiracy. If he's asked, encouraged, or paid someone to commit a criminal act, that's criminal solicitation. If he even *knew* about the plan or helped in any way to facilitate it—which seems pretty likely given that Georgi Argyros is the licensed driver of that Caddy—"

"Jesus Christ." I closed my eyes. *"Geo used to work for the judge.* In fact, that's how he got out so fast after he went to jail for stealing a car. Judge Baldwin interceded."

"I'm guessing Geo still works for the judge. Though maybe not in an official capacity."

"I can't believe it."

Finn said nothing.

I opened my eyes, looked at him. "I don't know, Finn. I don't see how we prove any of this. It's all guesswork and speculation. It's all circumstantial."

"We don't need ironclad proof—just reasonable suspicion in order to point out to Baldwin that he's got a lot to lose, too. If we approach this right, we might be able to pressure him into admitting the truth. Our goal is to get him to back off. Even if he doesn't confess his involvement, if we can stop this from spiraling any further out of control, that's mission accomplished."

"But if he had Milo killed?"

"I still don't think Milo's dead."

Neither did I, really. I thought it over and had to admit, "I don't believe Geo would kill Milo. He wouldn't have anything to do with that." I smiled without humor. "In fact, I could see him offering me up in place of Milo."

"Geo may not know the truth. He may think you really did kill Dominic. He might even think you had something to do with Milo's disappearance."

I sat motionless, feeling mostly numb.

Finn said quietly, "It's up to you, Keir. There is a risk. I won't lie to you. But I think it's our best shot at ending this now before any more damage is done."

I had no idea what the right decision was. This was Finn's area of expertise. Not mine. His proposal terrified me. But it wasn't as though I had a better plan.

I let out a long weary breath, nodded. "Okay. If you think this is the way. When do you want to talk to him?"

"I don't want to give him a heads up. I think we pay him a surprise visit early tomorrow."

"What if he won't see us?"

"If we're right, he's absolutely going to want to see you. Even if we're wrong, he'd probably be willing to give you a few minutes of his time." Finn's smile was sardonic. "That smart kid he sent Christmas presents to? Hell yeah, he'll see you."

# Chapter Twenty-Two

The floor-to-ceiling windows cast angled blocks of moon-light across the room.

Building blocks? Cell blocks?

"I don't think I'm going to be able to sleep much," I admitted when Finn climbed into bed a few minutes after me.

He gave a funny laugh, reached out, and I moved into the circle of his arm. He smelled comfortingly familiar: soap, toothpaste, himself.

"I never thought we'd do this again," I said.

"Sleep? Me neither." I could feel his smile although I continued to watch the indigo dome of sky tilt and slide its bowl full of stars into the ocean, the glittery reflection spilling across the rippled black water. Beyond the harbor, dark silhouettes of fishing boats rocked gently in their slips, deck lights casting pale halos onto the inky water.

His words registered. I made a sound of amusement, turning my face up and, still smiling, he dropped a kiss on my mouth.

"I missed you so much," I whispered. I was happy in this instant, but that hole in my heart still ached a little.

Finn hesitated, said quietly, "I kept waiting for that moment when I knew I'd made the right choice. It never came."

The next time his mouth brushed mine, it wasn't a kiss so much as gravity—the force by which one body draws another toward its center. We closed the gap, held each other tightly, silently, breathing in soft unison.

Just held each other.

I closed my eyes, breathing in his scent, feeling the rebellious softness of his hair, hearing the roughness of emotion in his breathing.

"I'm so sorry, Keir." His voice was barely a whisper. "I never meant to hurt you. It kills me to think I'd be the one to cause you pain."

"It's okay," I reassured. "We're okay."

His instincts had been correct, after all. I had been harboring dangerous secrets, secrets that could harm him, too.

I slid my fingers into his hair, holding his face still, gazing into the colorless gleam of his eyes.

"I love you."

I'd only ever said it twice in my life, and my heart thudded as though I'd suddenly leaped from a balcony, dropped into empty sky.

He made a sound that seemed closer to pain than pleasure. His mouth found mine, his lips surprisingly soft. I opened to him, tasted his answer.

For a moment we stayed like that, lips barely brushing, eyelashes flickering, soft, unsteady breaths. When we kissed again, we were both tender, both reassuring. Yes, there was wear and tear. Damage had been done. But nothing that couldn't be repaired with time and patience.

At least the harm Finn had done had been inflicted without malice. Even before we'd thought of reconciling, he'd tried to undo some of the damage.

He pulled me in carefully, then more firmly, and I let myself be held, wanted to be held. It was lovely to be stroked and caressed, lovely when it was Finn, who knew when and where to touch lightly, delicately, when and where I liked his demands and urgency. From our first time together, he'd seemed to instinctively understand things about me I barely understood myself. That I did not like roughness or grabbing or surprises. I did not like to be rushed.

He whispered, "I've wanted to tell you that for years."

Tears started in the back of my eyes. I said shakily, trying for a joke, "That I love you?"

"That I love *you*." Finn said it steadily, seriously.

I shook my head, but he said gently, "Of course I do. You've known for a long time."

Yes. Although these last few days there had been reason to believe he'd changed, that I'd lost that love.

I'd done little enough to deserve it.

"It's terrible timing," I said.

"I don't agree." His mouth moved against mine with tender insistence, and we were kissing again. Kissing till we were out of breath.

Maybe he was right. If his plan didn't work, if I did end up in prison, the memory of this, the promise of this would probably be the only thing that could keep me sane.

"I don't want you to pay the price for my mistakes."

Finn said, "There's always a price for loving someone."

I wasn't sure what that meant—other than once you loved someone, anything that hurt them, hurt you. That was true.

Finn's hands continued to move over me, exploring, pleasuring. When his large capable hand closed around my cock, I pushed into it, making encouraging sounds, willingly giving up control, letting Finn set the pace, shoving into that sure and knowledgeable grip...*teamwork makes the dream work...*

It took almost no effort from either of us before I was spilling over in high tide, coming in pulses like the waves rushing the pilons beneath us. My heart pounded in time to each silvery surge. Distantly, I heard the sounds I was making, somewhere between laughter and tears.

Finn nuzzled me, making comforting sounds. I could hear that little thread of humor in his voice, but I didn't mind—had never minded—because he wasn't laughing at me. Or if he was, it was with affection. He did not think I was a joke.

We continued to kiss and touch. It was all nice. Everything with Finn was nice. But for me, this was the best part.

He said, "The first time you let me crash at your loft, I saw you had a very battered copy of *How to Make Friends and Influence People* in the back of your bookshelf."

"*Oh no.*" I laughed self-consciously.

"I think that's when I started to love you."

"Jesus. That's..."

"I finally felt like I was starting to understand you."

I shook my head. "I just wanted to be liked when I was a kid. That's all there is to understand."

"You *are* liked. You're kind and funny and smart. But mostly, you care about people and it comes through. You didn't have to organize that management buyout. You could have left early on."

"Well, it failed, so it wasn't much of an effort. Anyway, I'm not sure why everyone thinks I had so many options. I don't have any more options than anyone else."

"Bullshit." Finn said it gently.

I was silent for a moment, and then I admitted, "Rudolph told me he put my name before TM's board of directors."

It was Finn's turn for silence.

"Good," he said at last. "It's the obvious move for you."

I half sat up. "I can't *accept* it! Even if they do offer—and I don't think they would, especially if I end up going to trial—"

Finn sat up, too. "Whoa, whoa. What's all the uproar?"

"You know better than anyone what the uproar is!"

"Keir." He put his arms around me. "If you don't think they're going to make you an offer, why are you panicking?"

Until Finn pointed it out, I hadn't realized that I *was* starting to panic. I took a couple of deep breaths, shook my head. "It's just...a lot. We're going to talk to Judge Baldwin and then I'm probably going straight to jail do not pass Go. Lila fucking hates me. So even if— I'm not qualified for that job!" I heard myself babbling and shut up.

"You're not going to prison," Finn said. "I don't care what I have to do. You're not going to prison."

I gave a shaky, hopeless laugh.

"Secondly, Lila doesn't hate you. She resents the fact that you made choices she didn't have the nerve to make, and those choices paid off for you. She isn't happy at W&W but she feels trapped. Thirdly, you've been doing the job of editorial director without the commensurate pay for how many years now? You're a senior editor in name only and everyone paying attention—which includes Rudolph Dunst, as it turns out—knows it. You *are* qualified."

I swallowed.

"This is absolutely the right move. It's a fucking godsend, and I one hundred percent think you should take it."

"I can't just walk away in the middle of everything!"

"Keiran, look at me."

I raised my head, stared at Finn's stern face.

"Millbrook House is gone. It's over. You did what you could to save it, you failed, and that's the end of that story. Wheaton & Woodhouse is not the right place for you. It's not the right place for a lot of your authors. Including me."

"Wait. What does *that* mean?"

"It means the only reason I'm signing with W&W is you."

"But—"

"And I'm guessing a number of your authors feel the same way."

Some of them did, I knew that for a fact. But that didn't mean—

Well, what *did* it mean?

"I still don't think I'm qualified."

"Rudolph does. You seem to have a lot of respect for the guy. Do you think he'd recommend you for a job he didn't think you were qualified for? Especially *his* old job?"

Well, no.

I shook my head, but I had no idea what I was denying. The idea that there might be a solution for at least one of my problems? That despite not deserving it, I might get a happy ending after all?

"This is an awful lot of heavy lifting for this time of night," Finn murmured.

"I know. I wasn't going to bring it up now."

"Or at all," Finn said wryly.

"No, I'd have told you. I-I want your thoughts. It's just I'm not used to…"

"Having to take someone else into account?" He was teasing, but gently.

"Yes. That's true."

"You'll get used to it."

He said it with such confidence, I laughed.

But it was moving to hear it, to think that maybe I *would* have this—someone I loved who loved me back. He knew, understood that I was not a safe bet, might be going to prison for a long time, and even if they didn't throw away the keys, I wasn't great at this, at relationships, but Finn was willing to, well, work with me.

I was still wondering about it as he urged me over and onto my knees. This was his favorite part, and I liked being able to give him exactly what he wanted, what he needed. It was always easy and light with Finn. My thighs were widely parted, forehead resting on my folded arms, smiling a little as he took his time with warm fingers and oil that smelled like driftwood. When he began to press his very large cock into me, I concentrated on my breathing, on relaxing my muscles. I focused on the always strange, always confusing sensation of being filled—of being shared.

Finn pushed in, I gasped at the familiar shock, and he began to thrust, thrust, thrust—before withdrawing. And then all over again. The prod, the push, the piercing me with careful, calculated deliberateness, changing angle, thrusting more deeply, thrust, thrust, thrust.

I moaned in time to his deep grunts, the guttural sounds he made with each thrust.

"Uhn…"

"Uhn…"

"*Uhn…*"

It was such a bewildering sensation to be taken. I felt helpless. I *was* helpless. But I wanted it, too. Part of the helplessness was desire. I wanted this. I wanted him. Always.

"Your smell, your taste, the sounds you make," Finn gasped with each thrust. "You're perfect, Keiran."

He was always so loving, so sweet, trying so hard to reassure, but truthfully, I didn't need reassurance about this. I knew he loved fucking me, that my complete and total submission turned him on like nothing else. I loved having that power. But it wasn't about power. It was about the ability to make him happy.

It all felt so good. That was the truth.

The dangerously teetering world suddenly locked back into place.

Finn reached beneath my belly, found my penis and tugged it back into life—and that was unexpected. The scrape of his thick cock inside me, his hand rubbing me with unusual roughness, not hurting me, but less restrained than usual. It startled me, excited me a little. Those intense but different feelings created a sudden shock of fluttering, flustered sensation that spread, expanded, and suddenly rolled through me in a giant rush.

I yelled in inarticulate reaction, coming a second time, dimly aware of Finn's orgasm flooding me, hot, sticky. My thighs shuddered, muscles clenching tight around Finn who was coming in gasps of wet heat, groaning deep in his throat as though he'd been mortally wounded, his hands biting into me reflexively, and then trying to smooth away any hurt.

We collapsed in a hot, damp tumble. I was wet and wobbly, inside and out, and Finn's breath was coming in hot gasps against my ear.

Another of those funny shuddery half-laughs, half-sobs escaped me, and Finn wrapped his arm around me, pulling me close. "All right?" His voice was gruff.

I nodded.

"It was good?"

"Always."

"I didn't hurt you?"

"Never."

He leaned his forehead against my forehead, gently rubbed his nose against mine. *Kunik.* As kids we called it *Eskimo kisses.*

I smiled, made a sound of amusement in my throat.

He whispered, "I love you so much."

My throat closed. Inarticulate in the aftermath.

We drifted in a silence somehow more restful than sleep.


I listened to the waves.

The soothing beat and boom of the incoming tide.

I'd been awake for a while, thinking, trying not to worry. The sound of the ocean woke me before the alarm. Had we set an alarm? The night before seemed a long time ago.

It took me a moment to sort out the days. Right. It was Saturday.

We were going to see Judge Baldwin.

And after that, everything would be changed forever.

Granted, everything was already changed forever.

I sighed. I was really getting to hate change.

I glanced at Finn's sleeping face—*was* he sleeping? Not all change was bad.

Closing my eyes, I tried to pretend I could fall back asleep, tried to convince myself I didn't notice the slice of sunlight through the parted drapes. I wanted to spend every possible minute with Finn. I wanted to savor the moment without thinking beyond cool cotton sheets and sunlight on my face, the sound of the ocean, and the entirely pleasant weight of Finn's arm slung possessively around my waist.

Finn mumbled, "Morning."

I glanced over. One bleary green eye studied me.

"Good morning."

"Sleep okay?"

"Yes." I was too exhausted not to have slept okay.

His closed his eye, didn't say anything else. I smiled a little, studying him. He must have heard that faint sound of amusement. He opened his eyes again.

"What?"

I shook my head, then said, "I've been thinking, and I'm glad—well, relieved—that I'll have the chance to tell Judge Baldwin I'm sorry."

Finn said nothing.

"It's not that I expect it to make a difference to him. But I want him to know I regret my actions. Everything."

Still no comment from Finn.

"I used to think it was easier that he didn't know that Dom was dead. I believed it was better to have hope. For years I told myself that."

"No." Finn was definite. "Not knowing is harder."

Yes. I understood that now. After years of wondering why Milo had left. *If* he had left.

Finn said, "You were a kid. You didn't have a lot of life experiences. Sometimes cruelty comes from a lack of empathy. Sometimes it's a lack of imagination. But sometimes it's simply the lack of experience."

"It's still strange to me that someone like Judge Baldwin could have a son like Dominic. Because he really was a bully. Not to me. He didn't know I was alive. But to a lot of other people. He was horrible to the girls he dated. Milo gave as good as he got. But Dom used to roll over other kids like a Mack truck. Roll over them, back up, and roll over them again."

Finn said, "Too much freedom, not enough supervision. An only child with a tragically dead mother and a father who spent the majority of his time pursuing a busy and demanding career? My guess is that Baldwin tried to make up for a lot of things by spoiling the kid. It wouldn't be the first time that backfired."

True. That particular dynamic showed up a lot in fiction because it showed up a lot in real life.

"Judge Baldwin gave me my first mystery novel," I said. "*The Tower Treasure.*"

Finn's eyes crinkled at the corners. He said softly, "And the rest is history."

I nodded. "He liked mysteries. Classic mystery."

After a moment, Finn pushed up on his elbow, propping his head on his hand as he considered me. "You think U.N. Owen is Judge Baldwin?"

"It makes sense. If you're right and he's the one pulling the strings. Colby doesn't strike me as an Agatha Christie fan."

"Probably not."

"It's a pretty elaborate scheme."

"There's a lot of rage behind the calculation," Finn agreed. "The cruelty is the point, as we so often hear these days."

I sat up, pushed the covers back. "Do I have time for a swim? Or did you want to have breakfast and get going?"

"What time is it?" Finn peered at his watch. "My eyes won't focus. How much did I drink last night?"

I reached for my glasses, checked the clock. "Six thirty."

Finn groaned. "Go swim. We can have breakfast when you get back. Then we'll drive up to Steeple Hill."

I threw back the covers, glancing back as Finn's outstretched fingertips brushed my ass.

"Or—?" he suggested.

I chuckled, shook my head. "If I'm going to spend another three hours in a car, I've got to work some of these kinks out of my back."

"I'd be more than happy to help you work out your kinks."

"Hold that thought."

"I'd be more than happy to hold your d—"

I tossed the blankets over him.

Too early for tourists. Too cold for conference-goers nursing their second-degree hangovers. The Horizon Deck was quiet and deserted.

Just the way I liked it.

There were a couple of empty glasses on the deck by the hot tub. I raised my brows at a pair of plaid swim trunks discarded next to one of the mesh lounge chairs.

It was still damp and cool and gray this early in the morning. Mist curled over the glass safety barriers; the sky was a dull purple, as if bruised by the previous night. The only sound was the soft lapping of water against blue tile and the more distant thunder of the surf.

I dropped my towel over the back of the lounge chair nearest to the pool, left my glasses on the little table, and walked to the pool's edge. The surface was smooth, faintly steaming in the morning chill, light from the submerged lamps casting a soft green glow through the murkiness. The pool was empty, as expected.

I stepped out of my deck shoes, adjusted my goggles, and dove.

The lightly heated water embraced me in profound silence. I let myself sink, easily slipping into an almost meditative state. I kicked off the wall and swam two laps with long, clean strokes, my thoughts blessedly blank for the first time in days.

My awareness narrowed; I was solely focused on my breathing, my strokes, my kicks.

*Reach, pull, breathe. Long and clean. Don't rush the turn.*

On the third lap, I rolled into a breath, opening my eyes mid-stroke—and something shifted in my periphery.

A strange shape seemed to drift below me, hovering over the bottom of the pool.

I instinctively kicked closer, expecting pool equipment, a towel, light bouncing off the tiles, a hallucination—

Time stopped.

The blurred outline sharpened just enough: pale limbs drifting without purpose, silver hair fanning out like seaweed, a gray T-shirt ballooning spinnaker-like over a waxen torso.

My underwater yell was distorted, muffled.

His eyes. His eyes were wide open, unfocused, milky from hours in the water. The slow sway of hair and fabric and those terrible blank eyes. Like a ghost.

I froze mid-descent, lungs burning, still rejecting what I was seeing even as realization crashed in with all the force of hydrostatic pressure

I instantly understood two things: it was already far too late for Colby, and my touching the body would make everything worse.

I kicked hard for the daylight, broke the surface with a gasp, lungs burning, water sluicing from my face in sheets. I tore off my goggles. For a moment, I couldn't breathe— not from exertion, but from sheer horror. I swam to the side of the pool, my arms trembling as I clung to the edge of the deck, heart hammering.

*This can't be happening...*

I blinked hard, once, twice, but I couldn't get that image out of my brain. Colby, pale and suspended, floating just beyond reach.

Clumsily, I climbed out of the pool, grabbed my glasses, and padded across the deck to the pool phone.

I hit the emergency button.

*Don't get more involved than you already are.*

Yeah, good luck with that.

"Front desk," said a sleepy voice.

"You need to call security," I got out. "There's a body in the pool."

# Chapter Twenty-Three

Hotel security staff arrived within five minutes.

Five minutes is a long time when you're waiting with a dead body.

The minute I hung up with the front desk, I phoned Finn, and Finn arrived what felt like ninety seconds later—well, before security.

He wore jeans, tennis shoes, and carried the mostly decorative blue and gold afghan from the suite's living room

I had the confused idea that he was going to retrieve Colby's body and put the blanket over him, but the afghan turned out to be for me. He wrapped it around my shoulders, putting his face next to mine and saying very quietly, "Don't lie, but don't offer anything, either. Answer what they ask—no more, no less. You're in shock, you were swimming laps, you saw something in the water, and you called for help. That's it. Stick to what you know for sure, not what you think or suspect. And if they push, tell them you want to talk to your lawyer before going further."

I nodded mechanically. "There are security cameras everywhere. They're going to see my run-in with Colby last night."

"No. They're going to see a conversation. Which can be interpreted different ways. What they will also hopefully see is whoever followed Colby up to the Horizon Deck."

I stared at him. "You don't think it could have been an accident?"

Finn said grimly, "Until we hear otherwise, it absolutely was an accident. That should be your assumption."

"Right. Yes."

Finn hesitated. "If the subject of the manuscript comes up, play it like you did last night with Colby."

"I— You said not to lie."

"It's a decades-old missing persons cold case. Nobody's going to make an instant connection to what happened in Steeple Hill. We need some time to figure out what's happening. Right?"

I nodded.

He scrutinized my face. "You okay?"

"I think I need a vacation."

He grinned a little. "How's San Clemente sound?"

It sounded like heaven and about as far out of reach.

Security arrived at that point. They conferred, agreed that the victim was clearly deceased, and phoned 911. After confirming that Finn and I were guests at the hotel, we all waited the ten minutes it took Monterey Police to respond to the 911 call.

Finn sat with his arm around my blanketed shoulders. We didn't speak.

The first officers arrived and the scene was secured. I was separated from Finn and very briefly interviewed: What's your name? What were you doing in the pool? Did you touch the body? Did you see anyone else?

To my relief, they did not ask if I recognized the dead man, and, remembering Finn's instructions (and the thousands of mystery novels I'd edited) I volunteered nothing.

After about fifteen minutes and more conferring, the decision was made to call for a detective supervisor.

My heart sank, but it wasn't really a surprise.

It was still unclear—or at least, I was still unclear—as to whether Colby's body had visible injuries. But a sudden unexplained death at a mystery conference?

No chance in hell was there not going to be a complete and thorough investigation.

About ninety minutes after I'd discovered Colby's body floating in the Horizon Pool, Homicide Detective Robert Olivares strolled into the crime scene, and I finally caught a break.

Olivares was perhaps fifty, handsome, genial, and clearly experienced. He wore a gold wedding band and a small golden stud in his right ear.

"Mr. Chandler?" he asked. His voice was warm, conversational. "Detective Robert Olivares, Monterey PD."

I said automatically, "How do you do?"

"Better than you, I imagine. Anybody offer you coffee? Something to warm you up?"

"Yes. Thanks. My stomach's a little off."

He offered a brief sympathetic smile. "Understandable." He pulled a small notepad from his jacket. "I understand you discovered the body. Mind walking me through what happened this morning?"

I took a breath, trying not to glance back at the far end of the pool, where Colby's still floating body was currently being photographed behind crime scene tarps.

"I was swimming laps," I said. "Early. Around six thirty? Maybe a little after. I noticed something in the water at the deep end. I wasn't sure what it was at first."

"You were the only one using the pool?"

"At that time, yes."

"You enter through the east gate?"

I nodded again. "I used my key card."

"Did you see anyone else around? Anyone entering or leaving?"

"No." I hesitated. "I wasn't really paying attention. I took my glasses off when I got to the pool. I was focused on swimming."

Olivares jotted something down, then looked back at me. "So, you saw something in the water—what made you realize it was a body?"

"I didn't, at first. But as I got closer... The way it moved—didn't move, actually. The shape. Then I saw it—he—had a face." I shivered convulsively, seeing that face again.

"You touch the body?"

"No. I could tell he was dead. His eyes were..." I swallowed, admitted, "I couldn't jump out of the pool fast enough. I got to the nearest phone and called the front desk."

He watched me for a moment, then asked, "Did you know the victim?"

I hesitated. "I didn't get a close look at him, but I think it's Troy Colby. He was a writer attending the conference."

"Then you did know him."

"Only in passing."

It was alarming how easy it was to say too much.

Olivares raised an eyebrow. "And you're...another writer?"

"No. I'm an editor. Several of my authors are here this weekend."

"Right," he said, flipping a page. "Keiran Chandler. Senior editor. Millbrook House. You're staying in the Grand Bay Suite?"

That was a timely reminder that detectives often asked questions they already knew the answer to.

"Yes."

Another nod. "Did you have any disputes or disagreements with Mr. Colby?"

I gave a short laugh. "Disagreements? I'm sure I did. He was a writer."

Olivares smiled faintly. "I meant anything more serious."

"Not from my perspective."

His brows shot up. "That's an interesting comment."

It was, wasn't it? What the fuck was the matter with me?

"I've bumped into several authors this weekend who, it turns out, took offense at comments I made during evaluations or because I turned down a manuscript. Those decisions are part of my job. It's not personal to me, but, understandably, it is to writers."

He smiled, displaying perfect teeth. "I can see that. You rejected Mr. Colby's manuscript?"

"If that *is* Mr. Colby, his wouldn't be the only manuscript I turned down this weekend."

"Do you know if Mr. Colby had run-ins with anyone this weekend? Did he have any enemies?"

"Wasn't it an accident?"

Olivares shrugged. "Just covering all the bases. At the moment, it's a suspicious death. Would you say he had enemies?"

I hesitated again. "I can't answer that. I just don't know."

Olivares studied me for a long beat. "Okay. We'll follow up later for a formal statement, but I appreciate your cooperation this morning."

I nodded. I was abruptly out of words.

He clicked his pen and gave me another of those polite, unreadable smiles. "You might want to have a hot drink. Lie down for a few minutes. It's normal to be shocked."

"Yes."

"Different from books, right?" His tone was wryly humorous.

I nodded. There were no words for how different it was.

"You're not planning to leave town?"

"I— No. The conference ends tomorrow. I'm having a cocktail party for some of my authors tomorrow night. I can postpone my flight for however long is necessary."

"We appreciate that." He nodded in dismissal.

That was not the part where I caught a break. That happened as I was leaving the Horizon Deck.

Finn, who had been waiting over to the side, made his way over to Olivares and quietly introduced himself as a retired San Clemente homicide detective. That was all I was able to hear, but as I went through the security gate, I heard Olivares exclaim, "*Finn Scott*! No kidding. Man, I *love* your books!"

It was about forty-five minutes before Finn returned to our room.

I'd had time to shower, shave, dress, and consider burning *I Know What You Did* in the living room fireplace before I heard the electronic lock.

I couldn't read Finn's expression when he walked in, but he was good at concealing his feelings.

"Was he murdered?" I asked.

He grimaced. "They're not confirming or denying, but I got a glimpse of Colby when they dragged him out. There's a lot of bruising around his neck."

"Jesus. I don't understand." I leaned forward in my chair, carding my damp hair with my fingers. "Does this make sense to you?"

"No. It doesn't make any sense. You've been the target from the beginning. So why is Colby dead?"

I appreciated the importance of the question, although, frankly, I couldn't help being glad not to be the one floating in the swimming pool.

I studied his face. "Are we still going to see Judge Baldwin?"

"No." At my expression, he said, "I don't think you're under exceptional scrutiny, but you found the body and you did admit to some level of acquaintance with the victim, so you've attracted their attention. The last thing we want to do is point them in a direction potentially dangerous to you."

I closed my eyes. "Right."

"The best thing to do is carry on as normal."

What the hell was normal?

I opened my eyes. "Do you think I should destroy the manuscript?"

"*No.*" Finn was definite. "We don't know how many people have knowledge of that manuscript. We don't know who, besides Rachel Ving, saw Colby hand it to you or whether that exchange showed up on a security camera. We don't know how many copies are floating around out there or what records he kept. If it's discovered that you destroyed your copy of the manuscript, it will be viewed as an admission of guilt. Whereas treating it like any other submission you planned on rejecting, looks innocent."

I thought about that, and said, "What if I mark up the manuscript as if I'd actually edited it?"

Finn stared at me and then laughed. "You know what, that's fucking brilliant. Yes. You do that while I jump in the shower."

While Finn showered, whistling with what I couldn't help feeling was peculiar cheerfulness, I took a red pen and marked the hell out of Colby's partial manuscript and then tossed it back onto the small desk.

Finn, dressing in the bedroom, called, "What have you got scheduled for today?"

"Well, I was going to throw myself on the mercy of the court, but as it turns out..."

He stepped out of the bedroom, pulling down a forest green polo shirt. "Are you free for breakfast?"

"I should probably..."

I did not have breakfast scheduled with anyone, but there were any number of things I could and should be doing. I should check on Cherry. Reassure her that murder rarely happened at conferences—especially when there were no award ceremonies involved. I should touch base with Lila. I should contact the conference organizers and offer to...

What?

It all felt a little bit pointless. Every time I closed my eyes, I saw Troy Colby floating in the green-blue water.

Finn waited a moment, and when I didn't complete the thought, he came over and sat beside me. "What would you *like* to do today?"

I said honestly, "I don't think I can take any more panels or any more interviews or any more meetings."

"Agreed. I'm pretty much done with Noir at the Shore. Why don't we have breakfast away from the hotel and then figure out the rest of the day."

"Is that allowed?" I was only half-kidding.

"It's not only allowed, I think it's mandatory," Finn said, and he was not kidding.

Water + Leaves was quiet at that hour—just the occasional cyclist whizzing by on the coastal trail, the muted clatter of cups behind the counter, and the low murmur of two baristas trading sleepy gossip.

We grabbed a table near the window, facing the water. Outside, the bay was slate gray and barely stirring. A pair of sea otters bobbed in the distance, heads just visible as they floated belly-up, indifferent to the human attention they were drawing a few hundred yards inland.

Finn casually mentioned having had breakfast with Hayes there on Friday morning after our encounter at the pool.

I sipped my American, said casually, "Okay, you and Hayes are...what?"

Finn raised his brows. "Hayes and I are friends."

"Friends with benefits?"

"There are certainly benefits to having friends. If you mean are we having sex, no. I find him entertaining company. We've never had a sexual relationship. I seem to recall mentioning that I've been in love with you for about eight years."

I'm not prone to blushing, so I'm not sure why heat flooded my face. Maybe it was simply the open honesty of it.

"He seems pretty taken with you."

"I'm pretty damned loveable, in case you haven't noticed."

I sputtered a reluctant laugh. "I did notice. I just want to be sure I'm not—"

I ran out of steam in the face of his quizzical expression.

"You're not competing with anyone, if that's what you're worried about. I appreciate the fact that you're a grown-up. I want a relationship with you. If I haven't managed to communicate that yet, maybe I should start thinking about another line of work."

I said, "Sorry. I'm not usually so...needy."

"Nope," Finn said. "You're not. This is a nice change. After the last eight years, I don't mind hearing that I matter to you and that you're hoping for more than a conference weekend together."

Our breakfasts arrived. Avocado toast for me and a breakfast sandwich for Finn.

"Do you think Geo killed Colby?" I asked.

"The only thing we know for sure is Geo is somehow connected to the plot to intimidate and harass you. He seems the most likely person to have tampered with your car. Was that at the direction of someone else? Judge Baldwin? Or was it his own idea? Was Geo directed to eliminate Colby or was that a decision he made on his own? We don't know enough to do more than speculate."

"I'm okay with speculating."

Finn smiled faintly, but did not indulge me.

I said finally, "Did Olivares ask you if you thought I did it?"

"Yep." Finn's smile was sardonic. "I told him I knew you hadn't because you'd spent the night with me."

*"Oh."* I'd known Finn would supply an alibi if required, but I hadn't expected him to volunteer it at the first opportunity. But he was a straight-from-the-shoulder kind of guy. It shouldn't have been a surprise. "Do you think he believed—"

"Which will be confirmed when they do find that security footage. You never left the room after you spoke to Colby. I never left the room after I came upstairs."

"That's true. But if they start investigating Colby, they're liable to find out about *I Know What You Did.* God knows what evidence might be in his hotel room."

"Yes. That remains a problem. But right now, their priority is figuring out who murdered Colby." He added with that same cynical smile, "I told Olivares you were my editor as well as my partner. He found that *very* interesting." Finn's mouth quirked. "He's working on a book."

"He's…"

Finn chuckled.


The café was only a five-minute walk along the Monterey Bay Coastal Trail, and after breakfast we hiked the trail and talked and then eventually hiked back and sat for a long time watching the long waves roll across the beach and then retreat in sizzling, sparkling foam.

"I miss the ocean more than I realized," I admitted.

"Maybe we do six months in Manhattan and six months in San Clemente?" Finn suggested casually.

I smiled, not looking at him.

"Try not to worry so much," he said.

"I'm okay."

Mostly I was resigned to taking it—whatever it turned out to be—one step at a time.

Was going to prison still my biggest concern? I wasn't sure. I couldn't decide if my life really was in danger or if the idea was to frame me for Colby's murder. What had Colby done to turn himself from co-conspirator to liability? What had I done to turn myself into a potential murder victim?

On the walk back to the hotel I got a text and started laughing.

"What's so funny?" Finn asked.

"Mindy. She texted to thank me for sending flowers. She appreciates the gesture and she forgives me for standing her up. However, she isn't going to allow me to climb my way back to power on the coattails of CIA Operations Officer Bebe Bloom."

"What the hell?" Finn started laughing, too. *"Climb your way back to power?"*

"I'm glad the series is doing well for her, but..."

"Poor Min. You know, her boyfriend left her for a twenty-year-old romantasy writer."

I stared at him, aghast. "A *romantasy* writer!"

He grinned. "I love that you think that's the worst part of that story."

We were still laughing when we got back to the hotel, and the rest of the afternoon was as relaxed and casual as if we really were on vacation with nothing to worry about beyond where to have dinner.

In fact, we were dressing for dinner when someone knocked firmly on the suite door.

Finn moved me aside and went to peer out the peephole. He threw me a baffled look and opened the door.

Adrien English, Christopher Holmes, J.X. Moriarity, and Kyle Bari stood in the hall. They didn't say anything, although their expressions spoke volumes—if all in different languages.

More perplexing, J.X. wasn't even one of my authors.

"*Oh!* Cocktails are tomorrow night." I must have looked as confused as Finn. "But if you'd like to come in for a quick drink—"

"A drink is probably a good idea," Adrien said.

Which seemed rather cryptic, especially from him.

Finn's brows shot up. He made a sweeping *Come in gentlemen!* sort of gesture and stepped aside.

Adrien, Christopher, J.X., and Kyle walked into the suite. They seemed just a little bit wary, and I wasn't sure why.

Well, Adrien, Christopher, and Kyle seemed wary. J.X. seemed his normal sociable self.

"Very nice," he remarked, glancing around. "That view of the bay is incredible."

The others ignored him.

Christopher said, "Don't take this the wrong way, Keiran, because we're all agreed that you're a terrific editor and a good person. If you killed someone, you'd have to have a very good reason, and we're committed to helping you in any way we can."

# Chapter Twenty-Four

"*Kit*!" J.X. exclaimed.

Adrien gave Christopher a *Seriously?* look.

In apparent response to Adrien's look, Christopher said, "*This* is why I suggested it would be a good idea for you to stay in the bar with Jake."

In fact, the comment was addressed to J.X., who retorted, "And this is why I *didn't* stay in the bar."

Adrien, abruptly switching sides, said, "I think Jake would appreciate the company."

To which J.X. retorted, "I think Jake would appreciate *your* company."

Finn said—loudly, "What in *the hell* is going on?"

And Kyle said, "I'd love a drink."

There was no official bell, but that was the end of round one.

I said, "You think *I* killed someone?"

Our guests looked apologetic, but no one seemed to be backing down.

"You think I committed *murder*?" Before they could answer, I said, "Just out of curiosity, *were* that true, how do you imagine you could help me?"

Adrien said with touchingly misguided sincerity, "Keiran, it's obvious something's really wrong. You've looked sick with worry for days. It's more than the merger."

"Buy-out," Kyle corrected.

"And there's that body in the swimming pool," Christopher said.

"That's it? I look worried and there's a body in the swimming pool, ergo I committed murder?" I looked at Finn. "I think we do need drinks. I definitely need a drink."

"The body of Troy Colby," Christopher pointed out.

I drew a sharp breath and said, "Please. Don't stand on ceremony. Sit down. Share your thoughts." I gestured expansively to the elegant seating arrangement.

Adrien, Christopher and Kyle took their places in front of the fireplace. J.X. hung back.

"The more the merrier," I said.

"I'm truly sorry," J.X. said. He did look truly sorry. "They're determined to help you."

"Here." Finn thrust the empty ice bucket at him. "Make yourself useful."

J.X. headed for the door. Finn and I exchanged long looks.

I moved over to the chair nearest the fireplace, sat down and leaned back, casually crossing one leg over my knee in a show of relaxed confidence. "Okay, tell me what you imagine is going on."

Adrien said, "At first, we did think you were stressed out about the merger."

"Takeover," Kyle interjected.

Christopher said, "And then we thought it was that pompous little prick Hayes Hartman and you know..." He moved his head meaningfully in Finn's direction.

"I never thought that," Kyle said. "At no time did I think that."

"I'm right here, Christopher," Finn said. "I can both see and hear you."

Adrien said, "But it's obvious Finn—"

"Is crazy about you." Finn said to me.

Our gazes locked and I smiled at him, although I think it was kind of a wavery smile, because that instant, open affection caught me off guard every single time.

"Exactly," Kyle said. "And vice versa I knew it the first night we went to dinner."

"Right," Adrien said. "In fact, it became obvious that Finn was *also* sick with worry—about *you*."

I said, "You've used that phrase twice and I object. It's cliché. Vague and physiologically nonspecific. It's faux-vivid. It reads like placeholder emotion."

"*Ouch*," Christopher and Kyle murmured.

Adrien was unmoved. In the meantime, Colby had been dropping hints about how he couldn't wait to hear from you regarding his recent submission based on an actual still-open cold case that occurred in Steeple Hill some twenty years ago."

I didn't move a muscle. Out of the corner of my eye, I could see Finn standing motionless by the wet bar.

"What he didn't realize," Adrien said, "is that we had insider knowledge." He looked at Kyle.

Kyle met my eyes, his expression contrite. "Sorry, Keiran. I only know of one cold case in Steeple Hill. The disappearance of Dominic Baldwin and Milo Argyros. It happened about twenty years ago. You still lived here then. You'd have been the same age, gone to school with them, probably."

I said, "I'm aware of the case—cases." The penny dropped. I gaped at them, stammered, "W-W-wait a second. Are you doing a summation gathering on *me*?"

"What's a summation gathering?" Finn's frown transferred itself from the others to me.

"It used to be called the drawing room reveal. It's a Golden Age mystery trope. The sleuth gathers their suspects in a drawing room—well, any room. It could be a train car or-or a ship's cabin—"

"This is why I hate Golden Age mystery," Finn said.

At the heavy knock on the door, we all—well, not Finn—but the rest of us, jumped like Cub Scouts listening to ghost stories around a campfire.

Finn growled, "That's J.X., you menaces to society," and went to answer the door.

Kyle said, "We're not doing a summation gathering *on* you, Keiran. We're doing it *with* you. Because if you were involved in those disappearances, but you *didn't* kill Colby—"

"I did not kill Colby," I said. "I haven't killed anyone. So far."

"See, that's the thing, though," Adrien said. "If you're just a witness, then you're in a hell of a lot of danger. That drowning wasn't accidental. The police aren't giving out a lot of information, but we did get that much."

"Jake got that much," Christopher said, and Adrien nodded as if it was the same thing.

Maybe it was.

Finn opened the suite door, J.X. handed over the ice bucket and called, "Kit, I'll be in the bar when you're done torching your career."

"Save me a seat," Christopher called back.

Adrien said to me, "What you're not doing is denying receiving a manuscript from Colby. Or denying that you were a witness to...something."

"A witness to something," I said. "That narrows it down."

The clink of ice cubes dropped in glasses filled the sudden silence.

Christopher said, "Let's not forget. Keiran's not the only person at the conference Colby was obsessed with. He kept trying to attach himself to TM."

"Theodore Mansfield?" I had a sudden uneasy memory of Rudolph wandering in from the pool the night Colby had been murdered.

Granted, Finn had spotted three women heading out to the hot tub after that.

Still...I hadn't noticed the body immediately. It would have been dark. They'd probably been drinking.

Kyle clarified, "T. McGregor."

Somewhere in the distance I heard Christopher saying, "Now *there's* someone who reads his own PR. What an ego. J.X. doesn't think he was even on the force."

"Maybe he worked Dispatch," Finn drawled. "With that personality, he'd be a natural."

Christopher snorted.

"He does have a very weird accent," Adrien remarked.

"His bio says Outer Hebrides." That was Kyle.

"Outer space maybe."

"That's right. Your mother's English?"

"He's got the weirdest, coldest eyes," Christopher commented.

"They're contacts," I said. "Opaque color contacts."

It was like listening to them underwater. I could hear their faraway muffled voices, but the words no longer mattered.

"Excuse me." I rose.

Finn reached me as I picked my way through the ottomans and side tables. He handed me a drink. "Okay?"

I took the drink, knocked it back in a gulp, and handed him the glass. "I'll be right back."

"What do you mean, you'll be right back?"

I opened the suite door as Finn called, "Keir?"

I stepped into the hall, letting the door close heavily behind me.

Shock is not a plan.

I didn't have a plan.

I was moving with purpose, but the purpose was simply to get to that door, to knock on that door, to look him in the eyes.

I had no thought beyond that.

I knocked on the door of the Cannery Row Suite. Knocked again.

The floor creaked and I knew he was standing on the other side of the door, eyeing me through the peephole.

I stared stonily back at the small glass eye.

The deadbolt clanked, the lock clicked, the door opened, and I saw him as he really was.

A few months older than me, medium height, thicker than he'd been as a boy. That beard. It should have been my first clue: thick and carefully groomed in that trying-too-hard hipster style that suggested *I Know Exactly Who I Am* while obliterating recognizable features. His hair had thinned a bit, that was real enough. His eyes were the give-away, though they had not given him away at first.

It wasn't just contextual blindness. He'd changed a lot. Just as I had. He probably wouldn't have known me, either, if we'd happened to bump into each other on the streets of Manhattan.

I stared into his too bright, too blue eyes.

"How could you do it?" I asked. "How could you do that to me?"

Milo let out a pained sigh, scrunched up his face in an expression that, despite the beard and the lines, was unexpectedly familiar.

"I knew it. I knew you were going to figure it out. I could feel you starting to analyze in the elevator yesterday."

Had it only been yesterday?

*If* I had started to figure it out, it had not been consciously. I'd bought the whole eccentric author act. Plenty of authors *were* eccentric.

He stepped back into the large tiled foyer. I walked into his suite. He let the door swing shut behind us.

Low-slung modern furniture in soft grays and coastal blues. A gas fireplace flickered beneath a wall-mounted flat screen. The windows looked out over the bay, the waves lapping almost directly beneath the suite. To the left, Cannery Row unfolded in all its quirky, tourist-tangled charm—shuttered windows, weathered brick, and the ghost of Steinbeck in every salt-bleached sign.

One large suitcase already stood next to the door. There were stacks of books going into boxes. Empty gift shop bags were scattered around. He was packing for his flight home.

The door to the master suite was closed.

"Why didn't you just tell me?" I asked. "Why did you leave like that? I thought you were dead."

"*Dead*?" He looked astonished. "Why would I be dead?"

"Because you vanished without a trace. Your family filed a missing persons report."

"Well, they had to."

"Because you *vanished*."

"Well, I *had* to."

I suddenly remembered what an ass he could be in an argument.

"How much did you tell them?"

Milo's expression was blank. He said evasively, "Only what I had to."

Which meant what? I thought I knew now where Judge Baldwin had got a lot of the information he'd fed to Troy Colby: Geo.

Milo said, "I had to tell them something. I couldn't just—"

Leave without telling them anything? Leave them to worry and wonder.

Milo said instead, "It was only a matter of time before we—I—was caught. I had to leave the country."

"Why didn't you tell me? You let me think—"

He made a sound of exasperation and threw his head back in a kind of full body twitch of impatience—and that too was uncannily familiar. "Because you would have begged me to stay. Or begged to come with me." His expression was a blend of emotions: impatience, exasperation. A little guilt, too, and I remembered how he resented being made to feel guilty.

He was right, of course. I would have begged him to stay. I might even have begged to go with him, although I'd have known that wasn't really an option. I certainly would have begged him not to leave me with what we had done. With what I had done for him.

"I loved you."

I didn't say it in accusation or to make him feel more guilty than he did. I was honestly bewildered at the realization of how misplaced that love had been.

He shook his head as though he too were honestly bewildered. "We were kids, Keiran. We didn't know what love was."

I said, "I can't speak for you, but I think I knew what love was. Even back then."

It made him angry.

"I don't know what you want me to say. Could I have handled it better? Yes. I could have handled *all* of it better, including— Och, for feck's sake!"

*Och, for feck's sake*

He was never a good actor, but he did always throw himself into the role. I had to give him that.

"I was eighteen and terrified. If you think it was easy to leave everything I knew and create a life for myself in a fucking foreign country, you're wrong. I had to build a life out of nothing. My grandparents didn't leave a college fund for me. I was depending on scholarships and grants, all of which I *lost* when I had to flee."

It probably *had* been difficult and lonely and terrifying. His achievements were all the more impressive because of the obstacles. But he'd thrown those obstacles in his own path, and I found myself unmoved.

"Did you kill Troy Colby?"

Milo recoiled. "*Me*? Commit murder? You *know* Dom was an accident. You of all people know that."

"Self-defense, right?"

"Right! I accidentally killed him *defending* myself. How can you even ask me that?"

I said, "It turns out I didn't know you as well as I thought I did. Were you working with Colby? Were you behind that fucking fake manuscript? Did you get your brother to slash my tire?"

"Slash your— What are you even *talking* about?" He seemed legitimately dumbfounded. "Of course not! Are you crazy? You think I'd have anything to do with blackmailing you? That I'd be in cahoots with someone like Colby? How would that even happen? I never met the guy till he introduced himself. I didn't know about *any* of this at first."

My skepticism must have shown.

He protested, "I was just attending a conference. I'd no idea you'd even be here when I signed up. You think I'd have taken the chance of running into you? This was *all* Judge Baldwin. He's on this crazy *Vengeance is Mine!* trip."

"Why would he come after me? How would he have known I had any involvement? How would *anyone*?"

Milo got a very weird look on his face. He stopped blustering and said quietly, "He has my journal."

"He… What journal?"

"I kept a journal. I always kept a journal. Dom got hold of it."

"How would Dom—?" I stopped.

*How do you think Dominic knew to find Milo in the cemetery that night?*

"You and Dom were...together?"

"Yes. Sometimes. It wasn't... It wasn't a normal, healthy relationship. He was a fucking trainwreck. He hated being queer. He hated me because he wanted me. And I hated me, too, because I wanted him. Even though I knew he was a lost cause. He was a *bastard*."

Milo watched me and when I didn't say anything—because I literally could not find the words—he threw his head back and yelled, "*What do you want from me?*"

"The truth would have been nice."

"Listen, Keiran, you *had* the truth. I *did* care for you. What we had was sweet. It was wonderful compared to the catastrophe of being with Dom. You were a-a breath of fresh air in my life. I regret what happened. I wish I'd never called you that night. And I wish even more that I had not asked Dom to come to St. Bibiana's. He was supposed to bring my journal, which he'd stolen a week earlier. Stole it from my *bedroom* when he broke into our house because that's who he was."

I said scornfully, "You didn't ask him to come there to get back your diary."

Milo sighed. "No. That wasn't why I asked him to come there. And that wasn't why he came."

"Was *any* of what you told me true?"

Of all the times I'd imagined having this conversation—well, I'd never imagined this conversation. Never imagined anything like it.

"It was *all* true," Milo insisted. "He did try to strangle me. He was angry after we fucked. He was always angry. That night I was angry, too. I fought back." He drew a hard breath. "Anyway. Judge Baldwin found the journal. He had it for years. For *years*. He knew everything for years. But he did nothing with it. Because he knew his son was a sick fuck and it was always going to end badly."

Milo's face worked. "But now, he's sick. He's dying. And suddenly, out of the blue, he wants…justice. For a goddamned ghost."

"Why's he dragging me into it?"

"You're in the journal. He could put two and two together. Who else would have helped me that night?"

Yeah. Who else?

Milo added, "Plus, he thinks I'm dead."

*"What?"*

"Geo told him I was dead. Let him think…"

I said in disbelief, "Let him think *I* killed *you*?"

Milo nodded. "You were long gone. It didn't matter."

"Didn't *matter*?"

"It's not like anyone was going to the police. Or Baldwin wouldn't have come up with this crazy revenge scheme."

"No, God forbid anyone try to handle this through legal channels. So now what? Geo's planning to kill me so that I can't disagree with his version of events?"

"Of course not!" Milo seemed authentically indignant.

"He slashed my tire in the hopes I'd drive off a cliff. Did he kill Troy Colby?"

"You're crazy. My brother wouldn't slash your damned—"

The door to the master bedroom flew open and banged against the wall. Georgi Argyros charged out like a bull rushing into the arena.

*Him*, I would have recognized anywhere. Anywhere I could get a good look at him. Big and burly, with a face like a much-pummeled boxing glove. There were more grooves in his face, his shaggy hair was silver now, but those were the only real changes.

I'm not sure why, until Geo showed up, it hadn't occurred to me that I'd placed myself in a dangerous situation. Maybe because I hadn't placed myself in the situation, so much as sleep-walked into it.

Despite everything, despite hearing Milo's self-serving excuses, despite knowing Milo was capable of violence, I hadn't been afraid. Shocked. Sickened. Saddened. Not afraid. When Geo burst out of the bedroom, I was afraid.

In fact, I'd always been wary of Geo. Not that he'd ever done or said anything threatening to me. But something about the way he looked at me, his grim silences always reminded me of my father.

"*Why* would you tell him that? *Why* would you talk to him at all?" he shouted. "I can't believe what I'm hearing!"

"It's *over*," Milo shouted back. "For chrissake! How many times are we going through this? *You're on the security cameras*. It's *done*. This is what I've been trying to tell you. There is *no way out*. The only thing left is to come up with a believable reason—that doesn't implicate me—for why you thought drowning that asshole was a good idea."

I felt unobtrusively for my cell phone—and realized I'd walked out of my hotel room without it. I went cold. The only way out of this suite was the foyer door, and Geo and Milo were blocking my access.

"How about because he was going to tell *him*." Geo jabbed his finger at me.

"So what? *He* can't go to the police! He's as culpable as I am."

I hadn't thought Milo could say much more to shock me. The realization that he understood perfectly well the jeopardy he'd placed me in—oh, maybe not at first, maybe not back in the day—but for a good long while, was like getting punched in the gut.

*"Like hell!"* Geo was glaring at me. His face was scarlet with fury. His eyes were red-rimmed black holes. "I'm not confessing to anything."

"Yes. And you know why. Otherwise, there's an investigation and *I* get dragged into it. And then the money stops. You want to ruin Ma? You want to ruin Thea and Cora and Zoe? You want to destroy our whole fucking family?"

I was increasingly afraid of how this was going to end. Milo clearly thought he was winning the argument. But Geo had never been a big brain kind of guy. He did not look to me like someone who was going to let cooler heads prevail. To me, he looked like someone who would kill me and, if he saw no other way, his brother, before he'd go back to prison.

It was not a quiet confrontation, though, and as I listened, ears straining for any sign that neighbors were getting concerned, I thought I heard the low murmur of voices down the hallway—radio static, clipped commands.

Or maybe that was wishful thinking.

"I did this for you," Geo insisted. "My little brother. If his Honor knew—"

"The hell, Geo! I never asked you to do any of this. You did it all to keep the money flowing. Well, that still holds true."

Someone knocked with practiced force on the suite door. Milo and Geo froze. Finn called loudly, "Keiran, are you in there? Answer."

Even as my heart leaped in relief, Geo tried to grab me. I jumped back, putting the length of the glass coffee table between us. "Finn! I'm in here!" I yelled.

"Open the door!" Finn called.

*Uh, sure.* There was nothing I'd have loved to do more.

"Help!" I yelled.

"We throw him off the balcony. No one can say it wasn't an accident," Geo hissed. He nodded at the sliding glass door to the side of me.

Milo goggled at him. "You're insane. No. You're not laying a goddamned hand on him. There are cops all over this hotel. That's Finn Scott out there. His boyfriend. His boyfriend who used to be a cop. It is *over.*"

No, it was not wishful thinking. Booted footsteps pounded closer, hard soles thudding against plush carpet. Someone barked, "This one—open it."

Geo made another lunge for me and, heart pounding in alarm, I shoved the table forward full force with my foot so that he crashed down on top of it. I heard the glass break.

A voice shouted, "Police! Open up!" followed by a louder thump—then a bang as a shoulder—or possibly a small battering ram—hit the door.

Milo turned, sprinted across the tiled entrance hall, yanked open the door, and scrambled out of the way as the door slammed inward.

A stream of uniformed officers flooded in, weapons drawn. Shouts filled the suite: "Hands where we can see them!"

Finn followed the first rush, striding into the room. He was pale, grim-faced as he scanned the room with hard eyes. He saw me hovering near the small beige sofa with my hands up.

I stumbled forward to meet him and he grabbed me, gave me a little shake, and folded me into his arms. "What the hell was *that* about?"

I shook my head. Why does any idiot in real life *or* in fiction think it's a great idea to confront someone they believe capable of betrayal and violence?

Finn was clutching me so tightly I could barely squeeze out, "Annotation complete. Ending pending." Apparently, editor-speak for *I thought I was going to die thank you for saving me.*

Milo pointed at Geo, being lifted off the shattered table-top and dragged to his feet.

"That's the one, lads! Broke in here ramblin' mad—I've been tryin' tae talk him into givin' himself up!"

# Chapter Twenty-Five

"How did you know?" I asked.

It was much later that night. Finn and I were in the very comfortable bed in the very comfortable Grand Bay suite, quietly bringing each other up to speed on the events of the last five hours.

After the hostage rescue operation, the police took me, Milo—er, McGregor—and Georgi Argyros downtown—three separate cars, three separate interview rooms. I gave my statement twice, drank bad coffee, stared at chipped walls, and listened to the muted hum of a police station going through the familiar motions. It was close to three hours before they finally let me go, paperwork and apologies trailing after me.

My story—and *story* is the correct word—was simple. As both a fan and his prospective new editor, I wanted to informally introduce myself to McGregor and welcome him to Wheaton & Woodhouse. Perhaps invite him to dinner. Unfortunately, I'd stumbled into a hostage situation and had also been taken prisoner by the author's drunken and distraught captor.

It had only taken about 50 minutes to make my statement. My situation was straightforward: I was a victim.

Milo was still being questioned when Finn and I finally departed.

Geo had been arrested. Milo had been correct. Geo was all over the hotel's CCTV surveillance footage. Nobody had confirmed that he had been caught on camera killing Troy Colby, but there seemed to be a certain *We Got Him* buzz of excitement in the station.

How *many* hims was the question.

Milo's version of events was a more complicated sell: Even if police temporarily bought the story that Geo, hiding from the police after accidentally killing Colby in a drunken argument, forced his way into McGregor's room, I had to think there was a good chance cell phone activity and earlier security camera footage would indicate prior acquaintance.

Not my problem. Not anymore. My story only had to hold up for a few hours more. After that...

Well. That was the question.

But at least I would be done with the lies, with the hiding, with the fear of wondering what had really happened that night, what had happened to Milo. No more secrets.

Well, not many.

Not from Finn.

"Know what?" Finn's voice brought me back to the here and now. "That T. McGregor was Milo Argyros? Or that you were liable to get yourself killed?" He softly nuzzled my temple, which softened the harshness of his words considerably.

"Either. Both."

"You. Let's see. You turned as white as a ghost, slammed three ounces of whisky without taking a breath, and walked out of the suite like you were having a vision. Meanwhile, The Three Investigators were shouting things like *It's the grand reveal!* and *He's doing the final reckoning*!

I snorted at the 'Three Investigators' crack.

"As for T. McGregor…" He hesitated and said, "I'm sorry, Keir. That's all. Sorry it turned out like that."

I let out a careful, controlled breath. "I think I started to put it together when you asked me all those questions about things I should have asked myself. Like, how did Dominic know to come to the graveyard that night? There were red flags but I didn't want to see them."

Finn nuzzled me again. It was a consoling kind of kiss.

I said, "But it's not like I was mourning his ghost or anything. I felt affection for that boy I'd known—grief for what had happened. Or what I thought had happened. But I knew a long time ago that a big part of the attraction was that we liked the same things, that he loved talking about books and my writing and mysteries. But the main thing was, I was finally having sex with someone. Not great sex, not even good sex, but sex."

Finn made an amused sound. "I get it."

"And I don't blame him for what happened back then. He didn't force me to help him. I used my own terrible judgment. I wanted to help him because I loved him. He's not to blame for that."

"There we have a difference of opinion."

"He was only a couple of months older than me."

"And a hell of a lot more self-centered and heartless. But go on."

It was my turn to kiss him gently because it really did bother Finn: the way that long-ago Milo had treated that long-ago Keiran.

"He didn't come right out and say it, but I got the feeling that he's known where to find me for a while."

"I'm sure he did."

"He could have let me know he was okay. It's not like I would have wanted to start anything up. It would have been a relief to know there wasn't someone out there who wanted me dead, too."

Finn's expression was somber in the moonlight.

"How did you know McGregor was Milo?" I asked again.

"I knew for sure when you walked out looking like you'd seen a ghost. I had my suspicions about McGregor—not *that* suspicion. I had no idea Milo even existed before Friday. But I was pretty sure McGregor was never a cop. He just doesn't think like a cop. Nobody in his books thinks like a cop. Or talks like a cop. Or acts like a cop. Even a Scottish cop. Even a Scottish cop in the most outermost Outer Hebrides. In fact, that was something Hayes pointed out at McGregor's Smoking Gun interview. His accent's a wee bit fishy."

I huffed my disapproval that Hayes would be that observant.

"I didn't think a lot about it. In fact, I kind of put my antipathy down to you being so impressed by his books and his bloody prose."

I grinned faintly at that *bloody*. "Not *that* impressed."

"You don't talk about my books like that. If I heard one more soulful description of his *salient* use of metaphor I was going to clonk you with my thesaurus."

I laughed.

Finn's chest moved beneath my head as he chuckled, too. "Anyway. I thought he was a phony. And standoffish. Not that there's anything suspicious in being reserved. I also thought there was a possibility that Troy Colby had been on this floor trying to find McGregor, not you."

*"Oh."* That had not occurred to me.

"Anyway. When you walked out, I knew. I phoned Olivares and told him I thought Colby's murderer might be hiding in T. McGregor's suite."

"How did you know that?"

"I didn't. I was thinking Milo had drowned Colby in the pool when Colby tried to blackmail him, too. I had no idea the brother was hanging around. I was just trying to get you out of there safely."

I was silent thinking of the irony—or maybe the poetic justice—of that.

"I hate that we're lying to protect Milo," I said abruptly.

"We're not. We're lying to protect you. And we won't be lying for much longer."

"No." I said, "But."

He prompted gently, "But?"

"I know I said I was glad to have the chance to tell Judge Baldwin how sorry I am, and that's true. I owe him that. But after hearing everything Milo said; we don't have *any* leverage. If the judge is dying, he's not going to give a damn about his reputation or anything else. He wants revenge, end of story."

"I agree," Finn said. "We're not going to waste time talking to Baldwin. He's already going to have a pretty good idea of what's happened because I'd bet money Geo is desperate enough and dumb enough to call on him for help."

"Jesus. Then what are we doing?"

Finn hesitated and my heart dropped.

I shook my head. "Finn... I can't."

"Just listen for a minute. We have to control this narrative. It's only a matter of time before Milo's dumbass stranger danger story falls apart. Even if Geo is willing to confess to killing Colby, there are going to be questions. The police are already curious, they're going to keep poking around, and it's not going to be hard to find more than they ever dreamed of."

"But it won't necessarily tie back to me. There's no reason for Milo to drag me into it. It's not going to help his situation."

"That's how you look at these things. That's not how everyone looks at them. Milo is first and foremost concerned with Milo. He's going to jet back to Scotland and talk through his lawyers; he's going to stall telling the truth about anything and everything as long as possible. And one of those stall tactics might be cutting a deal and throwing you to the wolves."

That gave me pause.

"I don't think he…"

Actually, I had no idea what he might do. He was a complete stranger to me.

Finn didn't bother arguing. "We have to get out ahead of the narrative, whatever it's going to be, and we have to do that quickly. This is an evolving situation. It's not how I wanted to handle it. But we're out of options. I think our best bet is to go straight to whoever is your sheriff now and be absolutely honest."

"About everything?"

"All of it. Everything."

I could see the sense in what he was saying, but the idea of turning myself in—that my time might have just run out—left me feeling cold and hollow.

When I said nothing, Finn's arms tightened around me. He said fiercely, his breath warm against my ear, "I'll be with you every step of the way. Whatever happens, it's go-

ing to happen to both of us, and we'll work through it together. I promise you."

I had no words. Couldn't have dislodged them from the
vise my throat had become, if I had.

I nodded.


The Steeple Hill sheriff's station sat on the edge of town,
a small, white building with a cracked asphalt lot and a
flag that always seemed to hang half-mast, no matter the
weather.

Finn parked in the empty "visitors" lot and we got out
and went inside.

Indoors, it still smelled faintly of old coffee and pine
disinfectant. The front counter was more scuffed, the plastic plants more dusty, and the bulletin board more cluttered
with curling wanted posters, bake sale flyers, and a faded
handwritten note about a missing bike. A handful of desks,
a radio that occasionally crackled to life, and a coffee pot
that was surely a direct descendent of the one I remembered.

Nothing high tech, nothing fancy, but this wasn't a town
that required a large police presence.

Granted, there had been a few technological advances
since my day—or, more accurately, my father's day: flat-
screen monitors sat on the desks instead of the old CRT
monitors. A security camera feed, visible behind the front
desk, offered split screens showing different corners of the
town. (Nothing was happening as usual.) Body cam dock
chargers were lined up in the corner like they'd been sent
to detention hall.

Lunchtime on Sunday was never busy, but I honestly
thought there was no one in the station at all, until I heard

the slide and scrape of the filing cabinet in the sheriff's office.

My heart began to skip unpleasantly at memories I thought I'd forgotten.

"Hello?" Finn called, and I jumped. He patted my shoulder encouragingly.

Sheriff Rankin filled the doorway of his office. "Howdy. Can I help you folks?"

His voice was deeper, rougher. He was probably in his late fifties now. My father's most trusted deputy—and the nearest thing he had to a close friend. Up until my father had been recalled and Rankin was elected in his place.

Anyway, when I'd known him, Deputy Rankin had been tall, whip-thin, and brown. Brown hair, brown eyes, and sun-browned skin. He'd had a wide smile that reached his eyes and an easy, lowkey manner. He was thicker through the middle now; his face was more lined. He still wore scuffed cowboy boots and a stiff-brimmed hat, like he'd been hoping to join the Texas Rangers but had ended up in Steeple Hill instead.

I remembered that he'd told me to call him 'Jim,' which had flabbergasted my childhood self. He'd seemed genuinely kind though, not someone who was being nice because I was his boss's son.

I said, "Hi. You probably don't remember me. I'm Keiran Chandler."

He actually sort of rocked back on his heels. "*Keiran Chandler*? Now that's a funny thing. I was thinking about you today."

That answered the first question: would he even remember me?

"This is my friend Phineas Scott. I was wondering if I—we—could speak to you in private."

Rankin smiled that wide, genial smile I remembered. "Sundays are about as private as it gets around here. Step on in."

We stepped on in to his crowded office. I didn't think I'd been in that little room since my father had been sheriff. Rankin had a framed photo of his wife and daughters on his desk and an actual live potted plant on the file cabinet.

"Take a seat, boys. Keiran, I was real sorry about your daddy. Sorry I didn't get a chance to speak to you at the funeral."

I murmured something. Had he been at the funeral? I hadn't noticed. I remembered almost nothing of that day except my desperation to leave.

Finn and I took the two wooden chairs in front of his tidy desk. Rankin sat down, too, and closed the file on the blotter pad. He studied me with his shrewd brown eyes.

"I saw you put the house up for sale, lock, stock and barrel. Would you folks like some coffee?"

We declined coffee. I leaned forward and said, "Sheriff Rankin, I want to talk to you about something that happened twenty-three years ago. The night Dominic Baldwin...disappeared."

Rankin's unruly brows rose. He folded his arms across his chest and leaned back in his chair. "I'd be very interested to hear that, Keiran."

I couldn't help thinking he didn't seem as surprised as I'd have expected. I glanced at Finn. Finn gazed back, calm and serious. He gave a little nod like *let's do this.*

So, I did. I told Sheriff Rankin the whole story.

Everything.

Everything that had happened back then.

Everything that had happened in the last five days.

I relived the horror of that first sight of Dominic's face in the cemetery, the realization that he really was dead, that there was no going back. Milo's hysteria. The horror of dragging Dom's sodden, lifeless weight through the reeds, the wet fabric catching on every sharp rock and splintered root, of standing in the sucking mud of Pescadero Marsh, my shoes mired to the ankle, watching his body sink slowly into the muck, the dark water lapping over his legs, his face disappearing beneath a slick of green algae. Remembered my breath sobbing in my chest, praying that he would hurry up and sink.

I told Rankin about the shock of Milo's disappearance, the hurt that gradually gave way to the conviction someone must have done something to him. The grief and fear that followed.

And after years of...nothing, the bewilderment and alarm of receiving the implicit threat of the manuscript, *I Know What You Did*, with all that it had gotten wrong—and all that it had gotten right. I handed over the plastic bound binder. Rankin took it automatically, laid it on top of the closed file.

I detailed the drive to Steeple Hill, my effort to track down Troy Colby, and the harrowing trip back to Monterey, reliving again the blowout in the middle of nowhere, the night pressing in, the trees, thick with the hum of insects, the sharp scent of pine and hot metal. The doubt that turned to panic as headlights appeared. The sinister rumble of a V8 engine, the creak of the opening door, the blinding, glaring certainty that this wasn't a coincidence.

I talked about confronting Colby, of confronting Milo, of Geo's suggestion to throw me off the balcony.

I talked for three hours.

I talked until I was hoarse.

I don't think Rankin said anything the entire time except to ask for the occasional clarification and to offer me a glass of water.

Finn didn't say a word, but I felt his silent, steady support. On the rare moments I glanced his way, his expression was calm, approving.

When I had finally talked myself to a standstill, Rankin remarked, "That's... I don't know what that is."

"It's the truth," I said.

"I don't see what you'd have to gain by implicating yourself. You offered a clear and lucid account. You came in voluntarily. Funny thing. I was telling my wife the other night that nothing shocks me anymore. Guess I spoke too soon. So, Georgi Argyros is in jail for killing Troy Colby and Milo is..."

"Not going to corroborate anything I've said."

Finn said, "Keiran was a minor at the time."

"Yep."

"With a reason not to have a lot of faith in the justice system."

Rankin's eyes flickered. He said again, neutrally, "Yep."

"Most of the charges against him would have expired long ago."

"Most of them," Rankin agreed. "There's no statute of limitations on murder. Or accessory. And as far as Dominic's death, we only have Keiran's version of events."

Finn said, "Was the body ever discovered?"

"Nope." Rankin's smile was dour. "You must have driven a ways into the marsh, Keiran." And then to Finn, "You're no lawyer. Cop?"

"Former cop. I worked homicide for five years. One thing I learned is DAs don't like cases where there's no body."

Rankin nodded noncommittally.

Finn gazed steadily at Sheriff Rankin. Sheriff Rankin considered him thoughtfully, then reached down to pull open his desk drawer. He pulled out a very worn blue cloth-bound book.

I felt the hair prickle on my scalp. I hadn't remembered Milo keeping a journal, but when I saw that blue book, I remembered it. I'd thought he'd used it to organize his book notes. I kept a spiral notebook for the same purpose.

"Judge Baldwin's lawyer dropped this off this morning," Rankin said to me. "There was a letter which confirms a lot of what you told me. The judge did believe you'd killed Dominic and Milo both, and since his plans to punish you weren't working out, he wanted to make sure justice would be served."

I closed my eyes.

"Well, that's bullshit," Finn said briskly. "Seeing that Milo is still alive. Baldwin was off his rocker. I'm not sure how credible the dying declaration of someone plotting a blackmail and possible murder revenge plot will appear to a jury. I think you could argue that Baldwin is at least partially responsible for Colby's death. He dragged him into this scheme."

"I don't suppose Colby was an unwilling victim. The judge was always generous. Colby would have been paid handsomely to write that chapter."

I said, "It would depend on how the story was spun to him. If Colby believed he was helping to catch a murderer? Maybe he didn't think of it as participating in extortion. Maybe he thought he was one of the good guys."

Finn, who *was* one of the good guys, made a growling sound at the very idea. He said to Rankin, "Either way, you're smart enough, savvy enough to know Keiran's told you the truth, but if you want to waste tax-payer money trying to take this to trial—"

"Hold your horses, sonny boy," Rankin interrupted. "What I was about to tell you is Judge Baldwin died during the night. He's been on borrowed time for a while now and the clock ran out."

I dropped back in my chair. After a moment, Finn said, "Which leaves us where?"

Rankin said to me, "You didn't know Dominic well did you, Keiran? You didn't run with that pack."

"I didn't run with any pack." I said with self-mockery, "I was a lone wolf."

"You were a good kid," Rankin said gruffly. "All you needed was—" He didn't finish the thought.

"Keiran was never a suspect, was he?" Finn asked.

I guessed, "And neither was Milo?"

Rankin gave another of those sour smiles. "No. Oh, we knew Dominic didn't disappear all on his own. There was no question of foul play. The question was who, out of a very large cast of suspects, might have decided to take matters into their own hands."

"A very large cast of suspects?" I repeated.

"Dominic started getting into trouble with the law when he was thirteen. He must have been detained or arrested about twenty times by the time he disappeared. The charges were always dropped. A lot of it was petty stuff. Fist-fights, peeking in windows, taking stuff and forgetting to pay for it, sneaking into empty houses—"

"You mean assault?" Finn inquired. "Voyeurism? Theft? Breaking and entering?"

"Yep," Rankin said grimly. "It escalated as he got older. Why wouldn't it? He had years of learning the laws didn't apply to him. Judge Baldwin never saw it that way. He considered any trouble Dom got into as kid stuff."

My father would have been the sheriff during that time. Now there was irony. The man who never let failure to wash a dish or a "smart-aleck" comment go unpunished.

"Keiran, your pal Milo knew this—it's in his journal— but you might be surprised to learn that when Dom was in high school, he considered himself quite the lady's man. He was handsome, rich, on the football team. He didn't have trouble getting girls. Keeping them was a different matter because he was a bastard. There were complaints of physical and verbal abuse, stalking. A couple of charges were filed—but none of it came to anything. The thing is, those girls all had daddies, and several of those men weren't happy about the way their daughters were treated. They weren't happy with the failure of the law to protect their kids. They all, at one time or another, made threats."

Finn said, "So when Dominic disappeared, the investigation focused on the fathers of the girls who claimed Dominic had assaulted or abused them."

"Grandfathers, fathers, and brothers," agreed Rankin. "Milo disappearing the way he did raised some eyebrows, but he was never really on our radar. We took an extra close look at a couple of folks, but nothing came of it. The case went cold."

I said, "But now—"

Finn and I stared as Rankin picked up the journal, the plastic binder, and the manila folder on his desk and dumped them in the trash.

He read our expressions and said wryly, "Don't worry. I'm planning to incinerate all of it."

I said on a swallow, "But... Are you not going to pursue...this?"

Finn put a hand on my shoulder. I wasn't sure if it was reassurance or a warning to shut up.

Rankin grimaced. "I spent the morning reading your friend Milo's journal. There's a lot about Dom in there. A lot about you in there, too. Maybe the system did fail in finding justice for Dominic Baldwin, but it also failed those girls, and it failed you most of all."

That choked me up, and I'm not sure why.

"The only person still having sleepless nights over Dominic Baldwin is gone now. There's no fixing the past. Dom Baldwin got away with a lot worse than you ever did, Keiran. And maybe Milo, too." Rankin sighed. "Sometimes letting old ghosts lie quiet is as close to justice as we get."

I stared in disbelief from Rankin to Finn. I was afraid to believe what Rankin seemed to be saying.

Finn was smiling, his eyes light with relief and happiness.

"You're fine," he reassured me.

For the first time in my life, I knew it was true.

# Epilogue

"Milo is going to have to dig his own way out of the mess he created for himself," Finn was saying when we walked through the doors of the Monterey Plaza Hotel. "I've got zero sympathy. Not only did he leave you holding the bag—*his* bag—he knew you were being blackmailed, threatened, and he didn't lift a finger. He was only too glad to let you play decoy."

It was nearly five in the evening on Sunday evening and the hotel lobby was largely empty. The exodus of conference attendees had started early that morning, readers and writers alike returning to the "real" world, and now only a few die-hards or people with late flights remained.

I said, "I'm only concerned that Milo's story—or lack of a story—is liable to suck me back in."

"No. Colby's murder falls under the Monterey Police Department's jurisdiction. As far as they know, there's no connection to a twenty-year-old missing persons case in Steeple Hill. It was never their case. If Milo's smart—well, if Milo continues his usual self-serving pattern—he'll stick to the story that a drunken and distraught stranger forced his way into his hotel room and held him hostage for most of the day while he tried to convince the man to surrender to authorities."

"I don't see how his story can possibly hold up. Even if Geo goes along with it—"

"Geo's guilty. He's not being asked to confess to something he didn't do."

"Right. True. But nobody's going to believe that Geo was in this hotel for a mystery convention. I doubt if he's ever read one of Milo's books."

"Lucky him."

"I'm not even sure he can read."

"It doesn't matter. If they both stick to their stories, they might get away with it. Either way, it has nothing to do with you." Finn put a hand on my arm, stopping me. "Do you want to grab an early dinner? Or did you want to go upstairs and…"

"Nap?" I suggested innocently. "I haven't had much sleep recently, that's true."

He grinned.

A sharp shrill whistle cut across the cool silence of the lobby; a sound mostly heard by Border Collies herding stray sheep—or felons fleeing English bobbies through foggy London back alleys.

We looked around in surprise.

*"Yo!"*

The preemptory shout seemed to be coming from the lobby bar.

I stared into the gloomy, empty interior, stared harder, and sure enough, over by the far windows, a couple of comfy chairs and another table had been dragged together to create a larger seating arrangement. Several gentlemen—well, authors—seemed to be trying to get our attention.

"Oh *no*," Finn said. He didn't bother to lower his voice.

"Keiran! Finn!" Adrien English, Christopher Holmes, J.X. Moriarity, and Kyle Bari beckoned to us.

"Have they been drinking all day?" Finn asked.

I shook my head. "Shall we?"

Finn sighed, rested his hand on the small of back. "We may as well get it over with. Now that they know you're here, there's no escape."

I chuckled and we headed into the bar.

As we reached them, Adrien said, "We decided to have the cocktail party anyway. Unfortunately, only we were able to attend."

"Where have you two been for the last twenty-four hours?" Christopher demanded, as room was made around the tables for us.

"It's a long story," I said.

Adrien said, "We want to hear it."

Introductions were made. The tall, slender man with dark, curly hair was Adam, Kyle's partner.

"I didn't realize you were attending the conference," I said as we shook hands.

"I wasn't. But Kyle called on Friday."

"He's attending me," Kyle joked, but the look he gave Adam was pretty much adoring. And it seemed to be mutual, given the way Adam smiled and linked hands with him.

The tall, blond man with eyes the shade of a tiger's, and a muscular arm around Adrien English's shoulders, turned out to be the notorious former-cop-turned-PI Jake Riordan.

We shook hands. "I've heard a lot about you," I said.

His grin was sardonic. "Likewise. Especially over the last forty-eight hours."

"What's everyone drinking?" Finn questioned, moving toward the bar.

That they were—and had been—drinking for most of the afternoon was no longer in question.

"The Red Herring!"

"Smoke & Mirrors."

"The Femme Fatale."

"The Plot Twist!"

"Harp."

"Make it two."

Finn sighed. Looked at me.

"Plot Twist," I said.

He nodded and departed for the bar.

"Has anyone seen Grace Hollister since the banquet?" I asked suddenly.

Adrien said, "She left this morning. Cherry drove her to the airport."

"So, she got off all right. Good."

Kyle was staring at me with amusement. Christopher demanded, "Are you going to tell us or not?"

"Well, you must have heard by now. There was a drunken fight by the pool—"

They all made loud *Nnn* and buzzer sounds.

Adrien said, "We know that someone is being held in connection with the drowning death. And we know that T. McGregor took off for Scotland like a bat out of hell this morning."

"His wee wifey's giving birth in some undisclosed location." Christopher's accent was nearly as bad as 'McGregor's.'"

I blinked but managed to say nothing.

Kyle said, "And he's not signing with Wheaton & Woodhouse after all."

"Huh," I said.

"Zero interest," Adrien observed to Christopher.

"I noticed."

Finn returned from the bar, wisely tucking his credit card away. He sat on the edge of my chair and rested his hand on my shoulder. I smiled up at him. He smiled down at me.

Kyle said to his fellow snoops, "I don't think we're going to hear the real story. I suspect it all worked out in the end."

I laughed. All at once I felt completely, blissfully relaxed. It was a beautiful afternoon. In a little while, Finn and I would go upstairs and talk and laugh and make plans for a future I'd never really believed in until now.

I stared out the giant picture window at the long rollers crashing against the beach, and knew a moment of perfect peace.

Or maybe it was just simple, unadulterated happiness.

Either way, it was something I felt I could get used to.

I studied their faces, the expressions varying from curious to quizzical.

"Speaking of Wheaton & Woodhouse," I said slowly. "I might just have an idea…"

# About the Author

Author of 100+ titles of Gay Mystery and M/M Romance, Josh Lanyon has built a literary legacy on twisty mystery, kickass adventure, and unapologetic man-on-man romance.

Her work has been translated into twelve languages. The FBI thriller *Fair Game* was the first Male/Male title to be published by Italy's Harlequin Mondadori and *Stranger on the Shore* (Harper Collins Italia) was the first M/M title to be published in print. In 2016 *Fatal Shadows* placed #5 in Japan's annual Boy Love novel list (the first and only title by a foreign author to place on the list). The Adrien English series was awarded the All-Time Favorite Couple by the Goodreads M/M Romance Group. In 2019, *Fatal Shadows* became the first LGBTQ mobile game created by *Moments: Choose Your Story*.

Josh is an EPIC Award winner, a four-time Lambda Literary Award finalist (twice for Gay Mystery), an Edgar nominee, and the first ever recipient of the Goodreads All Time Favorite M/M Author award.

Josh is married and lives in Southern California with her irascible husband, two adorable dogs, a small garden, and an ever-expanding library of vintage mystery destined to eventually crush them all beneath its weight.

Find other Josh Lanyon titles at www.joshlanyon.co

Follow Josh on Twitter, Facebook, Goodreads, Instagram and Tumblr.

For extras and exclusives, join Josh on Patreon

# Also by Josh Lanyon

## NOVELS

### The ADRIEN ENGLISH Mysteries
*Fatal Shadows • A Dangerous Thing • The Hell You Say*
*Death of a Pirate King • The Dark Tide*
*Stranger Things Have Happened • So This is Christmas*
*Fatal Shadows: The Collectors Edition*
*A Funny Thing Happened*

### The HOLMES & MORIARITY Mysteries
*Somebody Killed His Editor • All She Wrote*
*The Boy with the Painful Tattoo • In Other Words...Murder*
*The 12.2 Per-Cent Solution*

### The ALL'S FAIR Series
*Fair Game • Fair Play • Fair Chance*

### The ART OF MURDER Series
*The Mermaid Murders •The Monet Murders*
*The Magician Murders • The Monuments Men Murders*
*The Movie-Town Murders*

### BEDKNOBS AND BROOMSTICKS
*Mainly by Moonlight • I Buried a Witch*
*Bell, Book and Scandal*

### The SECRETS AND SCRABBLE Series
*Murder at Pirate's Cove • Secret at Skull House*
*Mystery at the Masquerade • Scandal at the Salty Dog*
*Body at Buccaneer's Bay • Lament at Loon Landing*
*Death at the Deep Dive • Corpse at Captain's Seat*

## OTHER NOVELS

*This Rough Magic • The Ghost Wore Yellow Socks*
*Mexican Heat (with Laura Baumbach) • Strange Fortune*
*Come Unto These Yellow Sands • Stranger on the Shore*
*Winter Kill • Jefferson Blythe, Esquire*
*Murder in Pastel • The Curse of the Blue Scarab*
*The Ghost Had an Early Check-out*
*Murder Takes the High Road • Séance on a Summer's Night*
*Hide and Seek • Puzzle for Two • Ghosted*
*Kill Your Darlings*

## NOVELLAS

### The DANGEROUS GROUND Series
*Dangerous Ground • Old Poison • Blood Heat*
*Dead Run • Kick Start • Blind Side*

## OTHER NOVELLAS

*Cards on the Table • The Dark Farewell • The Dark Horse*
*The Darkling Thrush • The Dickens with Love*
*I Spy Something Bloody • I Spy Something Wicked*
*I Spy Something Christmas • In a Dark Wood*
*The Parting Glass • Snowball in Hell • Mummy Dearest*
*Don't Look Back • A Ghost of a Chance*
*Lovers and Other Strangers • Out of the Blue*
*A Vintage Affair • Lone Star (in Men Under the Mistletoe)*
*Green Glass Beads (in Irregulars) • Blood Red Butterfly*
*Everything I Know • Baby, It's Cold (in Comfort and Joy)*
*A Case of Christmas • Murder Between the Pages*
*Slay Ride • Stranger in the House • 44.1644° North*
*The Lemon Drop Kid*

## SHORT STORIES

*A Limited Engagement • The French Have a Word for It*
*In Sunshine or In Shadow • Until We Meet Once More*
*Icecapade (in His for the Holidays) • Perfect Day*
*Heart Trouble • Other People's Weddings (Petit Mort)*
*Slings and Arrows (Petit Mort)*
*Sort of Stranger Than Fiction (Petit Mort)*
*Critic's Choice (Petit Mort) • Just Desserts (Petit Mort)*
*In Plain Sight • Wedding Favors • Wizard's Moon*
*Fade to Black • Night Watch • Plenty of Fish*
*Halloween is Murder • The Boy Next Door*
*Requiem for Mr. Busybody*

## COLLECTIONS

*Short Stories (Vol. 1)*
*Sweet Spot (The Petit Morts)*
*Merry Christmas, Darling (Holiday Codas)*
*Christmas Waltz (Holiday Codas 2)*
*I Spy...Three Novellas*
*Dangerous Ground The Complete Series*
*Dark Horse, White Knight (Two Novellas)*
*The Adrien English Mysteries Box Set*
*The Adrien English Mysteries Box Set 2*
*Male/Male Mystery & Suspense Box Set*
*Partners in Crime (Three Classic Gay Mystery Novels)*
*All's Fair Complete Collection*
*Shadows Left Behind*